DATE DUE

A Hidden Affair

ALSO BY PAM JENOFF

The Kommandant's Girl

The Diplomat's Wife

Almost Home

A Hidden Affair

PAM JENOFF

ATRIA BOOKS

New York London Toronto Sydney

ATRIA BOOKS

A Division of Simon & Schuster, Inc.
1230 Avenue of the Americas
New York, NY 10020

First Atria Books hardcover edition July 2010

ATRIA BOOKS and colophon are trademarks of Simon & Schuster, Inc.

For information about special discounts for bulk purchases, please contact Simon & Schuster Special Sales at 1-866-506-1949 or business@simonandschuster.com.

The Simon & Schuster Speakers Bureau can bring authors to your live event. For more information or to book an event contact the Simon & Schuster Speakers Bureau at 1-866-248-3049 or visit our website at www.simonspeakers.com.

Designed by Davina Mock-Maniscalco

Manufactured in the United States of America

10   9   8   7   6   5   4   3   2   1

Library of Congress Cataloging-in-Publication Data is available.

ISBN 978-1-4165-9071-2
ISBN 978-1-4165-9795-7 (ebook)

For Benjamin, the Love of my Life

In water one sees one's own face;

But in wine one beholds the heart of another.

—French proverb

A Hidden Affair

chapter ONE

I GAZE ACROSS THE veranda, beyond the rows of yachts and sailboats bobbing in the Porte de Monaco toward the sparkling Mediterranean waters. To my right, the shoreline curves inward before jutting out to sea again at La Condamine, the cluster of tall gleaming buildings that rise against the steep, rocky hillside. A drop of perspiration runs down the glass carafe of water that sits before me and seeps into the white linen cloth. From the dozen or so other tables around mine comes the quiet murmur of conversation, mingled with spoons clinking against teacups and the gentle rustling of morning newspapers.

Inhaling the mix of salt air and coffee, tinged with a hint of citrus, I tilt my head upward. Above the canvas-and-bamboo umbrella, the sky is an unbroken blue. It is hard to believe that just two days ago I was in England. I took the last evening flight from Heathrow, rushing to the airport only to be predictably delayed by fog. We didn't land in Milan until almost three in the morning, and I briefly considered getting a hotel room there, catching a few hours of sleep. But eager to reach my destination, I decided against it. Instead, I took a taxi to the train station, loitering over cups of burned cappuccino in the all-night café until the ticket office opened at four thirty. Half an hour later I boarded the train to Monaco.

We traveled through the gritty outskirts of the city in the darkness, stopping twice at remote stations for passengers before picking up speed and moving through the rugged border region between Italy and France. As we reached the coast, the sun seemed to rise suddenly behind us, a floodlight on a movie set, revealing the jagged peaks above, blue waters below. The terraced hills were broken indiscriminately by grand mansions and simple cottages that seemed to share the breathtaking environs with egalitarian ease.

The train slowed again to a leisurely pace, hugging the mountainside, unfazed by the sports cars and lorries that raced along the thin strip of road beside it. As the sun climbed higher in the sky, a man opened one of the carriage doors facing the sea and hung carelessly by his arms from the top, open shirt blowing in the breeze.

It was not the first time I had taken this journey. I had been here as a student during the summer holiday between my first and second years at Cambridge, on a monthlong backpacking trip across Europe with a few of my British classmates. We spent three nights sleeping on the floor of an apartment owned by a friend of a friend whose mother had remarried a Monaco native. After weeks of tents and public campground bathrooms, the tiny flat, with its washing machine and real shower, felt like paradise. I remember being struck by the dramatic terrain of the Côte d'Azur, the idyllic tropical beauty that seemed so improbable in my American view of what Europe would be like. I left reluctantly, hoping to return again someday. But I certainly never expected to be here now. Not like this.

I take a sip of coffee, tearing my gaze reluctantly from the sea, and reach into the leather tote that sits by my feet. Feeling instinctively around the familiar contents, I pull out a manila file. My boss,

Maureen, gave it to me at the embassy in London, just minutes after she dropped the bombshell that would change my life forever: Jared, my college boyfriend, did not drown in the river a decade ago as I believed, but had faked his death and disappeared from Cambridge.

I thumb through the file, which I took with me when leaving the embassy after I resigned my State Department commission. It contains all of the information Mo had about Jared's whereabouts these past ten years, or so she claimed. Pictures, reports, and other notes form a tapestry of Jared's life after he vanished. There are little snippets about the places he had been, how he'd lived, what he had done after he'd left. A few aliases he'd used in the early years. Mo gave me the file in exchange for my silence. I wonder now if it was worth the price. Most of the details are months or years out-of-date. Only one scrap of paper, bearing the address of a Monaco apartment building, is of any possible use. That's what brought me here.

I close the file and take another sip of coffee, staring out once more across the water. The warm paradise is such a sharp contrast to gray, chilly England. It was just a few weeks ago that I requested the assignment to the London embassy in order to be by the side of my closest friend, Sarah, as she struggled against Lou Gehrig's disease. Then, it seemed that returning to England for the first time since Jared died, confronting my memories, would be the hardest thing I would ever have to do. But Sarah had summoned me, or so I thought, and so, steeling myself, I asked the Director to reassign me to the embassy in London.

It should have been straightforward: take care of Sarah, do my job, try not to get too buried in my memories. But then, shortly after my arrival, our classmate Chris approached me, stirring up the questions about Jared's death that I had always been too afraid to ask. What had really happened that night? The answer, we quickly learned once I agreed to help Chris do some digging, was not the one we had been given years earlier. Jared's death was not an accident. But that only begged more questions, darker ones: Who had wanted him dead, and why?

Jared. My breath catches as his face appears in my mind. I see him, as I always do, standing on the deck of the boathouse the day we met, tall and handsome, silhouetted against the pale, predawn sky. Ours was hardly love at first sight. We clashed horribly, him unable to control his frustration at my relative lack of experience as a coxswain, me at first terrified and later angered by his terse ways. With such intense dislike, I hadn't seen it coming, the heated kiss on the balcony overlooking the Thames months later. After, there was never any question that we would be together.

Together, at least, for a short while. We knew from the start that we had three months until my scholarship ended and I would be forced to return to America. And then, weeks before my scheduled departure, he was gone, purportedly drowned in the river. It was a story without an ending—until now. I still cannot believe that he is alive, that in hours or days I might see him again.

Might be alive, a voice in my head, not my own, reminds gently. He was last seen some time ago, perhaps, at a flat just minutes away from where I now sit. All I have is an address, no confirmation that he has been there recently or information as to the reliability of the source. But it was all I had to go on, and so I got on the plane. Finding Jared is the one thing that still makes sense, the only thing that matters.

But the revelation that he might be alive raised more questions than it had answered and even as I envision the reunion that for the past ten years had seemed impossible, nagging thoughts intrude: Why did Jared disappear without telling me? Why didn't he come back, or at least contact me to let me know he was not dead, instead of allowing me to grieve all of these years?

I tuck the file back into my bag. There will be time for questions later; first I have to find Jared. I signal the waiter over to sign for the bill, then walk across the terrace and into the lobby. The hotel, with its fifty-odd rooms, is exactly the kind I like, intimate, yet large enough for me to be inconspicuous.

"Mademoiselle Weiss?" As I pass the front desk, a voice jars me from my thoughts.

Surprised, I turn to face the clerk who helped me check in the previous day. So much for inconspicuous. "Yes?"

He is holding out an envelope in my direction. "For you."

I stare at his outstretched hand for several seconds, my heart pounding. No one is supposed to know I am here. Reluctantly, I take the envelope with my name typed on the front from him, tear it open. A card falls to the ground and as I scramble to pick it up, Maureen's familiar handwriting, long and flowery, seems to leap out toward me.

I'm sorry, the note reads. *Good luck, be careful, and thank you for understanding.*

I relax slightly. Maureen is not coming after me. At least not yet. Her note is another apology for her betrayal. But how did she track me down?

I feel inside the envelope once more. There is a thin stack of traveler's checks, held together by a paper clip. I thumb through them. There must be at least five thousand dollars. My anger flares. Does Mo think that she can buy my silence? But she did not intend it that way, I realize quickly. The money is a reaffirmation of our agreement: I will not report to the State Department the secret that would surely end her career when she is just a step away from becoming an ambassador. In exchange, she will not tell anyone else where I am, or stop me from doing what I have set out to do.

Of course, her note is wrong in one respect: I do not understand. Mo had been my mentor and friend. Yet she lied to me, and made me a pawn in her political game. My fury rises to full boil. I cannot imagine understanding or forgiving what she did, not now. Not ever.

My shoulders slump with fatigue. I suppose I should be grateful; in the end, she gave me the one piece of information that matters. Without Mo and her elaborate subterfuge, I might never have discovered that Jared is alive.

I approach the clerk at the desk once more. "Checking out," I say, thinking ruefully of my room with its crisp sheets, the small patio overlooking the harbor. But I cannot stay put any longer, not with Mo knowing where I am. No, I will move to one of the smaller pensions, somewhere nondescript that will take a cash deposit in lieu of a credit card without looking too closely.

I reach for my wallet, then pause, considering the traveler's checks. In principle I hate to touch them, to imply that my silence can be bought. But I don't know how long I will be on the road, how far my savings will go having quit my job. I hand the clerk three of the checks, accepting the change he hands me in euros.

"Would you like help with your luggage?" he asks.

"No, thank you." I have nothing other than the tote I carry. I've always been a light traveler, and the two suitcases I brought to London were destroyed in a gas explosion at my flat. In my mind I see the charred rubble, the rescue workers carrying a body bag from the site. Tears fill my eyes. I was supposed to have died in that explosion. Instead, my colleague Sophie lost her life when she stopped by to pick something up at my request. Guilt mixes with my anger. I will honor my agreement with Mo and not turn her in, at least for now. But she and the others will pay someday for the lives that were lost for their gain.

Swallowing my rage, I walk out of the hotel and start up the sloping, palm tree–flanked street, my sandals scuffing lightly against the pavement. The shops that line the sidewalk are a parade of expensive boutiques touting couture clothing, Swiss watches, fur coats that seem ludicrous in this tropical climate. Tanned tourists dart in and out of the stores with large shopping bags, ants carrying food back to the nest. The conversations around me are in a mixture of French and German and other languages I cannot quite discern.

I pause, catching a glimpse of my reflection in the window of a gourmet chocolate shop. Though my complexion is a bit pale, the white linen blouse and khaki capris I bought after arriving blend in easily. I put on one of my other purchases, a pair of oversized tortoise sunglasses, and continue walking. My gait slows, stride growing more relaxed. There is something comforting about being anonymous in this strange city, lost in the crowd. Of course, at some point I will have to check on Sarah, let my parents know I'm no longer in England. But for now, I am completely alone.

A few minutes later the street grows narrower and the throngs of shoppers thin, a rare quiet enclave in this crowded, tourist-soaked principality. The stores here are less grand, an easy mix of art galleries, booksellers, groceries, and wine shops. I turn a corner, then stop in front of a familiar café, weaving through the close-set outdoor tables, choosing one midway back to the left. A barista appears and takes my order.

When she has gone, I pull a notebook from my bag and lean back. I spent most of yesterday afternoon here, sipping cappuccinos. I placed the notebook in front of me, pretending to scribble in it like a traveler with a journal. In reality I kept my gaze fixed on the terraced building across the street to the right—number 12 rue des Lilas. It is the address in the file that Maureen gave me, the one where Jared was last seen months earlier.

The file did not contain an apartment number, though. Not knowing which unit in the four-story building might be Jared's, I fought the urge to pound on every door, instead taking a seat at the café to watch and wait. But there was no sign of Jared. The residents who came and went from the building were mostly old, leathery, hunch-shouldered seniors shuffling to the taxi stand at the corner or pushing wheeled shopping carts down the block. I found myself studying them, wondering what they had done to earn the millions of dollars needed to be residents here and afford this opulent life-style.

I didn't see anyone resembling Jared, and as the afternoon wore on, I grew frustrated. Did I really expect to find him here at a flat he might have happened to visit or occupy briefly some time ago? But the address was the only thing I had to go on, and I did not know where I would go next if the lead proved futile. So I came again today, ready to wait and watch the building like a dog hovering over a rabbit hole.

What was Jared doing in Monaco anyway, I wonder now, as the barista returns with my drink. He always hated places like this, crowded and pretentious. Even college life in bucolic Cambridge had been too claustrophobic for him. Jared was drawn to quiet, re-mote locations—the roof of the chapel where we perched so im-probably the night of the boat club dinner, talking and putting some of our initial dislike for each other behind us as we watched the party unfold below, or the spot by the riverbank where he would go to think so often in those final haunted days before he was gone.

When Jared was forced to be part of a group, he was usually listening, taking things in quietly from the outside. That's why he loved being on the water, I realize now, picturing him in the seven seat of the boat behind Chris, face locked in grim determination. There was an escape, a meditative quality to the rhythm of each stroke that communicated without speech. No, I conclude, taking in the street once more, it is impossible to picture Jared here.

Stirring the drink, I observe the other café patrons: a group of women clustered by the periphery, babies on their laps, miniature dogs half-sleeping at their feet; an elderly couple sharing a croissant, not speaking. At the far edge of the patio a man sits by himself, holding an open newspaper in front of him. He does not belong, I decide instantly, taking in his profile. Though his skin is appropriately bronzed, his features are strong, the square jaw and pronounced brow more Slavic than Mediterranean. His white T-shirt clings just a shade too closely to his raw, masculine frame to be fashionable. Of course, Monaco is a city of foreigners. But this thirtysomething man, with his broad shoulders and close-cropped brown hair, looks more military than tourist.

The man turns slightly and his gaze catches mine. I drop my eyes hurriedly to my notebook. Did he notice me watching him? Unlikely, I remind myself, remembering my sunglasses. But I can feel my cheeks redden as a surge of warmth runs through me. The stranger is more attractive than I anticipated from studying his profile. I push the thought away. In the years since I was with Jared, I almost let my guard down once, becoming close to Sebastian, the Scottish agent assigned to our investigation team in London. But I allowed my feelings to cloud my judgment—a mistake that nearly cost me my life.

No, there is only one man I am interested in, and he is Jared. I've pictured it a thousand times in the past few days, finding him again, seeing him alive. The vision, banished from my mind for all of the years I thought he was dead, comes unbidden now with every breath. I imagine his face breaking into one of its hard-won smiles that crinkled the edges of his emerald green eyes, strong arms encircling me. But what would our reunion really be like? Would it be awkward or would our feelings, easy and unspoken, resume as though uninterrupted by the years?

I glance up once more, avoiding the direction of the stranger, watching the apartment building as I sip my tea. A blond woman in a flowing print skirt strides down the street and opens the gate to the building. I saw the same woman leaving the previous day, her hair pulled back in a sleek chignon. She stuck in my mind because she was so much younger than the other residents that I wondered if she was visiting a grandparent. But she carries a bag of groceries, unlocking the door to the building with an ease suggesting she lives there. Her hair is loose today, falling straight just below her shoulders.

Watching her, my pulse quickens slightly. Easy, I think. Though the woman stands out among the elderly residents, there is no reason to assume that she is connected to Jared. But something, instinct or my training or perhaps some combination of the two, makes me think she could be a neighbor, someone who has seen him.

When the door closes behind the woman, I turn away, studying the man at the nearby table once more out of the corner of my eye. He continues to focus on the newspaper in front of him. But even from this distance, I can tell from the bold print of the advertisements that it is still open to the same page as before, despite the fact that several minutes have passed. Something is not right. What is he doing here, sitting alone in the middle of the day? Is he following me?

Though Mo promised she would leave me to my hunt for Jared in peace, there are others she cannot control who might try to stop me.

I force myself to breathe normally, fighting the urge to stand up and leave. Paranoia has never served me well. There could be lots of reasons why the man is sitting here. Still, this will be my last visit to the café. Varying one's schedule and route is a basic counterintelligence rule; repetition is the easiest way to get caught. And I cannot keep returning here day after day, just waiting. If Jared isn't here and the trail has gone cold, I need to know so that I can decide what to do next. I have to figure out if Jared is still connected to this address.

I think once again of the blond woman, who has disappeared into the apartment building. Should I try to speak with her to see if she knows Jared? It's a long shot but seems as good a way as any, and better than sitting here indefinitely.

I put some coins on the table, then stand and walk from the café. As I cross in front of the man with the newspaper, I feel his eyes on me. My stomach twitches. Easy, I think. He could just be, as the kids say nowadays, checking me out. Men in the Mediterranean tend to be much more unabashed in their admiration of women, I remind myself, remembering the catcalls on the streets during my student travels through Italy and Spain that intimidated me so. But I will not approach the apartment building directly, just to be safe. I go to the corner and make a left. As I turn, I glance over my shoulder at the man, who seems engrossed in his newspaper once more.

At the next intersection I turn left again, continuing around the block. The sun has climbed higher in the sky now, the late morning May air as hot as a midsummer afternoon in Washington. I pick up my pace, completing the circle. When I reach the corner by the apartment building, I stop, scanning the café across the street.

The man with the newspaper is gone.

My suspicion rises once more. If he was watching me, he would have had no further business at the café once I left. I search the street for the man but don't see him. Perhaps he just finished his drink and went on his way. In any event, I cannot worry about him now. I need to speak with the blond woman.

Taking a final look in all directions, I start toward the iron gate of the apartment building and slip into the front garden. I try to walk normally down the path, to appear as though I belong there to anyone who might be watching. I reach the door and turn the handle, but it is locked.

Hesitating, I study the dozen or so buttons beside the door. Each is labeled with a surname. None, of course, is Jared's, and I cannot tell which might belong to the woman. For a minute I consider pressing all of them, but that would attract too much attention. And what would I say, that I am looking for a man who might have been here once, for anyone who might know him?

There is a scuffling sound on the other side of the door and I step back quickly as it opens, moving to one side to let an elderly man exit. His eyes flick in my direction. "Bonjour," I say, managing a smile, hoping to disarm any suspicions. A look of confusion crosses his face and I instantly regret not remaining quiet, fearful that my abysmal French accent will only make more obvious the fact that I do not belong. But foreigners are more the rule than the exception here, and the man nods, then shuffles down the walkway.

I move swiftly toward the door of the building, grabbing it before it closes. Inside, the lobby is simple and elegant, with a black-and-white tiled floor, a marble staircase curving upward. A large bowl of gardenias sits on the table in the center of the foyer, their perfumed aroma trying unsuccessfully to mask the musty older-building smell.

I peer up the staircase uncertainly. Despite my earlier hesitation, I have no choice, it seems, but to simply begin knocking on apartment doors. But where to begin? The top floor, I decide, picturing the elderly residents I've watched come and go these past two days. Perhaps since the building has no elevator, they are more likely to occupy the lower levels, leaving the upper floors to younger residents like the blond woman.

I start up the stairs, my heels echoing loudly. Each level has two separate apartments, I notice as I pass the second floor, then the third. But when I reach the fourth-floor landing, the apartment door farther down the hallway is open, painters working on ladders, readying an empty space for new residents. Only the near apartment appears to be occupied.

I pause before the mahogany door. I do not know if the woman lives here, or what I will say to her if she answers. But I have to try something. I raise my hand, lightly tap the brass knocker twice.

"Oui?" a young female voice calls. The door opens and the blond woman appears before me. I inhale sharply. So it is her apartment after all.

A look, surprise or confusion, maybe, flashes across her face before disappearing again. "Bonjour . . . "

I hesitate, wondering if I should try to speak French, then decide against it. "Hello . . . " I am suddenly at a loss for words. Behind the woman, the apartment is large, a sprawling open room with smooth wood floors, trim, modern furniture giving it an even more expansive feel. The far wall is lined with glass doors opening up to a balcony, framing a distant view of the sea. Jealousy washes over me as I imagine Jared here, sipping drinks on the balcony, laughing with this woman beneath the sparkling sun.

"May I help you?" the woman asks in accented English, now with an edge to her voice.

I study the scalloped edge of her crisp white blouse, trying to think of an alibi for my presence, a way to ease into the questions I need to ask. Finding none, I decide to be direct. "I'm looking for a man called Jared Short."

"I'm not familiar with him," she says, a second too quickly.

"Or maybe he isn't going by that name. Michael Laurent? Joseph McVey?" I ask, reciting the aliases I'd memorized from the file Mo gave me. I reach into my bag and pull a photo of Jared, taken on a crowded street sometime in the years since his disappearance, from the file.

She opens her mouth, eyes darting from the photograph to the ceiling, then back again. "I told you, I don't know him," she replies, her voice wavering.

I take a deep breath. "I know that Jared was here." The bluff is a calculated risk.

"You're wrong," she says forcefully, regaining her footing. Her terseness is more than mere annoyance, I decide instantly. She is nervous, perhaps hiding something. "This is my grandmother's apartment. I came here alone on holiday." For a second I almost believe her. But the décor does not bespeak an older person's home. "Now I really must ask you to leave."

I look down, contemplating my next move. Jared apparently isn't here and I can't force her to admit he has been. "Okay, but please tell Jared that I am looking for him." She starts to reply, but before she can deny knowing him again I raise my hand. "It's vitally important that I find him." I reach into my bag once more and hastily pull out the cell phone I purchased shortly after my arrival yesterday, then scribble the phone number on the back of an old receipt. "Ask him to call me," I say, handing the paper to her. "My name is Jordan Weiss."

She does not respond, but takes the paper from me and starts to close the door. Before she can disappear, I catch her gaze again.

This time, the look of fear in her eyes is unmistakable.

chapter TWO

I STRETCH ACROSS THE wide bed, watching the blades of the ceiling fan rotate slowly. The hotel, a few blocks west of the one I left this morning, is considerably less opulent, yet still comfortable in a relaxed sort of way. The smaller, sun-drenched room is modern and minimalist, with a cubed desk and beige chaise lounge. A fresh orchid sits in a lead crystal vase on the nightstand.

I run my hand along the smooth white duvet, picturing the blond woman as she stood in the doorway to the apartment. Who is she anyway, and what is her connection to Jared? From the time Mo told me Jared is alive, I have consciously avoided thinking about how he spent the years after we parted. Now jealousy rises in me unabated. Is she a girlfriend or lover? She could be just a friend—a very attractive friend. But the fear I saw in her eyes tells me there is something more. She wouldn't risk what it takes to protect Jared without a reason.

Of course, I don't know why a person does anything anymore. The illusion of logical motive was shattered for me a few nights ago when I crept into Mo's office at the embassy and learned the truth about Jared's death, the full extent of the conspiracy to bring me to

England. I had already found out through those last desperate days of investigation about the doctoral research that had put Jared's life in jeopardy. But only when confronted with proof of her involvement did Mo tell me everything: Jared had not drowned in the river that night a decade earlier but had faked his own death, disappearing steps ahead of the powerful forces determined to silence him. Fortunately their plan did not work; I found the information Jared had hidden and was able to turn it over to the authorities. And Jared himself is still out there somewhere, alive. At least that is my hope.

Mo, I think again, propping up my chin in my hands. A breeze blows in from the open patio door, rustling the sheer linen curtains, sending the wind chimes above jangling. How is it possible that one of my closest friends (one of my few friends, in point of fact) had lied to me and nearly gotten me killed? Not that hers was the only betrayal: Sebastian, the first man in a decade I could have really loved, proved to be a traitor, too.

Sarah's face pops into my mind. One person, at least, who I know with virtual certainty would never betray me. I cringe, picturing her lying in the hospital bed, pale and weak. She's had a hard enough time of it, fighting the disease that is ravaging her body with slow, calculated determination. But then she tried to help me find out the truth about Jared's supposed death, and it nearly got her killed.

She's home from the hospital now, thankfully. But I need to call her, see how she's doing. I roll over and grab my bag from the nightstand, pulling out the cell phone. I almost didn't buy it. The store did not have the prepaid type; it required a credit card, which would make me easier to track if anyone is looking for me. But I couldn't keep going indefinitely without one—Sarah, and my parents at least, need to be able to reach me. So I purchased the phone, swallowing my natural inclination to buy the cheapest model and splurging for a BlackBerry that gives me access to my email as well.

I dial Sarah's number from memory, tap the receiver as it rings a second time, then a third.

"Hallo," a male voice answers.

For a second I consider hanging up; Sarah's boyfriend, Ryan Giles, is a British police officer. Will he report my call if someone is looking for me? "Hello, Ryan," I say, deciding to take the chance. "It's Jordan Weiss."

"Jordan, how are you?" Hearing his concerned, affable tone, I am flooded with relief. He isn't going to turn me in. Of course not. His first loyalty is to Sarah, has been since the moment they met in the hospital a few weeks ago.

"I'm well. Is Sarah there?" I glance at the clock, remembering the afternoon nap that sometimes helps reinvigorate her. "I don't want to wake her if she's sleeping."

"Not at all. One moment."

There is a shuffling sound as the phone is passed and Sarah's crisp, South African accent crackles over the line. "Jordie, are you all right?"

"Absolutely fine," I reply quickly, wanting to erase the worry from her voice. I fight the urge to tell her where I am, for her protection as well as mine.

"Have you . . . ?"

Though she doesn't finish her question, I know she is asking if I've found Jared. "Not yet."

There is silence on the other end. Sarah has always been the friend who would never judge me, the picture of unconditional support. I could call her in the middle of the night and tell her I wanted to rappel down the side of the Empire State Building and she would

respond by asking what time should she be there, how much rope
should she bring. But I can tell that she's worried: she thinks my
quest to find Jared, hopping on a plane with nothing more than a
scrap of information is crazy, and she is concerned about me getting
my hopes up for what could be a fruitless search.

"I had Ryan check on Chris for you," she says at last, changing
the subject.

Guilt rises in me as I picture Jared's best friend, captain of our
close-knit college rowing team. Chris was the one who had brought
the mystery of Jared's death to me in the first place, insisting that
Jared's drowning in the river did not make sense. And he was right.
But as we searched for the truth behind who killed Jared, I grew
distrustful of Chris's motives. The fact that we slept together in the
middle of our search didn't help. I avoided him after that night, my
suspicion fueled by false clues fed to me by Sebastian. In the end, I
almost killed Chris, shooting him before learning that Sebastian had
set him up. Fortunately, the wound hadn't been fatal. "How is he?"

"He's getting much stronger. Should be out of the hospital in a
few days. He's been offered a chance to do a freelance piece by the
Times on what happened to him. Just the shooting and recovery
experience," she adds quickly. "Not the underlying investigation
stuff."

"That's amazing." Chris had been a world-class journalist until
his career and marriage were derailed by the ghosts that dogged us
both. "He deserves a fresh start."

"We all do," Sarah replies pointedly. I do not answer. I know
that she wishes I would give up my search for Jared and move on
with my life. "Anyway, Ryan told Chris you'd been called away for
work."

"Thanks," I reply. I hate that others have to lie for me, but I cannot share what I learned about Jared until I find him and see for myself. Then I'll be able to call Chris, tell him the truth, and put those ghosts to rest for both of us once and for all. "More important, how are you?" I ask.

"Really well," Sarah says, her voice brightening to the point where I almost believe her. "Maureen contacted me about the clinic in Geneva, told me that the arrangements and payment had already been made." She pauses and I hold my breath, praying that Sarah will not fight me on going for what might be her best and only chance against the disease. "Jordan, you didn't have to . . . " Her voice cracks. "I mean, in the middle of everything else you've been dealing with, to do this for me . . . "

"It was nothing," I say. Getting Mo to secure and fund Sarah's trip to the clinic had been part of the bargain, another concession I extracted in exchange for my silence. "So you're going?"

"Yes. Ryan's been able to get leave from work. We're leaving tomorrow."

I exhale quietly. "That's great news."

"Thanks to you." Her voice is full and sincere.

"Sar, can you do me a favor?"

"Of course," she replies quickly. "Anything."

"Call my parents. Tell them I've been sent somewhere else and that I'm fine. Don't tell them I've left State, though, okay? I'll call them myself as soon as I can."

"No worries; I'll do that right now. Promise me you'll be careful?"

"I will." I can tell that she is thinking of the thugs that were chasing me in England, the danger we both faced. "Talk soon, okay?"

"Love you," she says, hanging up before I can respond.

I hold the phone in my hand for several seconds, imagining

Sarah curled up in her flat with Ryan. Only days before she met him, she seemed so certain of never finding anyone, resolved to spend whatever time she had left alone. And then in the hospital she met a man who seemed to love her instantly and without hesitation, despite the challenges her condition brings. They never would have found each other without the attack that hospitalized her, the investigation that brought me to England under false pretenses.

Despite my tremendous happiness for her, I cannot help but feel a slight tug of jealousy. She, at least, is not alone whereas I . . . sadness washes over me, catching me off guard. What's wrong with me? I've spent the past decade on my own, except for an occasional fling, and it's never bothered me before. Is it my recent brush with Sebastian, the way I nearly opened up and allowed myself to like him? No, it's something more than that—the realization that Jared is alive, the possibility of seeing him again, has stirred emotions in me that I'd long forgotten: desire, hope. And those feelings are more terrifying than anything I can remember.

But alongside my excitement at the prospect of seeing Jared again, negative thoughts intrude. The fact that Jared is alive means that the past ten years of my life, every thought I had and decision I made, was predicated upon a flawed assumption. An image flashes through my mind, quick and unbidden: the bright lights of a doctor's office, a metal table icy cold beneath my thin gown. I hold up my hand as if to shield my eyes from the vision, banished from my conscious mind for years. Stop. I push the memory away. I cannot do this. Not now.

I put the cell phone back in my bag. Sarah's skepticism at my quest echoes back at me. What am I doing here? I hopped on a plane at a moment's notice, driven by impulse and an address where someone claimed to have seen Jared once in the near past. Hardly the solid lead or thorough investigating my training as a State Department intelligence officer had taught me to rely upon.

I reach for my bag once more and pull out the file Mo gave me to recheck the documents, to see if there is anything I missed. The envelope with the traveler's checks slides out with it and as I start to return it to the bag, I feel something hard inside. I turn the envelope upside down and a ring tumbles onto the bed.

I pick it up hurriedly, recognizing it at first touch. It is an engagement ring, the one Jared had purchased but never given to me. I found it in the bank vault in Cambridge when I was searching for clues about his supposed death. At first, I thought it was just sentimental, evidence that his feelings for me had been deeper than a college romance, that we might have had a life together if given the chance. It was not until Sebastian confronted me that final night by the Thames and demanded I give the ring to him that I realized the truth—Jared had left it behind as a message, engraved inside with the bank account number that would lead me to the information he had hidden.

I study the ring now, puzzled. What is it doing here? I turned it over after the police came to apprehend Sebastian, knowing that it would be an important part of the investigation. I can't imagine the strings Mo must have pulled to have it released from evidence and sent to me, further proof of her repentance for what she had done.

I turn the ring over in my palm. It is a simple white gold band, a single perfect stone. Exactly the style I would have picked, one that would feel more like a part of me than the jewelry I seldom wore. But beyond the physical beauty, it is all that the ring represents—the life that Jared and I might have shared, the promise unfulfilled—that takes my breath away.

I hold the ring a moment longer, contemplating what to do with it. I don't feel right wearing it on my finger; after all, Jared never actually proposed. But I would like to keep it close and safe.

I tuck it away in my pocket, turning my attention to the file. I've been through it all a dozen times, of course, at Heathrow before my flight took off, on the plane, and again when I arrived here. There isn't much to it, just a few intelligence reports as to Jared's whereabouts over the years. Putting them in chronological order, I can trace a vague path of where he had been: in Buenos Aires about six months after his purported death in 1998, then Belize and Chile and Paraguay. There seems to be gap of a few years before he turned up again in 2003, this time in Zimbabwe. Was he just moving around to avoid being caught or was there something more? What had he done for work, for money?

There are a handful of photographs as well, grainy black-and-white images either affixed to the photocopied reports or freestanding. I fan them out across the bed, studying the images. Most are of a Jared I do not recognize, with longer hair and a thick beard, often wearing sunglasses or a cap pulled low at the brow. But there is a picture, the one I had shown to the blond woman, of Jared on a crowded street, where he is clean shaven, his face exposed. I run my hand over his cheeks, his haunted eyes. Is he as afraid now as he looks in this photograph?

Holding it closer, I notice for the first time that there is something on his shoulder, close to his neck. A hand. I scan the image of the crowd behind him. Though it is out of focus, I can make out a woman peering over his shoulder. My breath catches. Her hair was shorter and her eyes eclipsed by sunglasses, but the shape of her chin is unmistakable.

It's the blond woman from the apartment. The one who said she had never seen Jared.

I sit up, my suspicions confirmed. The woman was lying. She was with him when this photograph was taken. Confronted with the image, she won't be able to deny knowing him. Grabbing my bag, I jump up and race from the hotel room, the photo still clutched in my hand.

On the street, I retrace my steps hurriedly. The address Mo gave me is proving to be a good lead after all. Perhaps Jared is even here in Monaco. I stop, nearly thrown backward by the thought. Doubtful. If he had been at the apartment, he surely would not have remained hidden from me. Maybe he is close, though, somewhere in this very city.

I start walking again, fighting the urge to break into a run. When I reach the block where the apartment building is located, my eyes flick toward the café, then down the street in both directions, searching for the man I'd seen earlier, checking if he has returned. But he isn't there.

I hurry to the door of the apartment building and scan the buzzers, too impatient to wait for someone to open the door this time. *Boucheau,* the name beside the bottom button reads. Is that the blond woman? I press the button twice quickly, holding my breath as several seconds pass. Hearing no response, I push the button second from the bottom, marked with the name *Martine.*

The speaker beside the buttons crackles. "Oui?" The voice is female, but deeper and too old to be the same woman I met earlier.

I hesitate, disappointed. Perhaps it is the bell for another apartment. But it doesn't matter; I just need to get into the building. "Delivery," I say, crossing my fingers. There is a pause and then a click as the door unlocks.

Breathless, I climb the stairs to the top floor and knock at the apartment door for the second time today. There is a heavy shuffling sound on the other side, growing louder. My heart pounds. Those could be a man's footsteps . . . perhaps even Jared's.

But the door opens and a stout, white-haired woman in a housekeeper's work dress appears. "Oui?" she says again. She wipes her hands on her apron, then holds them out expectantly for the delivery.

I take a deep breath, hoping she understands English. "The woman who lives here . . . " I raise my hand to my own dark locks. "Blond?"

The housekeeper's forehead wrinkles and she shakes her head, not understanding. Then I remember the photograph I am holding. "Her." I hold out the picture and point. The woman's eyes flicker with recognition. "Is she here?"

She chews on her lip and for a minute I wonder if she will try to lie as well. "Nicole?"

Now the blond woman has a name. "Oui, Nicole." She looks over her shoulder and I hold my breath, waiting for her to step aside and summon Nicole to the door.

But she shakes her head again and raises her arms, flapping them as though flying. Then she points to the sky, managing a single word in English: "Gone."

chapter THREE

G ONE?" MY VOICE rises with disbelief.
     The housekeeper's eyes narrow, her face suspicious. "Excuse me," I say, forcing a smile and trying again. "I'm a friend of Nicole's and she mentioned she would be home today." Her expression remains unchanged. "May I use the toilet?" Before she can answer, I slip past her, my gaze locking on the bedroom that occupies the left end of the flat. The bed is impeccably made but the rest of the area is a mess, doors of a wood armoire flung wide open, clothes hanging out of the drawers. I try to recall the flat as I'd seen it over Nicole's shoulder earlier. It had been neat, no indication of such disarray. No, wherever Nicole went, she packed and left in a hurry.

I start toward the bed, ignoring the protestations of the maid behind me in French, presumably informing me that the toilet is at the other end of the flat. Studying the mess, my mind races: Where had Nicole gone? But the strewn clothing, arbitrarily scattered, offers no clues.

I step back, exasperated. Something dark catches my eye, sticking out from beneath the bed. I kneel down. It is the toe of a man's brown oxford.

"Oh, grandmother," I mutter, pulling out the shoe and holding it up. "What big feet you have." The shoe is a size eleven—Jared's size.

Easy, I think. There's no telling if it is Jared's shoe, or how long it has been lying there. I set it down and stand up, then turn back to face the maid. "Where?" I ask, mimicking her flying gesture. But she stares back mutely, either not knowing or refusing to say where Nicole has gone.

I walk to the bathroom at the other end of the flat and close the door. Inside, the sink has been swept clean of all toiletries, but the hand towel is damp and freshly used. Continuing my charade, I flush the toilet before stepping out of the bathroom, scanning the room once more for clues. Nicole could not have gotten too far. Without speaking further, I walk quickly from the apartment.

Outside, I turn right and race toward the taxi stand at the corner where the street intersects with a larger thoroughfare. I climb into the backseat of the first awaiting cab, which is clean but smells faintly of stale cigar smoke. "Côte d'Azur Airport, please." It is a calculated risk, assuming that Nicole really was planning to fly somewhere, as the housekeeper said.

As we pull out into traffic, I sink back against the seat, my mind racing. Nicole disappeared, not an hour after I confronted her. Maybe her trip was planned. But the woman I saw, carrying groceries into the apartment, gave no indication of an imminent journey. No, her hurried departure was almost certainly a result of my conversation with her. I wonder where she is going, whether Jared will be waiting there for her when she arrives.

Forty-five minutes later, we near the airport. Traffic slows as we approach the terminal, a line of cars and vans snaking their way beneath the DEPARTURES sign. Hurry, I think, digging my nails into my palms, willing the queue to move more quickly. The air is warm and thick with exhaust fumes.

The driver glances in his rearview mirror, asks me something in French. I shake my head. "Terminal One?" He points to the building closest to us. There are two terminals, and I have no idea from which Nicole might fly.

"Oui," I say, resigned. I have a fifty-fifty shot at being right.

Finally, we reach the curb and I pay the driver and leap out, weaving through a group of Japanese tourists clustered around a guide. Inside, the terminal is modern, walls of large paned glass, a ceiling of exposed steel beams. Business travelers toting laptop cases and compact rolling suitcases scurry in all directions, passing the young backpackers who lounge on benches and on the floor against the walls. Over the loudspeaker a woman's voice announces flight information in French, then English, last call for a plane to Amsterdam.

I search the terminal. Where is Nicole? With her head start, she could already be boarding a plane, or even gone by now.

Across the concourse, my eyes lock on a blond head bobbing through the crowd, a woman moving toward the security checkpoint. I begin pushing my way toward her but as I draw closer, the woman half turns and I can see that, although well preserved, she is about three decades too old to be Nicole.

Pausing, I contemplate my next move. I need to get past security to the gates and that will require buying a ticket to somewhere in order to get a boarding pass. I scan the ticket kiosks, starting toward the far end, where the lines appear to be shortest.

I approach the Air France counter. The woman looks up. "Oui?"

"A ticket . . . to Paris," I say, trying to come up with the least expensive destination. "One way."

The woman clacks at her keyboard for several seconds. "Seven hundred twelve euros," she says finally.

My eyes widen. I had not anticipated spending so much money on a plane ticket I wasn't even going to use. But I have no choice. As I reach for my wallet, I remember the photograph of Nicole, still clutched in my hand. I smooth it and hold it up to the woman behind the desk. "Have you seen her?"

Her eyes flick to the photo, then back to the computer screen, and she shakes her head. "Or perhaps you can look her up for me," I say, seizing the idea. "Her name is Nicole . . . " I stop, realizing I do not know Nicole's surname, then decide to take a chance on the name I saw on the door buzzer. "Martine. I need to know her destination."

The woman looks up, visibly annoyed. "I can't do that. A passenger's information is private."

"But . . . " I notice then a young baggage handler behind the counter, watching us out of the corner of his eye.

"Do you want to purchase the ticket or not?" the clerk asks impatiently.

There's no point in buying a ticket, I decide, without knowing Nicole's destination or even which terminal she is departing. "N-no, thank you." I step aside, looking once again at the baggage handler, who has moved several feet to the right but is still watching me out of the corner of his eye. I inch my way through the crowd to the end of the row of kiosks, my gaze locked with his. A minute later he sidles toward me, holding out a bag. "That's not mine . . . " I start to say, then realize he is pretending to help me.

His eyes dart in both directions. "You are looking for someone?" he asks in accented English.

I nod, holding up the photo. "Have you seen this woman?"

"Two hundred euros."

I hesitate. I'm loath to spend more of my quickly disappearing cash, but if this man can really tell me where she's going, it will be worth it. I open my mouth to protest, then close it again and reach in my bag, hand him one hundred. "The other half after you help me. The name is Nicole Martine." He starts to type on the keyboard, then stops, looking up again. "If you could please hurry . . ."

The man does not respond, but stares over my shoulder. My frustration grows. "Look, if you can't—"

"There." He nods and I follow his gaze. "Is her, no?"

At the far end of the concourse, smoothing her hair as she emerges from the ladies' room, is Nicole.

I start after her, hearing the protestations of the baggage clerk, demanding the rest of his money, behind me. "Nicole!"

Seeing me, she stops, her hand suspended in midair. She glances over my shoulder, calculating whether there is an escape route, how quickly she can get away. Her face falls. "Jordan . . ." There is a familiarity to her voice that tells me earlier today was not the first time she heard my name.

"You said you didn't know him," I say, blocking her path and holding up the photograph, now nearly a crumpled ball in my sweaty fist. "You lied."

Several expressions seem to cross her face at once, surprise, denial, then finally resignation. "You would have done the same."

I know then that Jared has told Nicole who I am, what we were to one another. Who is she to have his confidence and trust?

But there is no time for jealousy. Nicole is looking over my shoulder again toward the security checkpoint, clutching her passport with white knuckles. "Is Jared all right?" I demand. "Where is he? Can I see him?"

She glances in both directions and exhales sharply. "Jared's fine," she says in a low voice.

My heart leaps. Jared is fine. Alive. "Where is he?" I repeat.

"I can't tell you that. But he's nowhere near here. And if you care about him, if you ever cared about him, you'll leave him alone."

I watch in disbelief as she starts toward the gates, handing her passport to the security official and placing her bag on the conveyor belt. "Wait," I call as she starts through the metal detector. She turns back. "Will you tell him, at least, that you saw me? I mean, that I'm trying to find him?"

A look I cannot decipher crosses Nicole's face. Without answering, she spins and steps through the metal detector.

"Wait!" I cry, louder this time. But she is already on the other side, too far away to hear me even if she were willing to listen. I take a step forward, then stop again as she vanishes into the crowd. I'll never get through security without a ticket and by the time I buy one, she'll be gone.

I look up at the DEPARTURES board, scanning the flights bound for various points in Europe and North Africa. But there is no way to guess which one might be Nicole's. I turn back toward the Air France counter, but the baggage handler has disappeared.

I hesitate, then start toward the door; leaving the airport means acknowledging that Nicole has gotten away, but there's nothing more to be learned here. Resigned, I climb into a cab and give the driver the address to the hotel.

As the taxi pulls from the airport, I gaze up at the sky, watching a plane ascend through a lone cloud. I imagine Nicole disembarking at some nameless destination to find Jared waiting for her, see her enveloped in Jared's welcoming arms. My jealousy grows. Being re-united with Jared is *my* dream; the woman in the vision is supposed to be me, not her. Easy, I think. I do not know the nature of their relationship, whether they are involved.

I bring my hands to my temples, pressing against the pinch of a headache. My chase was not a failure in one respect: Jared is okay; Nicole had confirmed that much. But her acknowldgment that he is out there somewhere makes not being able to find him even more painful. The dull ache that has been gnawing at my stomach since leaving Mo's office the other night seems to swell and burst open.

What now? My only hope is to go back to Nicole's apartment, see if I can learn anything more from the maid.

When we pull up in front of the apartment building, I pay the driver and step out onto the street. The sun has dipped behind the tall buildings, and the palm trees silhouette coolly against the pavement. Across the street, the café is bustling now, filled with afternoon patrons. I scan the crowd, half-expecting to see the man sitting at the table behind his newspaper once more. But he is not there.

At the entrance to the building, I press the buzzer for Nicole's apartment, hold my breath. A second later, I push it again, but there is no answer.

The housekeeper must have gone for the day. I lean wearily against the doorframe as the pinch in my temples swells to a throb. There is a slight creaking sound. Looking down, I see that the front door to the building is slightly ajar. Whoever left last (it could have been me, rushing to the airport) had not pulled the latch securely. This one break, the first I have had today, fills me with renewed energy.

I enter the building, take the stairs two at a time to the fourth floor, and knock on the door to Nicole's apartment, listening for the housekeeper's heavy gait. I rap my fist against the door, harder this time. My own knock echoes back at me, followed by silence.

I step back, leaning against the railing to the stairway below. I need to find out where Nicole has gone and I can't afford to wait until tomorrow to see if the housekeeper returns. Time is of the essence: with every minute that passes, Nicole is farther away, my chances of finding her diminished. And if the man from the café really is following me, then staying in Monaco much longer is surely a mistake. No, I must see if there are any clues to Nicole's whereabouts and get out of this town one way or the other. If only I could look inside the apartment, search for information as to where she has gone. I reach down, twist the doorknob, but it does not turn.

Can I get in? The sudden thought catches me by surprise. I have broken into places twice, not counting Mo's office at the embassy when I sneaked in to review my file last week: once to an apartment in Liberia, another time to an office building in San Salvador. Unlike this, both were for assignments, sanctioned at least by some part of our government. Do I dare try it now on my own?

I reach down, try the knob once more. But the lock is brass plated, the door solid oak. I cannot break in here.

A strange odor tickles my nose. Fresh paint. I turn toward the vacant apartment down the hall, remembering the workers I had seen there earlier. Perhaps if one of them has a master key, I can persuade him to let me into Nicole's apartment. Cautiously, I make my way toward the open doorway. "Hello," I call, my voice echoing in the emptiness. I push the door open slowly. Inside, it is the same layout as Nicole's in a mirror image, the bedroom to the far right instead of left.

I step inside, my skin prickling as I wait to be confronted as to why I am here. But the paint trays have been cleaned and neatly stacked in the corner, the workers gone for the day. I walk gingerly around the ladders, across the tarps that cover the floor, aiming for the terrace.

I open the door and peer outside. The balcony is long and narrow, running several feet in either direction beyond the opening. To the left sits Nicole's apartment, the wrought-iron fences of the two balconies separated by a few feet of space. A fountain bubbles in the courtyard below.

I could climb over, I think, try to get into Nicole's apartment that way. But the gap is nearly three feet wide, with a four-story drop to the ground below. And even if I do make it, the other balcony door is probably locked. The French doors look old, though, with a lock that is probably not that hard to break into.

I stop, caught off guard by the callousness of the thought. Who am I? Once, not long ago, I had boundaries and principles, despite the dangers and ambiguities of my line of work. But that changed when Mo told me the truth about Jared and what they had done to me. It was as if the sky fell and everything I knew was turned upside down. Now, standing on the balcony of this strange apartment days later, the magnitude of the shift crashes down upon me. The person I became that night would do whatever she had to do in order to get what she wanted, without regard for the rules, because no one else played by them and doing so only put her at a needless disadvantage.

Of course, what I am contemplating is not some theoretical moral debate. The risks are real and deadly serious. If I can cross to the other balcony and get in, I will be breaking and entering in a foreign country, this time without the protection of diplomatic immunity. But I've come too far to turn back.

I look through the palm trees, scanning the apartment building across the courtyard to check if anyone is watching. Seeing no one, I go to the end of the balcony closest to Nicole's and throw my bag across, wincing at the loud thumping sound it makes as it lands. I hoist one leg over the railing, climb carefully onto the ledge. Taking a deep breath, I reach out and jump, aiming for the far side of Nicole's balcony. I fall short, smacking painfully against the outer edge, clinging to the top of the railing with both arms. Groaning, I hoist myself over, one leg at a time.

The housekeeper really needs to clean out here, I think, trying unsuccessfully to brush the large dirt streaks from my pants. I check the opposite building once more to make sure no one is watching, then turn toward the glass door, peering through the thin, filmy curtains into Nicole's apartment. The housekeeper seems to have straightened up, and put the scattered clothing back into the armoire. But otherwise the room appears unchanged, empty.

There could be an alarm system, I realize. I've had a little training in disarming those, a quick tutorial by my colleague Lincoln, who is one of the best at it, but I'm by no means an expert. I cannot see any sensors or other signs that the door is alarmed, though.

I push against the door, but it does not move. I reach into my bag for a credit card and slide it into the doorframe. Too hard, I realize, rummaging in my wallet for another card that will bend enough to get around the bolt yet still be firm enough to move it. I pull out an old VIP card from a rental car agency and try again, wondering as I maneuver it if it will work. Finally I hear a pop. Flinching at the loud noise, I tug hurriedly at the door, which opens with a squeal.

I pause, holding my breath, listening for voices or other signs of life on the other side of the door. Then I step inside, scanning the apartment. A hint of perfume that I recognize as Nicole's mixes with the lemony scent of a freshly washed floor. My gaze stops on a desk that sits along the far wall and I start toward it. The top of the desk is bare, an unused planner in the upper right corner, a cup of pens to the left. I open the lone drawer, but it is empty except for some rubber bands and a box of staples. I picture Jared's desk at college, piled high with books and notes. Clearly he has not spent much time here.

My eyes lower to the ground, fix on the wastebasket, which the housekeeper neglected to empty. Hurriedly, I drop to my knees. As I begin to rifle through the trash, there is a shuffling sound behind me, quick and light like a cat. I freeze. Someone is here.

Instinctively, I reach for my gun, then remember that I no longer have one. I start to straighten, but before I can fully stand, hands grab my throat, close around it.

A man, I can tell, from the size and strength of the grip. My mind reels back to the nighttime confrontation at Embankment in London a few weeks earlier, Sebastian's hands pressing hard on my carotid artery as he tried to strangle me.

Desperately, I lurch backward, feeling for my attacker's instep. Caught off guard by my movement, he loosens his grip. I pull away and he falls into me, his weight heavy on my back. We hurtle forward together, and as we crash toward the ground, I see the corner of the desk rising up to meet me. I try to raise my hand, but before I can shield myself, my head crashes into the hard wood, exploding with searing white pain.

For a second I am too stunned to move. Then I bring my hand to my throbbing temple and blink several times, willing the bright spots to clear from my eyes. The man lies heavy on top of me. Inhaling a mixture of aftershave and sweat, I remember his hands around my throat.

Panicked, I scramble to get out from beneath him. Weight lifts off me as he rolls away. I struggle to sit up, and as I do, a wave of recognition washes over me. Lying sprawled across my legs is the man from the café.

What is he doing here? I wonder whether he could possibly live in the apartment, too, if he perhaps attacked me thinking I was a burglar. I try to come up with a plausible explanation as to what I am doing, why I have broken in. But he does not seem to be angry or even interested. Instead, he stands up, eyes darting between me and the doorway, contemplating the best way to flee. No, he doesn't belong here anymore than I do. He must have followed me.

"Wait," I say as he starts for the door. Though my initial instinct is to get as far away from him as possible, my curiosity wins out. Why would he attack me one minute, then flee the next? He stops, turns back. "What are you doing here?"

"I could ask you the same thing," he replies evenly, his English accented. "The balcony is a most interesting entranceway."

We stare at each other awkwardly. "I saw you earlier at the café across the street," I offer, rubbing the spot on my forehead where a lump has begun to form.

"I was reading the newspaper and having a coffee. People do that."

"You were *pretending* to read the paper," I correct. "But you were really watching this building. Now you're in an apartment that isn't yours, knocking strange women unconscious."

"You don't belong here, either. And you startled me coming in that way." Despite the situation, his tone is challenging, a refusal to back down. But he still hasn't explained what he is doing here, or why he tried to strangle me. "I didn't mean for you to fall and hit your head," he adds, a hint of remorse creeping into his voice. "I was just trying to put you out long enough for me to get away." Put me out. Nice. "Are you all right?"

He takes a step toward me and I rear back. "Why are you following me?" I persist. He opens his mouth but before he can answer, I raise my hand. "Don't deny it. Just tell me who you are working for and what it is that you want."

The man hesitates and his expression is so sincerely confused that for a moment I wonder if I am wrong. "I'm not following you."

Middle Eastern, I decide, listening to the thickness of his vowels. "Then what are you doing here?"

"The woman," he replies. "The one you were watching from the café. You followed her into the apartment building."

He had noticed me also. My surveillance skills really must be getting rusty. I open my mouth to deny that I was following Nicole. Then, remembering where we are, the fact that I just broke in, I realize it is futile. "Yes," I admit. "I'm looking for the woman who lives here. I spoke to her earlier but then she took off, and I don't know where. I was searching for clues."

"As was I."

So he is following Nicole, too, or so he claims. But how did he get in here? And why? He could be trying to find Jared, I remind myself, and not for good reasons. "She's gone," I reply.

"I know. Any idea where?"

I shake my head. "I saw her for a second at the airport." I feel foolish admitting that I got that close and let her slip away. "I don't know where she was going, but she had a passport," I offer.

He waves a hand. "This isn't the States, where people show a driver's license at security on their way to Disneyland. Everyone in Europe travels with a passport." His tone is dismissive and condescending, causing me to instantly dislike him. At the same time, I am relieved that he thinks I am just another bumbling American. He does not seem to know who I am or the kind of work I have done. "Anyhow, it's just a few kilometers to the border. She could have been traveling by bicycle and odds are she would have been going somewhere international."

I decide to ignore his sarcasm. "Now why don't you tell me . . . " I begin. I stop again, noticing a folded paper in his right hand. "What's that?"

He looks at me evenly. "And why, exactly, should I tell you?"

I falter, searching for an answer. He has a point. "Because we both seem to be searching for the same thing," I reply, changing tactics, recalling the skills that I used to persuade foreign agents to work as assets for our government. The key was always to establish common purpose. "Maybe we can help each other."

He purses his lips, causing dimples to appear in his right cheek and chin. "Maybe. I guess that depends on what we are looking for and why. Something, I think, that neither of us are prepared to discuss here. Why don't we talk about it over dinner tonight?"

"No," I blurt. "I mean, I don't know you. You just attacked me, for God's sake . . . "

"How about drinks, then?" he persists.

I stare at him in disbelief. The nature of the social occasion is not really the issue here. Anyway, I don't have time. I have to find Jared.

"Like you said, maybe we can help each other. You don't have any idea where to find this woman," he continues. "I am, as they say, your best lead."

"No thanks," I reply firmly. I have no intention of spending any more time with this man who just attacked me.

His shoulders lower slightly and he reaches into his pocket, pulls out a piece of paper, and scribbles something on it before handing it to me. "Call me if you change your mind."

Then, before I can respond, he turns and walks from the apartment.

chapter **FOUR**

A HALF HOUR LATER I enter my hotel room and throw myself across the bed, still shaken from my encounter with the man in Nicole's apartment. I lingered only for a minute after he left, rifling through the wastebasket but finding nothing. Then I left hurriedly, fearing that someone might have heard the commotion, and I took an indirect route back to the hotel in case the man decided to follow me. But I had seen no sign of him. Who was he, and what did he really want? Perhaps he was, as he said, just looking for Nicole.

My temple begins to throb. I need to take some aspirin before this thing turns into a full-blown migraine, and I know better than to do that on an empty stomach. Eyeing the room service menu that sits on the night table, I pick it up and flip quickly through, cringing at the higher-than-expected prices, the exchange rate that is so much worse than I remembered. I can feel my bank account back in Washington beginning to creak under the weight of my newfound independence.

Not that money has ever been a comfortable subject for me, I muse, as I set down the menu and rummage through my bag for the half-eaten package of crackers I stashed there yesterday. Growing up, I didn't give much thought to whether we were rich or poor—we lived in a modest but comfortable subdivision outside town where one house was indiscernible from the next, and I wore the same sturdy, nondesigner clothes from discount stores as most of the other kids at my public school.

It wasn't until I got to college in Washington and found myself living among classmates with foreign cars and elaborate stereos in their dorm rooms that I first understood the different financial strata. I quickly became self-conscious about my own lack of means. In the end, the struggle was a good one: I worked at part-time jobs at law firms and think tanks that exposed me to the vibrant political side of the city instead of joining a sorority and drinking at parties. But there was always a sense of being chased, searching for the cash machine that would let you withdraw a ten dollar bill instead of a twenty, consulting the checkbook before agreeing to split a pizza. Only later at Cambridge, living on a generous graduate fellowship, was I able to blend in among the wealthy students and be free from those worries.

The State Department had proven to be a good deal financially, too—with my housing costs covered overseas, I paid no rent for most of the past ten years, which enabled me to sock away a small nest egg, even on my modest government salary. But the eight months I spent in Washington before being reassigned to London had been pricey, the steep cost of living eating into my savings.

And now I have no income at all. For the first time in years, the specter of financial trouble comes crashing down upon me. How long will my savings last, and what will I do when the money is gone?

I lift the engagement ring, which now hangs from a white gold chain around my neck. As always, my heart quickens. I could pawn it, live off the money for weeks or even months. I considered the idea on my way back to the hotel, going into a store that bought jewelry and antiques. But I'd lost my nerve, instead buying the chain to hold the ring.

Studying it now, my desire to find Jared is stronger than ever. But how? I reach into my bag and pull out the cell phone. I hold it in my palm, contemplating. I need another lead. There has to be something I can do, someone I can ask for help. For a minute I consider calling Mo, raising the stakes of our bargain, demanding more information from her in exchange for my continued silence. But I don't want her to know that I have come up empty so soon after starting out on my search, and I doubt she has anything else to tell me, even if she wanted to help.

The Director, I think, seeing his thinning hair and Coke-bottle glasses. Paul Van Antwerpen was my other mentor at State, one of the most senior intelligence figures in government. An image pops into my mind of the last time we met, when I stormed into his office a few weeks earlier, demanding to be reassigned from Washington to London to be near Sarah. He seemed genuinely surprised, not at my desire to leave the prestigious assignment as his liaison to the National Security Council (he knew I belonged overseas), but at the request of a post I had always avoided.

What assignment had he planned for me next, I wonder, if I hadn't insisted on the transfer to London? He would have known, of course. Van Antwerpen was like a great chess master, thinking a half dozen moves ahead, months or even years down the line, his strategy calculated but malleable in case contingencies changed the options or objectives. Though I fancied myself a key piece on his chess-board, I am certain that when I took myself out of the game to be with Sarah, he would have simply used another piece for his next move. Yet despite the cool, professional distance Van Antwerpen kept, I always knew I could count on him if I were in real trouble. But I had resigned, left the Department without so much as a phone call. No, contacting him is out of the question now.

I need help. There has to be someone else I can call.

Lincoln, I think suddenly. His smiling brown face pops into my mind. Lincoln Heller was in my A-100 class, the group of new officers with whom I'd entered the Foreign Service almost a decade ago. We spent nine weeks together in an orientation consisting of lectures on everything from surviving a motorcade ambush to working a room at a reception. Our group of thirty new recruits, ranging from young people just out of college to older folks pursuing second careers, had bonded well despite our diverse backgrounds, cooking meals at one another's apartments, taking weekend excursions to sites like Gettysburg and Shenandoah. And most of us had stayed in touch over the years while scattered across the globe on various assignments.

Lincoln had been part of our A-100 class—except that he actually hadn't. On the first day, during an icebreaker exercise where we had to interview the person seated beside us and introduce him or her to the group, he revealed to me that he was in fact CIA, the first of several operatives I'd meet using State Department as a cover. His identity was soon shared with the class, kept a trusted secret by all of us.

Though our roles were different and our assignments continents apart, Lincoln and I had stayed close over the years. He had risen quickly through the agency since then, been successful on a number of key jobs in the field. A few years ago, he reluctantly accepted a desk job back in Washington because he couldn't bear the lengthy separations from his wife, Arlene, and their two daughters that field-work necessitated. I had been to their house in Bethesda for dinner last year, a few months after I arrived in Washington.

I dial his number at Langley from memory, hesitating before entering the last digit. I don't know if he can help me, but at least I can trust him not to tell anyone we've spoken. I hit the send key. "Heller," he says a half ring later, his baritone rich but reserved.

At the familiar sound of his voice, I exhale quietly. "Lincoln, it's Jordan."

"Jordan!" His voice seems to expand, overflowing the cell phone and filling the hotel room. "How are you?"

I glance at my watch. It's nearly noon back home and I imagine him sipping coffee at his desk, reading the daily reports. "Am I catching you at a bad time?"

"Not at all. But where are you? I heard you left unexpectedly."

Alarm rises in me. How does he know? The Department is a small world; a requisition to terminate my housing or return my laptop could have set the rumor mill spinning. Still, I had not counted on word getting around so quickly. "We would have liked to have you over before you went," he adds.

He's talking about my departure from Washington for London, I realize with relief, not the more recent news that I subsequently resigned altogether. "I'm sorry I didn't get to say good-bye in person; it was all very sudden. It's a long story and I promise to fill you in sometime." I pause, wondering how much more to share. I need to level with him to some extent in order to ask for his help. I take a deep breath. "There's more to it, I'm afraid: now I've left London . . . and State, too."

"I don't understand."

"I've resigned."

There is no response. "We've got a bad connection," he says several seconds later. "Call me back at 703-555-7976. Give me five minutes first, okay?"

"All right." I push the disconnect button, staring at the phone, confused by his abrupt change in demeanor. Was it a mistake to call him? Perhaps Lincoln is too much of a company man to talk to me when I'm out on my own. And even if he is willing to help, I never should have put him in this position. For a second I consider not calling him back, but it's too late for that.

Two minutes pass, then three. Finally, I dial the number he gave me, hold my breath as it rings several times. "Jordan?" His voice comes over the line, breathless. "Sorry, I wanted to get off my work phone." I can tell by the background noise that he has stepped outside with his cell. "What happened? Are you okay?"

"I'm fine," I say. It's mostly, if not entirely, true.

I hear him light one of the cigarettes he was supposed to have given up long ago. Arlene would kill him if she knew. "Then why on earth did you leave . . . ?" he asks, after taking a long drag. His tone suggests that he finds the notion of quitting inconceivable. There were people in our A-100 class that we knew wouldn't stay long, dilettantes trying out diplomatic life for a tour or maybe two, who had the credentials but not the stamina for the transient lifestyle in the long run. But Lincoln and I had been different. We were lifers from the start; we had found our place in our strange, respective institutions, taken naturally to the work. We were willing to make the sacrifices that constantly moving around the globe entailed as the price for the excitement and high of the job, and we would ride the career as far as it took us. Or so we thought. Now he was working a Washington desk, living vicariously through the younger officers out in the field. I, on the other hand, had quit entirely. He knew it had to be something very big to get me to leave.

"Um, it's kinda out there." I bite my lip, trying to come up with a short version. "I asked for London to be with a sick friend from college. But it turns out that someone set me up."

"Seriously? Who?"

I hesitate, wanting to say more than I am able. "Let's just say it was people well above our pay grade."

"Now why would anyone do that?" he asks patiently, as though talking to a young child, more than a trace of skepticism in his voice.

"It's a long story, but it has to do with my college boyfriend, Jared Short."

I can hear him light another cigarette. "Jared," he says slowly. "Isn't he the one who . . . ?"

"Died? Yeah, that's what I thought." I can hear the coldness in my own voice. "Only it turns out that was a lie, too." But that was Jared's lie, I think, suddenly angry at him for the first time.

There is silence on the other end and I imagine Lincoln struggling with my explanation, wanting to tell me it cannot possibly be true. But he's been in this business long enough to know that it is entirely plausible—each of us is expendable for the right price in someone else's game.

"So I quit the Department and now I'm going to find him," I say finally.

"Wouldn't a leave of absence . . . ?" he begins, then stops again. Lincoln will not, I realize gratefully, try to talk me out of it, even if he thinks I am crazy. Like Sarah, he's one of the few people I could count on that way. "What do you need me to do?" he asks, knowing without my having to say so that I am calling for help.

"I need you to run a profile for me—if you can do it. I don't want to get you into trouble."

"No problem; who is it?"

"Nicole Martine," I say, going with the surname on the door buzzer, the only one I have. "I think she's French. She was staying at apartment number 12 rue des Lilas in Monaco. She knows Jared, though how I'm not yet sure. I'm interested in information on her activities, whereabouts, known addresses, everything."

There is a pause and I know he is wondering who she is, her connection to Jared. "Do you want me to run a search on Jared, too?"

I quickly measure the risk. Jared's research clearly put him on intelligence radar years ago, and there might be more out there than what Mo had to give me, but I don't want to draw attention to him. "If you can do it without raising any red flags. Mo said she gave me everything she had, but it can't hurt to check."

"I'll be discreet," he promises. I give him Jared's aliases from the file as well. "Okay, I need to get back inside for a meeting, but I'll run the profiles as soon as I can. Shall I call you?"

"Sure. And if there's anything you want to send, here's my email." I recite the address of my Hotmail account, the one I created last year in Washington so I could keep the jokes my parents liked to send separate from my official business. "Thanks so much. My love to Arlene and the girls."

I hang up, then roll over to stare at the ceiling, curious what he will find. Maybe nothing, and then what? The man from the apartment appears in my mind and I wonder for the hundredth time who he is, what he wants with Nicole.

On impulse, I pull out the scrap of paper he handed me, then hesitate, remembering his invitation to meet. The last thing I want to do is see him again, but I'm not likely to get anything else done tonight and it's probably worth an hour of my time in a public place to see what he knows.

I dial the number. I don't even know his name, I panic. But before I can hang up, there is a click and the man's now-familiar, accented voice comes over the line. "Oui?"

"This is Jordan," I say, consciously giving my first name only, and struggling to keep the tremor from my voice. "We met earlier today . . . "

"Ah, yes," he says, not sounding at all surprised by my call.

He's not going to make it easy for me, I realize, as several seconds of silence pass between us. "You mentioned possibly meeting up. To share information," I add quickly, cursing my own awkwardness.

"Le Grill at eight o'clock." He does not wait for a response. "See you then." There is a click and then the line goes dead.

chapter FIVE

I HURRY ACROSS THE Place du Casino, past the Casino de Monte-Carlo, a behemoth rococo palace framed by manicured gardens that occupies an entire side of the square. I had seen the Casino during my student visit to Monaco, but only from a distance as the friend who let us camp on her floor drove us breezily by before taking us up the coast to the smaller towns of Antibes and Cannes. We had not gone inside—the frayed jeans and flannel shirts that filled our worn rucksacks did not come close to passable attire. Now, taking in the elegantly dressed patrons streaming up the palm tree–flanked entranceway, I feel as out of place as the disheveled student I once was.

Fortunately, I don't have to try to enter the Casino—Le Grill, according to the guidebook in my room, is located on the top floor of the neighboring Hotel de Paris. I walk through the opulent hotel lobby, making my way to the elevator. The doors open to reveal a dining room of royal blue and white leading to an open-air terrace. I enter the lounge and scan the patrons, a young, stylish crowd, sipping cocktails as they wait for tables. But I do not see the stranger.

It is already ten past eight, I note, looking at the clock over the bar; perhaps he is not going to show. My shoulders sag with fatigue. I should be plotting my next move to find Jared and getting on a plane. But I don't know where Nicole has gone, and I have no more leads, no one else to turn to for help. Talking to this man is my best chance—assuming he doesn't stand me up.

A familiar figure appears behind me in the mirror. Startled, I spin around. The stranger is more striking than I remembered from earlier in the day, tan set off against a light linen sports coat. His frame seems less brawny now, streamlined.

"Good evening," he says. I wait for him to apologize for keeping me waiting, but he does not. Faint annoyance rises in me as I recall his dismissive, condescending tone at Nicole's apartment. I don't have to like his company, I remind myself; once I find out what he knows, I can leave.

The maitre'd approaches. "Monsieur Bruck," she says, using the name with a familiarity that tells me he has been here a number of times before. "Your table is ready."

I look at the stranger, puzzled. I only agreed to drinks, not dinner. Surely he cannot be that presumptuous. But the maitre'd leads us through the restaurant to the veranda and seats us at a round cocktail table with a breathtaking view of the sea, the molten orange sun dipping low to the horizon.

"I thought it would be easier to talk out here," he says, when the maitre'd has left.

My annoyance subsides. "I would have asked for the reservation, but I didn't know your name," I say pointedly.

"Of course. We haven't been properly introduced. I'm Aaron Bruck." He extends his hand across the table. I cannot help but notice how the pale blue of his open-collared shirt accentuates his azure eyes. "Friends call me Ari."

"Jordan Weiss." His expression as we shake hands makes me wonder if he already knew my surname.

I decide to get right to the point. "So why are you looking for Nicole?" A guarded expression flickers in his eyes and I instantly regret being so abrupt. Moving slowly in order to get more information is a basic rule of intelligence work, though unfortunately not indigenous to my personality.

"I . . . " he begins, but before he can speak further a waiter appears and looks at us expectantly. "What would you like?" Aaron asks.

A good stiff martini, I think, after the events of the past few days. Maybe two. But with the exception of a scotch on the rocks during my short flight from London, I've avoided the temptation to numb myself in drink, and I need to keep my wits about me. "White wine," I say.

"Do you like champagne?" he asks. "They've got an excellent selection."

"That sounds good." I watch as he expertly orders a bottle, not bothering to consult the wine list. Closer now, I notice that his brown hair is flecked with gray.

"Have you been to the Casino?" he asks a moment later, forgetting or choosing to ignore my earlier question about Nicole.

I decide to let it go for the moment. "Yes. I mean no, not inside," I correct myself, feeling instantly unsophisticated.

"You should have a walk through," he says. "The gaming salons are quite remarkable, though, as you probably know, only for the tourists."

"High-end tourists."

He fidgets with his watchband. "Yes, of course. Not the sort of crowd you would usually see in Las Vegas. I just mean that by law the Monegasques, the local citizens, aren't allowed to enter."

"I see." I lean back, allowing my gaze to wander to lights that twinkle in the distance.

The waiter returns with a bottle, pops the cork. "Where are you from?" I ask, my curiosity getting the better of me as Aaron samples the champagne.

He nods his approval, and the waiter pours two glasses, setting the bottle in a silver bucket before disappearing. "That's complicated," he replies when we are alone again.

I tilt my head. "Seems like a pretty straightforward question to me."

"My mother was a sabra, native-born Israeli." His English is fluent, but there is a slight hesitation, an effort to the way he constructs his sentences before speaking that, coupled with his accent, belies the fact that he is not a native speaker. "My father's family came from Poland. My grandfather survived Belzec, but his first wife died there. After the war, he stayed in Poland and opened a store in Warsaw. That's where he met my grandmother and where my father was born. They moved to the States when things got bad again during the communist purges of the sixties. My mother happened to be an exchange student at Johns Hopkins and that's where she met my father." His delivery of his family history is perfunctory, as if reading from a report.

"So you were born in America?"

"Yes. I'm a dual citizen, Israeli and American. I was raised in Haifa, but I spent most summers with my grandparents in Baltimore."

"That must have been interesting," I remark, holding back the many other questions I want to ask. Why hasn't he asked anything of me? He must wonder why I am chasing Nicole as well—unless, of course, he already knows.

From inside the restaurant, a piano begins to play. "I'm Jewish, too," I say, as if offering my bona fides. He does not seem surprised. Perhaps it is because my surname sounds Jewish. But is it something more? I appraise myself anew, considering my dark curls, the slight arc to my nose.

He hands me a glass, then raises his. "To shared interests," he proposes.

I lift the champagne beneath my nose, inhaling the aroma before touching my glass to his. The toast is an invitation to begin talking about Nicole. It is followed by a moment of awkward silence, neither of us ready to go first.

The bubbles tickle my nose as I sip the champagne. "Where do you live now?" I ask, shifting to an easier subject.

A strange look flashes across his face and he pauses, as if perplexed by the question. It is a reaction I recognize in myself, one that comes from a life lived out of a suitcase, a lack of a place that truly feels like home. "Tel Aviv," he replies at last, but there is no ownership behind his words. "I settled there after coming out of the army several years ago."

What does he do now, I wonder? Though the short hair could be a relic from his military days, his predatory gaze and the efficiency of his movements suggest something else. Perhaps he still works for the government. Could the Israelis be searching for Jared, too? It's a stretch, but nothing seems impossible to me anymore.

I clear my throat, raising my guard. "Are you staying nearby?"

"Sort of. I'm actually not in a hotel but on a friend's boat down at the marina. What brings you to the south of France?" He refills my glass.

I falter. I would rather ask questions than talk about myself, but information gathering is a dance of sorts, and I am expected to give something in exchange for what I have learned before he will say more. "I work for the American government as a diplomat," I begin, choosing my words carefully. "I mean, I used to. Now I'm on a leave, trying to figure out what to do next." It is not, I decide, exactly a lie.

"Chasing Nicole Martine through the streets of Monaco doesn't seem like much of a holiday," he observes evenly, challenging me.

I nod, recognizing the implausibility of my story. "I'm looking for a friend of mine. That's the reason I'm taking a break from work, at least in part. And I think Nicole might have some sort of connection to my friend, or know where he is."

"What is your friend's name?"

I hesitate. I almost led the wrong people to Jared once; I will not do it again. "Jared." I offer only his first name, then watch Aaron's face for any hint of recognition but see none. "And you?"

"It's Nicole herself with whom I'm trying to speak."

Before I can ask why, the waiter reappears with a plate of nuts, cheese, and olives to accompany the champagne. As he sets the food in front of us, I consider Aaron's response. So far I have regarded Nicole only as an appendage to Jared, a lead to help me find him. I remember Sophie, my colleague in London, how I underestimated her as just a beautiful, vacuous blonde before learning that she had a doctorate in finance and was proficient in Arabic. I should not make the same mistake with Nicole. Who is she really, and what does she do that could possibly be of interest to Aaron?

"Nice," he remarks abruptly, gesturing toward the top of my dress.

"Excuse me?" I say, taken aback by his bluntness.

"The ring."

I glance down. I had not realized that it was visible above the lower neckline of the black sheath dress I purchased from a boutique by the hotel in order to have something suitable to wear this evening. "Thanks. It's a memento from a friend."

He does not press further but slides the plate toward me, an offering. My stomach twists. Though I've been too nervous to be hungry since leaving London, I take an olive and a few nuts to be polite. Aaron helps himself to most of the remaining snacks, tearing into them as though eating a steak dinner. There is something about the abandon with which he eats that speaks to time spent in hardship, an unshakable sense of not taking food for granted, of eating what is offered when it is available for fear that there might be none later.

Combat, I think suddenly. Though he hasn't said what he did in the military, I sense immediately that he has seen conflict and that it changed him. In some ways, I can relate. I have not been to war, of course. But there's something about having lived abroad, putting one's life on the line in corners of the earth that most people never read or hear about, that changes a person.

My mind reels back to my hospital stay in Washington last summer when I was recovering from the injuries I received in Liberia. There was a girl of seven or eight in the bed beside mine briefly who had been in a car accident, and I remember seeing her father use a latex hospital glove as a makeshift balloon, blowing air into it to form a chicken. It was a harmless gesture, designed to amuse the girl. But picturing the children in Africa who didn't have clean water or bandages, much less surgical gloves, I found myself growing angry at the frivolous waste, at how easy it was for us to take the abundance in our lives for granted. I tried to explain my frustration to my visiting mother, who nodded sympathetically, but there was a blankness to her eyes. In that moment perhaps more so than any other I came to appreciate how much I had been affected by my experiences, how they had changed me in ways that those closest to me could never understand.

Studying Aaron now, I suspect that he returned from war or some other military conflict as a misshapen peg, unable to refit into the life he left behind. Had there been someone waiting for him, trying to understand the changes?

"I'm sorry I was late," he says, interrupting my thoughts. I force myself to focus as he continues, speaking in between bites. "But I was busy confirming what I originally suspected: Nicole flew to Austria."

"Austria?" I repeat. I've assumed since leaving the airport that Nicole had fled to Jared, and when she said he was far away, I imagined Africa or South America, the remote locations that had given him anonymity for the past decade. Could he really be in Europe, somewhere so close? I fight the urge to leap from the chair and head to the airport immediately.

"Yes. I'm not sure if that's her final destination or just a transit point." He has not, I notice, given me the city to which she has flown. Does he really not know, or is he being purposefully oblique?

He continues, "She didn't have a continuing plane ticket, at least when she left Nice. I'm going to head to Austria myself first thing in the morning." He pauses, and I continue looking at him in a way that I hope will prompt further information. "You're welcome to join me."

"Oh." Surprised by his invitation, I push back from the table and stand. Why would he ask a complete stranger to travel with him? I take a step toward the edge of the veranda and gaze out across the water. Suddenly I am light-headed and warm. I lean forward, grasping the terrace wall.

Aaron comes up beside me, moving with surprising agility. "Are you okay?"

"Y-yes," I manage, embarrassed, straightening as my head clears. "Just a bit tired is all."

He reaches toward my face abruptly and I pull back, startled. "Sorry," he says, retreating. He gestures to his own head. "The lump—where you fell."

Where you pushed me, I want to say, but I do not. The earlier attack, and the ludicrousness of my being here with him, come rushing back. I take a step away. "It's fine. It'll be gone in a day or two." I stare out across the water at the lights sparkling in the distance. The air is cooler now and a faint breeze blows across the terrace, carrying with it a whiff of something tropical and fragrant from the unseen gardens below.

"To leave one's job to find a friend," he says softly, moving toward me again. "One must have a very good reason."

His voice is equal parts comforting and beguiling, beckoning me to speak. Yes, I think, as Jared's face appears in my mind. He was the only man I ever loved. That is reason enough.

My vision clears. I look up at Aaron, who is staring down at me intently, and for a moment I am seized with the impulse to tell him everything. But I cannot let my guard down. I swallow. "Speaking of reasons, you haven't told me why you are searching for Nicole."

Now it is his turn to pause. "I'm working for a client who needs to find Nicole for reasons related to his business interests. I'm really not at liberty to say anything else now, but I'll tell you more tomorrow—if you decide to join me."

"I don't . . . " I begin, then stop again, studying his face, wondering how much of the little he has said is true, what he is not telling me. Could he be setting me up, using me to find Jared like the others tried to do? But he stares out over my shoulder at the skyline, his expression blank, seemingly disinterested in whether I choose to go with him or not.

I consider his offer. Traveling to Austria with a man I've just met, whose purpose I do not know, a man who attacked me just a few hours ago, seems absurd. And I've always preferred to work alone, an instinct that is stronger now than ever since I've been betrayed by the very few people I should have been able to trust. But while I don't like the idea of going with Aaron, I'm not sure what I will do otherwise. I don't have any other leads. And though I hate to admit it, I'm curious about Aaron—his reasons for wanting to find Nicole, his sources of information.

Take the risk, a voice inside me says. In my intelligence work, some of the best leads I've ever followed were those based on instinct, even when it seemed illogical to my rational mind and other, more conservative officers thought I was crazy. But it was that willingness to take the leap that had given me my edge. Of course, a few times it had nearly gotten me killed.

"Aaron . . . " I begin.

"Ari," he corrects, cutting me off, instructing me to use the name reserved for friends. I notice again that he is standing closer to me than is necessary, gazing deeply into my eyes.

I look away, my suspicions bubbling up anew. Why is he offering help? "You don't know me, or why I'm trying to find my friend."

He flicks his hand dismissively. "Irrelevant. You have your reasons and I have mine. Whether we can help each other is the only thing that matters." The waiter returns to the table with the check and Aaron leans over to sign it. "I have to excuse myself," he says, his tone so businesslike I wonder if I imagined the intimacy a minute earlier. "The flight leaves tomorrow morning at seven ten on Tyrolean Airlines, should you decide to join me. And if not, it was a pleasure speaking with you." Then, not waiting for me to respond, he stands and walks across the restaurant, leaving me to swim in a tide of confusion and intrigue in his wake.

I T IS NEARLY six thirty as I make my way across the main concourse of Côte d'Azur Airport. Though not as busy as it was yesterday afternoon, the terminal is brisk with early morning business travelers talking on their cell phones into unseen earpieces, juggling briefcases and cardboard cups of cappuccino.

I scan the ticket kiosks. At the far end sits a lone counter for Tyrolean Airlines. I walk to it, tapping my foot as the clerk serves the man in front of me. I glance at the clock on the wall above the counter; now that I have decided to go with Aaron, I don't want to miss the flight.

When the man shuffles aside, I step forward. "Jordan Weiss," I say, handing the woman my passport. "There should be a reservation in my name."

She types on the keyboard. "Right here, Ms. Weiss. Any bags?"

"No." I pull my credit card from my wallet and hold my breath, wondering how much a last minute flight will cost, but she waves it away. "The ticket has been paid in full." She hands me a boarding pass. "You're departing from gate twelve after you pass through security. The flight will be called at six fifty."

I pause, studying the pass. Vienna, I note. Had Aaron purchased a refundable ticket, or simply presumed that I would show? Despite my relief at not having the additional expense, I don't like feeling indebted to anyone, especially a strange man whose motives are still unclear. But there is no time to worry about that—the flight boards in less than twenty minutes. I proceed toward the security line.

As I shuffle forward in the queue, winding through roped stanchions toward the metal detector, my doubts about traveling with Aaron grow. I almost hadn't come at all. When I woke up a few hours earlier, I saw his blue eyes and muscular forearms as he leaned across the table, asking me to join him. What was his real motive? I am sure he knew, as I did, that having someone else along when you are on the move can only slow you down. And it wasn't as though I had any information that could aid his search for Nicole.

I lay in bed, resigned to stay in Monaco and do some more investigating on my own. Just then my cell phone began to buzz. Picking it up, I saw that there was an unread email from Lincoln. Inside, he wrote no message but simply forwarded an attachment containing the profile information he found on Nicole Martine. I scanned the information hurriedly: twenty-nine years old, born in Lebanon. I would not have expected that, given her blond hair. An art dealer by profession, she had lived in Johannesburg, Belize, and Buenos Aires. Jared had lived in Belize, too, I recall. Is that where they met? Pushing my jealousy down, I moved to the next entry, a note that she was seen in Namibia in May 2004. I tried to scroll down but there were no further entries. It was as if since then she simply dropped off the map.

I hit reply and jotted a quick note thanking Lincoln. Then, after a moment's consideration, I sent him a second message, asking if he could run a report on an Israeli-American citizen named Aaron Bruck.

I remained in bed for several minutes, studying the report on Nicole. If she was an art dealer, then it was plausible Aaron's client was seeking her out for that reason—which meant that he was telling the truth when he said his interest in her was unrelated to Jared. And Lincoln's report did not provide any additional recent information that would help me continue my own search for Nicole. Since I had no other leads, I decided to go to the airport and join Aaron on the flight. There was nothing to lose; if the trip proved to be a bad idea, I could always bail out after we arrived. So I quickly showered, then checked out of the hotel and made my way to the airport.

Approaching the gate now, I spot Aaron sitting behind an open newspaper. His eyes peer over the top edge of the paper, and he pretends to read, as he had done at the café, while scanning the terminal. Is he looking for me? Maybe, but it's something more than that, I realize: his gaze is animal-like, as though he expects to be attacked at any moment, even as he himself is searching for his prey. Is this, too, a relic from his military days? Or does it have something to do with his present work, his search for Nicole?

Aaron sees me then and his eyes meet mine. "Good morning," he says as I near. He refolds the newspaper and when he looks up his face is relaxed, no trace of his intensity a moment earlier. He is even more attractive this morning, I think, taking in his freshly shaven jawline before I can stop myself.

"Cappuccino?" He picks up one of two cups from the seat beside him. "I bought an extra, in case you decided to join me."

I try to decide if the gesture is considerate or presumptuous. Choosing the former, I take the warm cup from him and take a sip.

"Thanks." It is unsweetened, I notice, but there are two brown packets of sugar and one artificial sweetener beside the cup, planning for all contingencies. "You paid for my ticket," I blurt out. "That wasn't necessary. I'll reimburse you as soon as we reach Vienna."

He waves his hand, as though swatting away a mosquito. "Did you check your bags?"

I pat my tote. "This is it." He raises one eyebrow and for a moment I expect him to ask about my lack of luggage. Instead, he picks up his own coffee to clear the seat beside him for me and puts it on the floor beside a khaki rucksack. But before I can sit, a female voice comes over the speaker, announcing that our flight will board.

The plane is a turboprop, a single row of beige leather seats running eight deep down either side. A handful of other travelers, mostly men in suits, are scattered throughout the cabin. I follow Aaron midway down the aisle, taking the seat on the right he indicates. As he stows his bag overhead and occupies the seat across from mine, I am oddly grateful for the few feet of space between us.

"So," I say a few minutes later, as the flight attendant completes the predeparture checks and we begin to pull away from the gate, "any idea where to look for Nicole when we get to Vienna?"

"I have a few leads." He does not elaborate. He is willing to have me along for the ride, but that does not extend to trusting me with information that I might take and use on my own.

Neither of us speaks further as the plane taxis to the end of the runway and noisily picks up speed. I gaze out the window as the wheels lift from the ground. A moment later we clear the tops of the buildings and trees, and the shoreline becomes visible on the horizon. As we climb above the coastal mountains, a sharp breeze sends the small plane wobbling.

Glancing at Aaron out of the corner of my eye, I am surprised to see that he grasps the armrests tightly, his face uneasy. "What is it?" I ask, turning to him.

"Nothing." But I hear him exhale slowly, as though counting silently to himself.

"So about your suitcase, or lack thereof . . . " he says a moment later, when we have risen above the clouds and the turbulence has smoothed. Inwardly I groan. I had hoped he would have forgotten. But he is focused, with a certain tenacity I recognize from myself.

"I lost it," I say vaguely, looking away. It is not exactly untrue. "Before I came to Monaco. I just haven't had time to replace it."

"In the explosion at your flat?"

I look back at him, stunned. I had not told him about that. "How did you know?"

He shrugs. "You didn't think I would travel with you without checking into your background, do you?"

No, of course not. I had done exactly the same thing, or tried to anyway. "And?"

"Jordan Weiss. Thirty-two, American, never married. You served the State Department in Warsaw, San Salvador, Manila." He raises one eyebrow. "A really brief, poorly timed stint in Monrovia." I fight to keep my face neutral. I'd been on the ground in Liberia less than two weeks when the coup exploded. "How am I doing?"

Now it is my turn to shrug. The revelation that he has information on my background was not an accidental slip, but a power play, designed to let me know he has the upper hand. I won't validate that further with a reaction. He continues, "You worked in intelligence, but your exact role with the government was a little vague. I say 'worked' because you aren't on holiday or sabbatical. You quit, Jordan." His voice drops with recrimination, whether at my resignation or the fact that I hadn't been forthright with him, I cannot tell.

"You asked for an assignment in London, and a week later you resigned."

My mind reels. How had he learned all of this? I'm not naïve—I understand that with the vast quantities of information available electronically, it's impossible to keep quiet all but the most highly classified material. Still, the notion that my supposedly confidential background is so readily available gives me pause—and makes me question whether Aaron is really just the private investigator he claims to be.

He continues watching me expectantly, waiting for my reaction. He's a stranger, I remind myself; I don't owe him any explanations. Our conversation is interrupted by the flight attendant coming down the aisle with a beverage tray. "I'm sorry I didn't mention my resignation," I say when she has gone again, leaving us with glasses of orange juice.

"I'm not saying we have to tell each other everything," he adds. "But let's keep what we do say true, okay?"

Truth, I think. I've spent the past few weeks learning that I couldn't count on the truth from those closest to me, that the past decade of my life has been premised on a lie. And yet this man who I've known for a day expects candor. My stomach twists at the irony. Still, he isn't asking for full disclosure, just the absence of deceit. I struggle to find the flaw in his proposal but cannot. "Sure."

"You had such a promising career. I tried to find out why you left, but there was nothing."

No, they don't put those kinds of things in files, not when the very reason for my leaving implicates those keeping the records. I imagine the entry: resigned after being deceived by ambassador and deputy chief of mission. How would the out-processing folks back at State code that one?

Aaron is still watching me, his expression probing. But I'm not ready to tell him about Mo's betrayal, the revelation that set me on this path. "Like you said, we don't have to talk about everything, right?" He nods, acquiescing to his own rules.

"Well, that is quite a dossier you've built," I remark. I wish that I had heard back from Lincoln already, that I had some information about Aaron to level the playing field. "Surely there's something more you can tell me so I'm not at quite such a disadvantage."

He averts his eyes, and I can feel him weighing how much to say. Then he leans back, lacing his fingers behind his head. "I told you quite a bit last night. I'm an only child; parents deceased. A year older than you," he adds with a half smile.

I am surprised; with his smattering of gray hair and the crinkles at the corners of his eyes, I would have put him closer to forty. "Married?" I ask, squirming inwardly at my own question.

A shadow passes over his face. "I was. Her name was Aviva. We met when we were eighteen, wed within the year, and later had a daughter." He pulls a snapshot from his wallet of a stunning, raven-haired woman with olive skin and luminous, almond-shaped dark eyes. On her lap sits a young child of two or three, a replica of her mother but for Aaron's strong chin and full lips. "That's Yael."

"You have a child." I am unable to keep the surprise from my voice. I had not pictured Aaron as a husband, much less a father.

"Had." His jaw tightens. "My wife and daughter were killed."

I gasp involuntarily. "I'm so sorry."

"It was a freak accident. They drove over stray unexploded ordnance just outside an army base. Yael died instantly, thank God. But my Avi . . . " He pauses, catching his breath. "She lingered for days before I had to let her go."

"I'm sorry," I repeat, fumbling over the inadequacy of my words. I remember the pain when I thought I had lost Jared years ago. But the death of a child seems unfathomable.

He clears his throat. "Anyway, after they were gone, I began working as a private investigator. I've been doing this ever since, traveling on assignment."

And moving as far and as fast as you can, I think, trying to outrun your own pain. It's a familiar behavior, one I engaged in myself until returning to London just weeks ago. "And now you're trying to find Nicole . . . ?" I prompt.

He looks up, eyes clearing. Even lost in his memories, he will not fall into the trap of discussing more than he should. "Yes."

"Aaron . . . " I say.

"Ari," he corrects.

"Ari," I repeat, my exasperation growing. "I respect your privacy. But I just got on a plane with you. The least you can do is give me some indication as to what you're doing here."

He leans back once more, exhaling through his teeth. "Do you know anything about the wine industry?"

"Wine?" I don't know what I expected him to say, but it wasn't that. What can that possibly have to do with Nicole? "No, nothing really."

"Let me back up." He leans across the aisle, lowering his voice. "You've met Nicole, right?"

"Briefly."

"How much do you know about her?"

"Not much." I'm not about to share the profile I obtained from Lincoln, which is the only advantage I have on Aaron at the moment.

The plane bounces slightly with some turbulence and I reach out to steady the drink on the tray in front of me. Grimacing, Ari continues. "Nicole Martine is not just beautiful but brilliant. She studied finance at the Sorbonne and in another life she could have held a teaching fellowship at Oxford or Harvard. But she wasn't raised with a silver spoon, as they say. She grew up on the streets of Beirut before fleeing to Paris. She funded her way through school by working as a black marketeer, selling everything from cigarettes to firearms. In her twenties, she turned to items with a higher profit margin: jewelry, antiques, art."

I nod, remembering Lincoln's email. "Stolen?"

"Some items have what you might call a dubious origin. Other times the sales are just attempts to avoid taxes. The idea is to be able to buy or sell a high-end item without having to answer too many questions." His voice drops to just above a whisper. "But recently she became involved in a wine fraud operation."

"Wine fraud?"

"Yes, it's become big business in the past decade, people passing off bottles as valuable vintages that aren't authentic."

"I remember reading something about it in the paper. A man claimed that he had bottles from Thomas Jefferson's collection, or some such thing."

He stretches. "That was one case, yes. It's much more common than you think. Beyond the high-profile stories, there's a whole market where expensive wines are being faked in large quantities. Let's say, for example, that you have a good Burgundy that retails for two hundred fifty dollars a bottle. If you can substitute a much cheaper wine and replicate the label—"

"You can ship out thousands of bottles at a huge profit," I finish for him.

"Exactly. And it can be virtually impossible to tell the difference between a good fake and the real thing. Anyway, that's the kind of thing that Nicole is involved with, though how deeply I'm not sure."

I look out the window at the unbroken blue sky, processing what he has told me, unable to reconcile the beautiful blonde I had met in Monaco with the picture of the black-market operative Aaron had just painted. And how is she connected to Jared? He was always so upright in his principles; it's hard to imagine him associating with someone like that.

I turn back to Aaron. "And your client is interested in this because . . . ?"

I watch him struggle with my question, trying to decide if he can avoid answering it. While I am annoyed by his reticence, at the same time, I understand. He doesn't want to reveal his client's identity or purpose any more than I would be willing to disclose one of my intelligence assets. Then his face droops with resignation. "Industry professionals are very concerned with counterfeiting. It's a huge problem for the wine business—if someone is out there imitating their labels with subpar quality wine, it is going to dilute the brand, and the business can lose millions. There have even been cases of poisoning and other contamination in the fake wines, and the manufacturers worry about liability. They hired me to find Nicole to see what she knows. Hopefully she can direct me to whoever provided her with the counterfeits so we can try to stop it."

"That's it?" I ask skeptically.

"Yes. Only it isn't that simple. Nicole is constantly on the move between countries, with no known permanent address or residence, at least none that we've been able to identify, other than her brief stay in Monaco."

My heart sinks. Without knowing where she lives, how can I ever find Jared?

"One of my sources learned of a planned meeting in Vienna," he adds.

"So why didn't you leave last night, as soon as you knew where she was headed?"

"She can't take care of business and leave that quickly. And I was waiting on some additional intelligence regarding her specific whereabouts."

"That makes sense." I sit back, relaxing slightly. Aaron seems to have a good reason to be searching for Nicole, and it has nothing to do with Jared. Perhaps this partnership will work well after all. "I appreciate your telling me about this."

He bites his lip and a strange look crosses his face. "Jordan . . . " He pauses. "There's one other thing you should know." He averts his eyes. "After we spoke last night I made some inquiries regarding the man you are looking for, this Jared. Jared Short, no?"

"Yes," I manage, surprised. I had only given him a first name.

"Like I told you last night, I didn't know anything about him, but after you gave me his name I thought it would be prudent to do some checking." He hesitates. "And by looking into Nicole's known associates, I was able to learn his full identity and some information about him."

I cannot breathe. I brace myself, waiting for him to tell me that there was a mistake and Jared really is dead. "What is it?" I press.

He looks down, fiddling with the armrest. "He's definitely connected to Nicole, and I'm afraid it's more than just professional. Jordan, Nicole is the wife of the man you are looking for. She and Jared Short are married."

chapter SEVEN

"I'M SORRY," AARON says again as our taxi moves through the thick traffic on the autobahn outside Vienna. Rain falls sideways in sheets against the windshield.

I shake my head, still unable to speak over the freight train of questions roaring through my mind. Since Aaron first told me on the plane, the phrase has been playing over and over again like a bad commercial jingle: Jared is married. I sat numbly in my seat as Aaron waved over the flight attendant and requested two scotch on the rocks, both of which I promptly downed, ignoring the fact that it was not yet ten in the morning.

I don't know why it hadn't occurred to me before, I thought, as the liquor burned my throat, scorching the truth into my psyche. I fleetingly considered, of course, after meeting Nicole, that she might have feelings for him, even that Nicole and Jared might be somehow involved. But I never guessed, despite the photographic evidence that they had been connected for years, that they were married. Perhaps because until a few days ago, I still thought that Jared was dead. And in the thousands of scenarios that had played out in my head since then as to where he had been, what he had been doing all these years, I imagined him alone on the run, not establishing ties. Because even after learning he was alive, I stubbornly believed that if he could have come back, he would have. Because I always pictured him waiting for me. I am an idiot.

I draw my coat closer to ward off the damp chill that permeates through the closed cab windows. Beneath my shirt, the engagement ring presses icy against my skin. I picture Nicole at the door of the apartment, try to remember if there had been a ring on her finger. Surely I would have noticed.

"It appears they met in Central America," Aaron offers now, as the cab turns onto the wide expanse of the Ringstrasse. Belize, I think, remembering Lincoln's report. "They wed about four years ago," he adds.

Four years ago. My mind reels back. I was in San Salvador then, pushing away a DEA agent who wanted to date me, realizing yet again that I couldn't make it work because of my unhealed wounds, the fact that I was still not over Jared. Where was I the day he put aside his feelings for me and married Nicole? Presuming that he had not gotten over me years ago, that there hadn't been others in between. Immediately I am aware of the brevity of our time together. I hardly knew him at all.

"This Jared," Aaron asks, as we pass the imperial Opera House. "I take it he was more than a friend?"

"Yes," I admit.

"And he gave you that?"

I notice for the first time that I have been fingering the engagement ring around my neck. "A long time ago." But Aaron is still watching me and I realize that at least a brief explanation is owed. "Jared was my college boyfriend. More than that, actually," I hasten to add, as a dismissive expression flickers across his face.

He gazes out the window silently for several minutes. "Have you been to Vienna before?" he asks, changing the subject.

"Yes. I first visited when I was backpacking as a student. It always seemed a bit, um . . . " I look out at the columned museums, searching for the right adjective, " . . . antiseptic."

"And unapologetic," he adds. "From the war, I mean. To me, Austrians are just Germans who never apologized for what happened."

Caught off guard by the bluntness of his words, I glance quickly to the front of the cab, but the driver seems not to have heard. I have always eschewed the notion of collective guilt with respect to the Holocaust, but at the same time, there is a certain undeniable truth to what Aaron has said. "I also passed through Vienna a few times when stationed in Warsaw," I say, ignoring his comment. He wrinkles his nose. "What?"

"That's right; you lived in Poland."

"You have a problem with the Poles, too?" He does not answer. "You know, Poland didn't start the war," I continue, feeling myself grow defensive. "It was an occupied country. Three million Poles died."

"And the rest helped the Nazis put the Jews on the trains. Not to mention the centuries of anti-Semitism before the war, the pogroms after."

I hesitate, trying to decide whether to respond, how far down this path I want to go right now. It is a conversation I've had with Jewish friends and relatives many times over the years, and for those like Aaron whose families suffered through the Holocaust, the views are particularly entrenched. I went to Warsaw with those same preconceived notions, but the reality I found was so much more complex and nuanced. "Have you been to Poland?" I ask finally.

"No. My father never wanted to go back and I've honored that. I'd skip Austria and Germany, too, if the job didn't require it. Look." He points out the window of the car to an elderly man crossing the street. "You know he was probably a war criminal, or at least a Nazi supporter."

"That's not fair. Anyway, he's about a hundred. Do you really want to punish old people for what they did so long ago?"

"Every last one of them," he says, his expression grim, voice infuriatingly stubborn.

I try to reconcile his black-and-white view of history, find a way to argue. Then I decide against it, realizing it is useless. I don't have the strength for a political debate.

The cab weaves through the old city center, skirts the edge of a square. In the distance I can see the dome of St. Stephen's Cathedral muted against the gloomy gray sky. We turn onto a narrow side street, slowing before a small, nondescript hotel.

"Is this where Nicole is staying?" I ask as Aaron pays the driver.

But he ignores my question. "Come on." Thick drops pelt down, soaking through my hair and clothes on the few short steps to the front door.

Inside the lobby, Aaron leads me to a chair. "Wait here." Too weary to argue, I drop down, watching as he walks to the front desk and confers with the clerk, then produces a credit card. My heart sinks. I had hoped that we would be able to find Nicole immediately. I hadn't planned on an overnight stay.

A minute later, Aaron returns. "Our rooms aren't ready yet."

Inwardly I groan. If we do have to stay here, I desperately want to curl up in a fetal position and disappear into the oblivion of sleep, or at least a hot bath. I notice a restaurant on the other side of the lobby. "Drink," I say, pointing to the only escape available.

"I don't know if . . . " he begins, but I am already making my way toward it.

At the far end of the deserted restaurant, which smells of stale cigarette smoke and beer, a mustached man dries glasses behind the bar. "Scotch," I say. He stares at me, not moving. Climbing onto one of the bar stools, I point to the bottle on the wall of liquor behind him. *"Bitte,"* I add, but he is still looking at me strangely. It is not my English, but rather the fact that I am asking for hard alcohol for breakfast that seems to be giving him pause.

The bartender peers quizzically over my shoulder as Aaron comes up behind me, as though seeking permission from my husband. "Zwei, bitte," Aaron says.

He slides onto the stool next to mine as the bartender pours the drinks and sets them before us. Then he lifts his glass, clinking it to mine before taking a sip and grimacing. "So this Jared . . . you've gone to great lengths to find him. Does the fact that he is married change that?"

"No," I reply, indignant at the implication that I'm traveling the world on a schoolgirl's crush, trying to find an old flame. If anything, I need answers now more than ever about what happened ten years ago, why Jared faked his death and left without telling me.

But Aaron doesn't know any of this—or shouldn't, anyway. I study his face, wondering how much to say. "This is about more than finding an old boyfriend. Jared drowned in the river ten years ago when we were in college at Cambridge, or at least that's what we were led to believe."

"I don't understand."

I take a large gulp of scotch, the burning more muted than it had been on the plane. "Last month I came back to England and

found out that the whole thing was a lie. Jared faked his death because people were after him."

Aaron's eyes widen, his surprise seemingly sincere. "And you
never knew all those years?"

"No." I watch as he processes the notion. He's thinking of his
wife, I realize. Everyone who has ever lost someone close has imagined waking up one day and finding out that the whole thing was a
mistake, that his or her loved one is really alive. To Aaron, it must
sound like a dream. Of course in the fantasy, that person hasn't
moved on to marry someone else.

I finish off the scotch. The bartender, noticing, raises the bottle,
asking if I want another, and I nod. I should keep my wits about me,
but for the moment I do not care. "What else do you know about
them?" He bites his lip, reluctant. "Tell me," I press. I want, need to
know.

"They've traveled together as a couple for the past four years,"
he says.

Maybe it's a front, and they're pretending to be married for appearance's sake, I think. "It's a legal marriage," he adds gently, reading my thoughts. "And it appears to be real, not just for show."

Of course it's real. Nicole is a beautiful woman and Jared is, well,
Jared. Why wouldn't they love each other? Nausea rises in my throat,
brought on by the idea as much as the alcohol. "Excuse me," I
mumble, leaping from the stool and starting across the empty
restaurant.

At the lobby, I break into a run, finding the bathroom on the far
side. I slam into one of the stalls, just making it before I vomit,
bringing up scotch and bile tinged with the coffee and orange juice
I drank earlier. I retch again, but my otherwise empty stomach has

nothing left to give. Shaking, I straighten, then flush and walk to the sink, splashing water on my face and the back of my neck.

Aaron's earlier question reverberates through my mind: Do I still want to find Jared? I could give up. I know now that he is alive and well. And he's clearly moved on, started a life with Nicole. But somehow none of that matters, or if it does, it serves to make me even more driven to find him. I need to find out what happened. Why didn't he come back for me? At what point did he decide to move on?

I study my reflection in the mirror. My face is ashen gray, any trace of the light makeup I hastily applied this morning long gone. Dark circles ring my eyes and my hair is still damp and frizzy from the rain. I picture Nicole, elegant and well coiffed. Jared could hardly be blamed for choosing her over me.

Assuming that's what happened, another voice in my head, calmer and more rational than my own, seems to say. I'm speculating; what I really need are facts. I pull the phone from my pocket, checking for new email and finding none. Then I open Lincoln's earlier message and hit reply, then type, *Pls. check Nicole Short too.* I hate the idea that she might be using Jared's name. But the information contained in Lincoln's email ended four years ago—right around the time Nicole and Jared were married.

I press send and put the phone away. Smoothing my hair, I walk from the restroom and across the lobby. When I reach the bar, Aaron is gone. The scotch glasses have also disappeared and two steaming cups of coffee sit in their places.

I pull one of the cups toward me, then look around, wondering where Aaron has gone. Perhaps he decided I am too unstable, that he would be better off pursuing Nicole on his own. But a minute later he returns to the restaurant, closing his phone. "Sorry, I just had to make a call."

"No problem." As he tucks his phone into his pocket, his jacket pulls back and I notice the gun tucked low at his waistband. Uneasiness rises in me. How had he managed to bring that with him on the plane? Traveling armed on an international flight would require special permits, not something that a simple private investigator would be able to get. And why does he need a gun if his search for Nicole is related to some business interests? I wonder once again what he isn't telling me, how much of his story is true.

"My gun was in the hotel vault," he says, following my gaze. "I stayed here last week and they held it for me as a courtesy."

I study his impassive expression, unable to discern if he is lying. Several seconds of silence pass between us. "Our rooms are ready." He signs the bill that the bartender left on the counter. "Why don't we go get settled?" He holds out his arm to help me from the stool, but I ignore it, draining the rest of my coffee and stepping down myself.

In the lobby, he proceeds directly to the elevator, a tiny, old-fashioned lift with a grated door. Inside, it is barely big enough for the two of us and I face forward, breathing shallowly and trying not to notice his warmth pressed up against the side of my arm.

We exit at the third floor and walk down a dimly lit corridor. Through the closed doors come the sounds of television laughter, a couple arguing heatedly. Aaron stops before a door second from the end of the hall and unlocks it.

I turn to stare at him as he follows me inside. "You said rooms, plural," I remind him pointedly.

"I couldn't ask for a second room without attracting attention.

You're Jordan Bruck, by the way, in case anyone asks. We married four months ago in Milan after a brief courtship."

"I don't . . . " I begin, then stop again. The notion of pretending to be married to this man I just met seems bizarre. Did Jared and Nicole travel as a couple, I wonder, before actually becoming one?

"I don't like it any better than you do," Aaron says, more sharply than I have heard him speak, and I can tell that he is thinking of his wife. He brushes past me and puts his bag down on the floor by the window. The room is narrow, most of the space taken up by a single, queen-sized bed. A damp odor permeates the air.

I open my mouth to protest further about the shared accommodations, then decide against it. Hopefully we won't be here long.

Ari turns on a lamp that sits on the night table beside a telephone, filling the room with yellow light. Taking in the worn furniture, I cannot help but think longingly of the elegant hotel rooms in Monaco. "So what now?" I ask, sinking down on the edge of the bed.

"Now we wait." He opens his bag and rummages inside.

I tilt my head. "Wait for what, Ari? I thought you knew where Nicole is."

He looks up. "I do. She's staying at a flat north of here in the Brigittenau district."

I try to place the location in my mind but cannot. "I don't understand. If you know where she is, then why are we waiting? Why aren't we going after her immediately, before she gets away?"

I feel him yet again calculating how much to say. "Well, for one thing, I'm still awaiting confirmation of the actual address. More important, she has a meeting scheduled for tonight with one of her key associates. It will be better if I can catch her then."

"Better for who?"

"For me." He straightens. "For my client."

I stand up. "Why?"

"I really can't say."

"Dammit, Ari!" I explode. "How can you expect me to just sit here?"

"Because this isn't all about you, Jordan." Walking toward me, his voice remains even but his cheeks redden and a vein bulges slightly at his neck. "I brought you along, shared the information I had with you, against better judgment, some might say. But there are things at stake here besides you finding your ex-boyfriend."

"I told you, he wasn't just—" I begin.

He raises his hand. "Bigger things."

We are standing toe-to-toe now, neither willing to back down. "Like what?"

He presses his lips together. "She isn't going to leave before her meeting," he replies, avoiding my question. "She doesn't know we're here."

"Unlike in Monaco," I say, finishing his unspoken thought. "She might not have fled there, either, if I hadn't spooked her, right?"

I wait for him to deny the accusation, but he does not. "Ari . . . " I stop, caught off guard by my use of his nickname. It is not, I realize, the first time I have called him that. How long have I been doing it? I swallow, feeling my face grow warm. "What if you're wrong?" I press. He looks confused, as though the idea is not one he has previously considered. "What if Nicole does get away?"

"She won't," he replies confidently. "And if she does, we'll figure out where she's going and follow her."

"But . . . "

He cuts me off. "Trust me. I got you this far, didn't I? If it wasn't for me, you would still be sitting in Monaco."

He has a point. So far, he hasn't steered me wrong. But stubbornness rises up inside me. We need to go after Nicole now, to not lose her again. My unwillingness to bend to someone else's judgment is just one of the reasons I've never worked with a partner when given the choice.

It's futile, I decide, to argue further. I fling myself across the bed. "We have time," he says. "Do you want to go out somewhere for more coffee or some food?"

I look out the window at the rain-soaked street, then shake my head. "Tell me more about the wine fraud," I say.

Ari unfolds himself across the other side of the bed, keeping a comfortable distance between us. "The wine industry has become huge in recent years in the States and Europe. And developing countries have gotten into the wine business, too: Bulgaria, Georgia—"

"Georgia?" I echo, incredulous.

"Yes. In fact, one of the things that makes wine more complex is stressing the grapes, and some think that vintages from war-torn regions are particularly good. Even Israel has gotten into the wine game, and I mean the real thing, not just Manischewitz."

I laugh, imagining the sickly sweet wine we used to have at our Passover seders. He continues, "At the same time, the consumer market for wine has grown exponentially, especially in places like China, Russia, India, where there's a new middle class, with more young professionals than ever eager to pick up the tastes and lifestyles of the West."

He clasps his hands behind his head, and as he stretches out on his back, I try not to notice the way his T-shirt stretches across his chest. "There are secondary markets, too," he adds. "Wine tourism has become a lucrative business, vacations centered around trips to the vineyards. And then there are the investment funds."

"Investment funds?"

"They're just like mutual funds, only their holdings are wines." He yawns. "People buy in, for anywhere from twenty-thousand dollars to many millions. The funds purchase wines that they think are likely to hold their value, Bordeaux, maybe, or Burgundy, and then store them while they appreciate. There's even an exchange in London that values the funds. Oenophiles consider it a sexy investment, even though they may never see, let alone taste, any of the wine. Also, some people feel that it's not as volatile as the rest of the market these days because, as I explained, the demand for wine is likely to continue to rise."

"And the counterfeiting problem . . . ?" I prompt, trying to bring him back to Nicole.

"People want expensive wines, but everyone wants them at a bargain. So, like we discussed on the plane, if you can fake a really good vintage and introduce it into the market at a slightly lower price point, you can sell a ton and clear a healthy profit. Winemakers hate it but it's kept quiet, because if consumers lose confidence in the value and quality of the product they're buying, the whole industry will suffer. That's why counterfeiters have been able to operate beneath the radar for years—the winemakers were willing to let some amount go unchecked in order to keep the issue from becoming too public."

"What about Nicole?" I ask. "How does she fit into all of this?"

"Someone sold a counterfeit of a very valuable bottling. Nicole brokered the transaction. If I can see who she is doing business with, it will help to find some of the players higher up the chain."

Without speaking further, Ari closes his eyes and a few minutes later begins to breathe evenly. His arms, I note, are flung back over his head in a gesture that seems to replicate surrender. Not bothering to stop myself now, I study the contour of his muscles beneath his shirt, the place behind his ear where his hairline meets his neck. His sensuality is not groomed and self-conscious like some men, who seem to use their good looks to their advantage; it is raw and natural in a way that makes him even more dangerous.

An image flashes through my mind, sudden and unbidden, of reaching over and kissing him until he wakes, his arms coming to life, strong around me. I struggle to push the vision away. What's gotten into me? It's just my wounded pride, I tell myself, the need to revalidate my womanhood since learning that Jared chose someone else. Even if my attraction to Ari was legitimate, I cannot afford to complicate things. No matter where the years have taken Jared, my first priority is still finding him and learning the truth.

Jared is married. Despite what Ari said, it could be just a front, a union for the sake of his hiding, her work. But as I think this, I know that it isn't true. Jared would not wed for the sake of appearances. Then again, I never imagined he would fake his death, either, so perhaps I didn't know him as well as I thought.

A chill runs through me and I reach down, pulling the blanket that is folded at the foot of the bed up over both of us. My eyes grow heavy and the room begins to slip from beneath me.

Then I am in Cambridge, standing on Midsummer Common, gazing north toward the River Cam. Behind me, the towering spires of St. John's, Trinity, and Kings rise against the late day sun.

It is from this direction that the ringing comes, a sweet, gentle bell. Slowly the bicycle comes into view and, as the rider's distinctive shape registers, my heart fills. "Jared!" I shout, but he does not see me as he nears. Green eyes fixed, he pedals rapidly on a straight trajectory forward, his open black gown flapping in the breeze. He does not slow or swerve, and for a moment I fear I will be struck.

Flinching, I close my eyes. Bike and rider pass through me, as though I am not there. I spin around quickly, but his retreating image fades like dust and, before I can blink, he is gone.

"Jared!" I call again, this time aloud as I awake from the dream. The hotel room is nearly dark now, the lamp extinguished, gray sky weak through the half-drawn curtains.

I close my eyes once more, willing myself back to the place where I left the dream, hoping that if I fall asleep quickly enough I can return to Jared. But now I find myself in an unfamiliar room. A doctor's office, I recognize, inhaling the antiseptic smell, squinting against the bright overhead light. The metal table is icy cold beneath my thin gown. There is a sudden sharp pain in my lower abdomen and I cry out, jarring myself awake.

I clutch the blanket tightly, trying in vain to stop the uncontrollable shaking. It was just a dream. But there's more to it than that. I have been there before, in that doctor's office. It is a place I have not allowed myself to recall in ages, a memory buried so long that it had ceased to be real.

I open my eyes, blinking to adjust to the dimness. As I look around the hotel room, the day's earlier events come rushing back: the flight from Monaco, the revelation that Jared and Nicole are married, the scotch. My head throbs. Totally unprofessional of me. Ari must think I am a total hack.

Ari. Had he noticed me shaking or heard me cry out in my sleep? I roll over, but the space beside me is empty, a slight wrinkle in the sheets the only indication that he had been there at all.

I sit up, looking toward the bathroom. "Hello?" I call, but there is no response.

I switch on the night-table lamp. Beside the telephone is a note scribbled on a pad of white hotel stationery: *Went to check something.*

Back shortly. Food on table. A.B. His handwriting is slanted and craggy, the initials a scrawl that seems to fly off the page, as though he had finished writing the note while actually running from the room.

Swallowing against the stale taste of liquor in my mouth, I climb from the bed and walk to the table, where two cappuccinos sit beside a paper bag. Inside are a bottle of aspirin and a few still warm rolls, filled with salami and hard cheese. I bite into one of the rolls. The hearty, satisfying taste immediately reminds me of backpacking through Europe as a student, arriving on the overnight train in a new city. I would spend a few precious coins on a sandwich like this and devour it as we plotted the sites we would see, which hostel or campsite would serve as our base for the night.

When I've finished the sandwich, I down two of the aspirin with a mouthful of coffee, then go into the bathroom and turn on the tap in the narrow stall shower. As I wait for the water to warm, my thoughts turn to Jared once more. I feel foolish for having chased him, for thinking he might still be waiting and have feelings for me. Ari asked yesterday whether I still planned to continue my search for Jared. I consider the question anew: Should I stop now? I could give up the quest, try to piece back some semblance of a life for myself. But I still need answers about why Jared left and never came back. And the thought of knowing that he is out there somewhere in the world, of never seeing him again, is unfathomable.

Twenty minutes later I step from the bathroom, drying my hair. "Ari?" I call, but the room is still empty. I am annoyed. He could have said where he was going, when he will be back. He can't just expect me to keep following his lead without telling me what he is doing and why.

Across the room, a flashing red light catches my eye. It is the message button on the telephone. The light was not on earlier; the phone must have rung while I was in the shower. I walk to the night table, then hesitate. Clearly the message isn't for me, and Ari said no one knows he is staying here. Someone probably dialed the wrong number. Curious, I pick up the receiver, press the message button. "One new message," a prerecorded woman's voice says. There is a pause before a man's voice comes over the line: "Denisgasse achtzehn." Then there is a click and the line goes dead.

Puzzled, I stare at the phone for several seconds. Then I hit the repeat button and listen to the message again, scribbling the words on the pad of paper beneath Ari's note. *Denisgasse achtzehn.* What does it mean? Achtzehn translates as the number eighteen. Is it an address?

I reach for my bag. Easy, I think, as I pull out my phone. The message probably isn't even intended for us. I click on the internet function, then go to MapQuest, punching in the information. A map appears, showing Denisgasse street. I zoom out to a broader view, and my breath catches. The address is in the Brigittenau district, where Ari said Nicole is staying.

Adrenaline surges through me. Why would someone leave a message like that on a hotel voice mail? Because Ari was supposed to be here alone.

I study the map, considering. I should call Ari, or at least wait to give him the information. But then I remember his insistence that we not approach Nicole until tonight. My every instinct tells me that waiting is a mistake—by then it may be too late and she will be gone. I cannot afford to take that chance.

I stand up, then hesitate. It is risky to betray Ari's confidence, to go there without him and jeopardize his investigation as well as my own search. Ari will be back soon and perhaps I can talk him into going to find her earlier than planned. But I know that it is futile. He is just as stubborn as me and no amount of cajoling will change his mind. And if I wait for him, I could miss Nicole and lose my only chance to find Jared again.

No, I have to go see Nicole now. Perhaps if I hurry I can get there and back before Ari returns and notices I am gone. My mind made up, I pull my hair back and grab my bag hurriedly. Then, taking one last apologetic look around the hotel room, I slip out the door, the paper clutched tightly in my hand.

chapter EIGHT

O UTSIDE, THE EARLIER downpour has dwindled to a faint drizzle, but the sky remains an ominous gray, heralding more storms to come. I peer down the street in both directions to make sure I don't see Ari before walking toward the corner. Then I hurry to the taxi stand at the intersection, climb in the lone awaiting cab. "Denisgasse achtzehn, bitte," I say in my best high school German.

As we veer from the curb, I gaze out at the unfamiliar street toward the deserted tables of an outdoor café. I think of Ari, my guilt rising. He brought me along; if he hadn't, I'd still be stuck in Monaco without a lead. But his elusiveness in response to my questions, his insistence upon doing things his way, has left me with no other choice than to see if I can find Nicole on my own.

If, I repeat inwardly, doubt flooding my brain. All I have is an address. I don't actually know whether Nicole will be there. And even if she is, she's no more likely to speak with me here than in Monaco.

The cab slows and pulls over abruptly. Surprised, I turn toward the driver. Ari said that Nicole was in another district, but we've barely gone a block.

I lean forward. *"Entschuldigen sie, bitte?"* I manage, but the driver does not respond. The hair on the back of my neck stands on end. Something isn't right.

Suddenly, the rear door behind the driver opens and, before I can react, a sandy-haired man starts to get into the car. I search my memory for the words in German to tell him the cab is taken.

But he looks directly at me, the shared space intentional. "Hello, Jordan."

I freeze. How does he know my name? Alarmed, I pull the door handle but it is locked. I reach again for my nonexistent gun, looking desperately around the interior of the car, searching for a means of escape. I could kick out the window, I think, scream for help.

"It's okay," he says, his English surprisingly crisp and unaccented. American. But given my recent experience in London, the realization is of little comfort. The man's left shoulder moves down, as though he is going for a gun or other weapon. I lunge forward to stop him, but he raises his other hand, warding me off. "Relax. Just getting some identification for you. I'm Tom Montgomery, from the Vienna station." He hands me a card.

CIA, I realize, recognizing the seal. My heart pounds. "How did you find me? Did Mo send you?"

"Mo? I'm afraid I don't know who you're talking about." His confusion seems genuine. But if Mo hadn't sent him, then who? I don't think Lincoln would have betrayed me, and even if he did, I hadn't told him where I am. It would have been virtually impossible for him to triangulate my location so quickly. "I was sent by Paul Van Antwerpen."

"The Director?" I sink back into the seat. "How do I know you're telling the truth?"

"He said you'd be suspicious. Asked me to remind you that the office you occupied at State had the creaky chair he'd used twenty years earlier. And that you had a mutual friend in San Salvador named Margaret."

I relax slightly. The chair was an inside joke between us, something only the Director would have known. And he would not have mentioned Margaret, a secretary at the embassy who was in fact an intelligence asset, to anyone who could not be trusted. "Why did he send you? What does he want?"

He looks uneasily out the window. "I'd rather not discuss this here. Do you mind if we go somewhere more private to talk?"

"I do mind, actually." Isolating a witness is one of the oldest intelligence techniques in the book—the last thing I need is to be cornered somewhere alone with this guy, even if the Director did send him. And I have to get to Nicole before Ari discovers I'm gone and comes after me. "I have to meet someone in ten minutes," I say, wishing I had not given my destination to the driver. "So we can talk here or I'm just getting out."

Montgomery leans forward and says something in German to the driver, who turns off the engine. Then he sits back again. "You resigned your commission with State." He does not overtly acknowledge my ties to his agency, the unique hybrid role I've played these past several years. "May I ask why?"

Part of me would like to tell him everything, to finish off Maureen and the others once and for all. But keeping their secret is the bargain I made with Mo in exchange for not disclosing my whereabouts. And though this man found me, he did so at the Director's behest—Mo has not, as far as I know, broken her promise. No, my fate is inextricably linked to hers, at least for the moment, and so I have to remain silent. "It's a long story," I say at last.

"There's out-processing that needs to be done," he replies coolly. "A certain protocol. If we could just debrief you . . . "

"The London embassy has all of the paperwork on my resignation." But he's talking about more than just some documentation for State. My intelligence work gave me a connection to the agency that is not so easily severed.

"Yes, however, the specifics were a little thin." Guilt rises in me as I imagine the Director learning of my departure, trying to figure out why the protégé he spent so much time and energy grooming had left him without notice or explanation. Mo, his longtime rival, would not have provided him with the details of my resignation, even if they did not implicate her. No, I should have at least called him. I couldn't face his questions, though, or bear to hear the disappointment in his voice. "Anyway, the Director was hoping you would reconsider."

"Oh." The notion that the Director would try to stop me seems at odds with his formal, detached style. I'm flattered, but it doesn't change my decision, or the events that caused me to make it. "I'm afraid that's out of the question. I'm not going back to State." I look out the window at a deliveryman trying to navigate a hand truck piled high with boxes around the puddles on the sidewalk.

"We weren't exactly thinking of State," the man replies quietly.

I fight to keep my reaction neutral. "I-I don't understand," I say. Of course, in truth I know exactly what he is saying but I am buying time, trying to process the information.

"We'd bring you in with us this time, Jordan. Place you under deep cover. Your current status, a disgruntled former diplomat who has resigned, is the perfect story. We can set you up with a private sector job as a cover, or on your own, if you'd prefer . . . "

He continues talking but I don't hear him. My mind reels. Go back in, only deeper this time. He's not talking about official cover, as Lincoln had when he'd posed as a diplomat. Agents like that were at least able to say that they work for the American government and enjoy the protection of diplomatic immunity if something went wrong. This would be something else entirely. Nonofficial cover, or NOC, as it's known, with its lack of governmental acknowledgment or protection, is the most dangerous role an agent can undertake.

Yet despite the risk, the proposal has a certain attraction. I could do the work I loved independently, freed from the bureaucracy I found so frustrating, the deceit that made me flee in the first place. And though I wouldn't be reporting to him directly, I'd be making good on my commitments to Van Antwerpen, not letting him down. But I can't do it, not now, after all that's happened. "I can't," I say finally.

A look of surprise flashes across Montgomery's face. "You can name your terms," he says, as though I had not responded and the matter is still up for debate. "I'm sure I don't have to tell you how unusual this offer is, the lengths the Director went to to make it happen."

"I'm sorry," I say. "But I'm not interested." I force a false air of certainty into my voice, knowing that any hesitation on my part will only prolong the conversation.

He shrugs, gesturing to the card he gave me. "If you change your mind, you can reach me here." I hear a click as the doors unlock.

I tuck the card into my pocket, then climb from the cab. Watching the car pull away, my legs wobble. The Director found me, wants me back, even after I abandoned my post. I will have second thoughts about refusing the offer, I am sure, many times in the days to come. But for now I have to get to Nicole.

Too nervous to try another taxi, I make my way to the U-Bahn station farther down the block, consulting the map on the wall downstairs before buying a ticket. I sink down onto the cracked plastic seat, still shaking from the encounter.

As the train clacks through the darkened tunnel, I consider the man's offer to join the agency. I'd been given the chance once before to cross over in my first days at State, approached during a field trip to Langley with my orientation class. Lincoln brought me to a conference room with a window I could not see through, where two men in dark gray suits were waiting. Did I want to become a CIA agent under diplomatic cover? I hesitated, considering the offer. The idea of intelligence work appealed to me, but I declined, fearing the isolation, a life of lies, secrets kept from those closest to me.

Eighteen months later, in Warsaw, the agency approached me again with a different proposition: remain a Foreign Service Officer, become trained in intelligence. The hybrid concept was a new one, designed for just a handful of carefully selected individuals. Weary from nearly a year on the visa line, I quickly accepted. Within weeks, I had been extricated from my assignment under the pretense of a sick relative and sent to train at the Farm.

But even after that my status was never clear. I wasn't true CIA, recruited from the agency by the outside world, then planted in the diplomatic service or elsewhere. I worked on my own, handling discreet assignments, dispatched as needed by the Director. I never checked in with a station chief or interacted with the rest of the intelligence community, except on a limited, need-to-know basis.

Do I want to go back inside? When I resigned from the government, betrayed by Mo and the others, I slammed that door hard in my mind. Now, with a couple of days and a few thousand miles of distance, I see that they were only one part of the system—a system of which I was once proud.

What would my career have been like if I hadn't quit? Few agents, and even fewer women, spend an entire career in the field. But I couldn't picture myself returning to Washington, growing fat and complacent at a desk job, telling war stories until colleagues had heard them so many times they became cliché. No, I would have kept going, taking assignments from the Director, though the nature and intensity of them would have changed, I am sure, with age.

Enough, I think, as the subway screeches to a halt at the Friedensbrücke station. I'm flattered that the Director had gone to such lengths to find me, but that chapter of my life is over.

I disembark, following the stream of travelers toward the exit. The passageway that leads to the street is surprisingly dirty for the otherwise pristine city, smelling of urine and garbage.

But this is not the Vienna I knew, I quickly realize as I step outside, following the street to a bridge leading over the canal. Brigittenau is an ethnic enclave, shop signs written in Cyrillic, foreign techno music thumping from an unseen source. It is a by-product of the European Union expansion; despite Austria's draconian immigration laws, workers from the former Eastern Bloc countries have found their way here in droves, lured by the promise of higher paying wages in this closest of Western capitals.

Taking in the gritty, working-class district, I am reminded of Brick Lane, the area of London's East End where I pursued Vance Ellis just weeks ago. I'd gone to Vance looking for Duncan, Jared's college research partner. Fear had silenced Duncan, even before Jared's purported death, and he and Vance were left to live their lives in peace—until I came back to England and started asking questions.

Terrified, Duncan fled the country and I followed Vance from the theater where he was performing to an underground gay nightclub in the Indo-Pakistani neighborhood to ask about Duncan's whereabouts. Later that night, Vance turned up dead. Though it appeared a suicide, I knew he was killed for knowing too much—and for talking to me.

I push away my guilt. As I turn the corner onto Denisgasse, the commotion begins to fade behind me. The rain has stopped completely, small puddles on the pavement the only remnant of the earlier storm. The buildings here are more dilapidated, once respectable apartments deteriorated to little more than block flats, laundry lines strung across balconies, satellite dishes littering the façades. I pause, studying the street sign, wondering if I got the directions wrong. It seems impossible to imagine Nicole staying here. Does Jared know that his wife travels to places such as this?

Number 18 is a nondescript apartment building with an empty storefront on the ground level, indiscernible from its neighbors on either side. I reach for the door handle, then stop. I wonder if Nicole will actually be at this address, whether she will be alone. Perhaps I should text Ari now that I am here. But I cannot bring myself to admit that I stole the information he had and risked his investigation for my own selfish purposes.

Inside the building, the foyer is tiny, a bare lightbulb revealing water-stained walls and a gritty tile floor, a hallway with several apartment doors. Turn around, a voice inside my head says. I have no idea what I might find here. I can return to the hotel and pretend this never happened, just tell Ari I went for a walk and go with him later to meet Nicole as planned.

A piercing scream, high and shrill, cuts through the silence like a knife.

I leap back. The scream, which had come from the floor above, reverberates in my mind. It was Nicole's voice, I am certain of it.

I freeze, uncertain what to do. It is madness to rush in unarmed, but if I go for help, it may be too late. I listen for further sounds. Hearing nothing, I start up the stairs, trying to move silently, staying low and close to the wall.

At the second floor landing, I see a door slightly ajar. I walk to it, trying without success to look through the narrow opening into the apartment. Taking a deep breath, I push the door slightly farther open, then stop, gasping.

A man lies motionless on the floor of the apartment, eyes open, a halo of blood circling his head and neck. Kneeling over him, clutching a knife, is Nicole.

"Nicole?" I say. She does not respond. I take a step into the apartment. Her arms and blouse are streaked with bright red. I move toward her, touch her shoulder gently. "Are you all right?"

Startled, she jerks upward, swinging wildly in my direction. I leap back, pulling my midsection away from the arc of the bloody knife, which misses me by inches. As she starts to slice back toward me from the other direction, I catch her wrist, holding her at bay. "Nicole, stop!"

She stares back, her eyes wild, too disoriented to recognize me. Behind her I notice a bottle of wine broken on the floor, its contents still dripping down the wall where it had smashed. "It's Jordan Weiss. We met in Monaco, remember? I'm not going to hurt you." Her eyes dart back and forth and she processes the information. Then her arm relaxes slightly beneath my grasp, but her distrustful expression remains. Her once well-coiffed hair is wild, her skin pale and clammy. "What happened?"

She does not answer. Her arm tenses once more and her eyes widen. But she is not looking at me, I realize, following her gaze over my shoulder.

Before I can turn, something slams into me with full force. I am thrown forward and Nicole jerks from my grasp, pulling away. As she does, the knife slices across my forearm. I scream as blood spurts from my wrist and I crash to the apartment floor, landing with a sickening thud on top of the dead man's chest.

I try to get up, but a foot kicks me, sending me sprawling face-first onto the corpse once more. Searing daggers of pain shoot through my arm. I raise my head. By the door of the apartment, I see Nicole standing uncertainly, eyes darting from me to the hall-way. "Nicole . . . " I say, imploring her for help. But she takes one last look back at me, then disappears through the door.

"Nic . . . " I start to call after her again. But before I can finish, hands grab me roughly by the collar, jerking me up. Out of the corner of my eye, I glimpse a large, swarthy man in a black leather coat.

Instinctively, I shoot my leg out behind me in a donkey kick, aiming for my attacker's groin as hard as I can. My kick misses its target, landing on his inner thigh. Momentarily stunned, the man releases me with a grunt. I spin around, and as I do, an elbow smashes into my jaw and I fly backward, hitting my head hard against the floor. Fireworks of pain explode bright white in my brain. Then the man is gone, running after Nicole.

I struggle to my knees, gasping for breath. Hearing footsteps at the door, I try to stand up and defend myself. Someone grabs me from behind.

"Jordan, it's me." It is Ari, arms strong and reassuring around me. I relax slightly, inhaling his now-familiar scent. He releases me. "What happened? Are you all right?" His voice rises with concern.

I notice for the first time that I am sprayed with blood—mine as well as the dead man's—making my injury appear much worse than it really is. "I'm fine," I say, holding up my still bleeding wrist.

"Did you . . . ?" His eyes travel toward the dead man on the floor.

"No," I reply quickly. "He was already that way when I arrived. But Nicole . . . "

"You saw her? She was here?"

I nod. "I don't know if she did this or not. There was another man. She took off and he ran after her."

He opens his mouth as though he wants to ask me something else, then closes it again. "We've got to get out of here in case someone heard the commotion and called the police. The last thing we want is to be hung up in a murder investigation." He stands and helps me to my feet before going to the dead man. Running his hands over the body, he pulls out a wallet and starts looking through it.

"Who is he?"

"I'll explain later." He returns the wallet to the man's pocket. Then he reaches underneath the body and removes a gun, which he tucks in his waistband. "Let's go."

"But what's going on?" I persist as I follow him into the hallway. "I mean, is it related to—"

"Shhh!" Ari hisses. He clamps his hand over my mouth, pressing me back against the wall. There are footsteps below, growing louder. He steps away, drawing his gun. Then he crouches low, gesturing for me to stay back as he advances toward the stairwell.

An apartment door closes and the footsteps fade to silence.

"We need to get out of here. Come on." Not waiting for me to follow, he grabs my arm and pulls me toward the stairs.

Outside, he releases me and scans the street in both directions. He starts walking quickly away from the building, seeming not to care if I follow. I struggle to keep up with his long gait.

When we are several blocks away, he draws me into the doorway of an abandoned building. "Are you okay?" He runs his hands over my shoulders and torso. But his touch is impersonal, a medic checking for injuries.

"Fine, just this." I hold up my arm.

He studies it, his brow wrinkling. "That's a deep cut. You almost sliced the artery." He pulls off his shirt, tying it around my forearm to stop the bleeding. Then he looks up again, concern replaced by anger. "Dammit, Jordan. What were you thinking?"

I bite my lip, dreading the inevitable confrontation, searching for a good explanation for my actions and finding none. "I wanted to get to Nicole right away," I manage lamely.

"So you just stole my information and went on your own?" he demands. I do not answer. "You should have followed my plan and waited. Instead, you went in, unarmed and alone . . . " He turns away. "You could have been killed."

"I didn't need you rescuing me," I insist stubbornly. "I could have handled it." But even as I say this, I know that it is not true. "Anyhow, I had no idea there was any danger." I recall that he did not seem surprised by the dead man on the floor. "Who were those men, Ari?"

I half-expect him to deny knowing, but he does not. "Let's get out of here first," he says instead. Looking both ways over his shoulders, he leads me from the alley and down the street.

chapter NINE

B ACK IN THE hotel room, Ari fills the electric kettle that sits on the low table and plugs it in. I sink to the foot of the bed. "Nicole's gone."

"Of course she is." He goes to his bag and pulls out a shirt and a small plastic case. He crosses the room, putting on the shirt before kneeling down in front of me. "Let me see your arm." His breath is warm on my skin as he examines my slashed wrist. He frowns and pulls a suture needle from the kit.

I pull back. "What are you doing?"

"You need stitches."

"And you're going to do them?"

"Unless you want to go to a hospital."

I consider the option, then shake my head. Too many questions, too much time. "I've stitched guys up a dozen times in the army," he adds, opening an alcohol swab. There is a stinging burn as he cleans the wound site. He raises the needle. "You might not want to watch this."

"I can handle it." But I avert my eyes, staring hard at the wall.

"I came back and you were gone," he says, his voice recriminating.

"How did you find me?" My guilt grows.

"I heard the message on the voice mail and figured it out."

"I didn't mean to listen," I say weakly. "I mean, I didn't know that's what the message would be, and then once I heard it and figured it out, well . . . "

"And now Nicole is gone."

"Even if I had waited for you, Nicole might be gone anyway—or worse." I bite my lip, willing myself not to scream at the searing pain in my arm as the needle cuts into my raw flesh.

"She would probably be dead by now," he admits.

"Dead?" Suddenly the gravity of the situation I encountered sinks in. Of course if Nicole were dead, then Jared would be single and . . . I stop, appalled by the callousness of my own thought.

I glance back in time to see Ari pulling the final stitch through my arm. The room starts to wobble. "Who were those men, Ari?" I ask, forcing myself to breathe.

He does not respond, but ties off the stitch, then cleans the wound site with another alcohol swab. "I'm sorry that I went out on my own," I say, grabbing his arm. I am thrown off balance by the intimacy of my own gesture, the warmth of his skin against mine. "You keep asking me to trust you, but how can I do that when you won't tell me the truth? I've been burned before by people who were supposed to be my partners and friends. I can't let that happen again. And if we keep going with these half-truths we're going to destroy our search and each other. So we're either all in or we're not. It's time to stop holding out on me."

He gazes at me for several seconds before pulling away. Straightening, he walks to the table and pulls out two tea bags. His hand shakes slightly as he sets them in cups. "There are two different answers to your question, one for the man on the floor, and one for the man who went after Nicole."

"They're not together?"

"I don't think so. The dead man was Friedrich Heigler. He worked with Nicole on the wine deal. He was who I was hoping to find her with at the meeting."

"But you said that transaction was supposed to take place later tonight."

"It was. They must have moved the meeting time."

"Or Heigler showed up unexpectedly," I suggest.

He picks up a teaspoon, twirls it between his thumb and forefinger. "True. They could have had an argument of some sort."

"Do you think Nicole killed him?"

He pauses, considering the question. "It's hard to imagine."

How can he be so certain, I wonder? It's not as if he knows Nicole. "She was holding the knife," I point out. "Of course, she could have told us if she'd bothered to stick around after I interrupted whatever was going on."

"She has a funny way of expressing her gratitude," he agrees.

"Or the man who attacked me could have stabbed Heigler. Who was he?"

He stops in front of me. Our eyes meet. "Have you ever heard of Marcos Santini?"

"I haven't. Was that him?"

"No, but it might have been one of his men."

"His men?" I tilt my head. "I don't follow . . . "

"Santini heads one of the largest criminal enterprises in northern Italy."

"The Mafia?"

"Not exactly. Santini is related to some mob types, and his aunt is one of the most powerful bosses in Naples. He—"

"His aunt?" I interrupt, surprised.

"Yes, female crime bosses are more common than you'd expect. Lucia Santini, or the Little Tiger, as she is sometimes known, took over when her husband was sent to prison, and she's as ruthless as any male don. But Marcos himself is much more of a businessman. You're more likely to find him making money from insider trading than extortion."

"What does he have to do with Nicole?"

"Like I said earlier, the wine fraud was a dangerous business. Remember the investment funds?" I nod. The kettle bubbles, steam shooting upward through the spout. "Nicole sold the fake shipment of Bordeaux to a wine fund based out of London. When the wine was proven to be fraudulent, the fund was devalued and lost millions."

"All because of one shipment of wine?" He nods. "Was it worth that much?"

"Not the Bordeaux alone. It was valuable, but not that valuable. But the fake sale had a ripple effect. Investors lost confidence in the fund and pulled out, and the principals who remained took a big hit." He lifts the kettle from its base and pours the water into the teacups, not looking up. "Santini was one of the fund's principal investors." He holds up the teacup. "Milk?"

"No thanks." I take the teacup he hands me, then wave away the pack of sugar he offers. "And Santini's after Nicole for revenge?"

He shakes his head. "Like I said, Santini's a businessman. More likely trying to extract the money he lost. Although I'm sure there's some wounded ego at work here, too. Santini fancies himself an expert on wines and he was likely furious that Nicole duped him."

"I'm not so sure about this kinder, gentler Mafia," I reply. "I mean, I didn't get a good look at him, but the man who ran from Nicole's apartment seemed like your standard thug to me."

"The old ways die hard with these guys," Ari agrees. "Don't get me wrong; Santini's not above using some muscle when he has to get the job done, and he can be just as ruthless as the Old World mobsters, if not more so. But he's not going to dirty his own hands to do it."

"So he sent that guy to try to get money from Nicole?"

"Probably. I could have found out if I caught him. But by the time I got there, he was running away."

Ari could have gone after Santini's man. But instead he had run into the apartment to find me.

"The mob's after Nicole," I say, processing.

"In a sense. Assuming that guy didn't catch her after leaving the apartment." Alarm rises in me. If something happens to Nicole, my chances of finding Jared are nonexistent. "Don't worry," Ari adds quickly. "Nicole's pretty resourceful. And I doubt Santini's man would have risked another confrontation so soon after what happened at the apartment. They're more likely to regroup and then go after her again."

Remembering Heigler's body on the floor of the apartment, I shiver, then wrap my hands around the cup and take a sip, scalding my tongue with the too-hot liquid. "It just seems so implausible," I say. "Killing over wine." But even as I say this, I know that it's not about the wine. It is about money, just as it had been with Jared's research and the secrets he threatened to expose.

"What about the authorities?" I ask. "Why not go to the police with this?"

"Impossible. The wine transaction was illegal in the first place, so involving the police would put everyone at risk for prosecution. Including Nicole," he adds, as though for my benefit. If Nicole is incarcerated, she won't be able to lead me to Jared. "And as I told you on the plane, my clients, the wine industry folks, prefer to deal with it off-line because they want to keep the fraud issue as quiet as possible."

"But if you knew that the mob was after Nicole, why did you want to wait to confront her?" I ask, taking another sip.

"I had no idea," he insists. "I mean, I knew she had angered some nasty people by selling the fake wine and that she had a meeting set up here related to the sale. But I didn't think that the mob would come after her here." Seeing my mistrustful expression, he reaches down and takes my hand. "My sources gave no indication. If I had known, I would have tried to get to her first."

I pause, considering his explanation. It makes sense. He didn't want Nicole killed any more than I did. "I believe you," I say finally.

"Of course, if you had just trusted me, instead of going behind my back . . . " He drops my hand and turns away.

"I'm sorry," I reply quickly. "I was afraid of losing Nicole again." Which happened anyway. "I went on an impulse. I didn't think."

"I've been burned before, too, Jordan."

"Oh." I am not entirely surprised. The fact that we have both been betrayed by those we trusted is one of the things that makes Ari and I understand each other so readily. But maybe it means that we can't trust each other enough to work together. My stomach twists at the thought. Ari is the only hope I have of finding Jared. "Let's make a pact," I say, standing up and taking his hand. "No more secrets, okay? We tell each other everything and neither goes off alone. We'll swear to have each others' backs."

I watch his face as he considers the proposition. "All right."

I remember the CIA agent who had approached me in the cab. Should I tell Ari about him? I feel guilty about keeping it from him so soon after we've promised to be honest with each other. But it isn't relevant to what we are doing here, and I do not want to answer the complex questions about my background the disclosure would raise. "So what now?" I ask instead.

"Back to square one," he replies. "Comb my sources, try to figure out where Nicole went from here, and get to her before Santini's men."

I consider asking what kind of sources he has, then decide against it, not wanting to overstep. "There's another issue, though," he adds. "The man in Nicole's apartment saw you and knows that you saw him. That makes you a target—and one that they likely want eliminated."

A chill runs up my spine. "Great. So I lost Nicole for us, and put myself at risk." I wait for Ari to disagree or tell me I am being too hard on myself, but he does not. "If these men are as dangerous as you say, I'll need one of those." I gesture to the pistol at his waist.

He raises an eyebrow. "Do you know how to use it?"

I quickly realize my error. Ordinary diplomats do not, as a matter of course, need guns—my firearms training was only a product of my special intelligence role. I search for a plausible explanation but find none.

"I wouldn't have thought you carried one," he adds.

I shift uncomfortably. "I had some unusual assignments these past few years. Before England, I mean."

"Oh." He does not seem surprised. No, of course not. He has already seen my dossier. How on earth does he know so much about me? His access to information suggests that he is something more than a private investigator, though perhaps he still has contacts from his military days. The imbalance of knowledge in our relationship creeps up once again, making me uneasy. I make a mental note to circle back with Lincoln, see what if anything about Ari he has learned, as soon as I am alone again.

My thoughts return to Santini's men and I look around the room uneasily. "Do you think they know where we're staying?"

He shakes his head. "I've never shared this location with anyone." Except the contact who called with Nicole's whereabouts, I think. He continues, "So we should be safe. But, all the same, I may try to find us another place."

"I'm not sure that we need to stay in Vienna at all," I observe, standing up. "Now that Nicole knows someone is after her, she's sure to take off."

He does not respond but sits down beside me and grasps my forearm, drawing it closer to him and resting it in his lap. I shiver at the unexpected touch. My pulse quickens. What is he doing?

Then I notice he's staring down, studying the stitches. "How's your arm?"

Embarrassed to have misunderstood, I look away, feeling the heat rise in my neck. "Fine."

But he brings my arm closer and his fingers remain, grazing the soft underside. "Jordan," he says, and as our eyes meet I realize that the attraction to him, which I've been trying to ignore, is not one-sided. My breath catches. He brings my fingers to his mouth. I am too surprised to respond as he presses them against his lips. An urge to protest rises in me, falls quickly again. He begins to suck gently on my fingertips, sending tremors of electricity through me. My knees buckle and he catches me, drawing me close until I am half-sitting on his lap.

I pull my hand away. "Jor—" he begins, his voice part apology and part plea. But before he can finish my name, I lean forward, putting my mouth on his, meeting his open lips with such force that he rocks backward on the bed. He wraps his arms around me as he falls, taking me with him.

As he unbuttons my shirt, a moment of doubt flashes through my mind: I don't know him, shouldn't trust him. But he is kissing me harder now, hands running down my body. Desire rises in me. There have been others, of course, my awkward night with Chris in London that was a mistake before it happened, my perfunctory trysts with Mark, the Secret Service officer I dated before leaving Washington. But neither was like this. This is the promise I thought I glimpsed with Sebastian, what it might have been had he not proven to be a traitor. I push the thought from my mind as I let myself be swept away by passion I haven't felt in a decade.

I reach down for him, first on the outside of his jeans and then beneath the fabric, and he groans, growing taut. He follows my lead, hands dropping lower, exploring. He touches me and in that instant I explode, all of the pent-up desire rushing forth in a single burst of light.

"Do you have a condom?" I whisper into his shoulder, as the initial waves of passion subside, practicality intruding upon desire. Though I want him beyond all reason, to let myself sleep with him unprotected is a mistake too costly to make again.

He groans. "No. I hadn't exactly planned for something like this."

I roll to one side, still holding him close. Somehow the fact that he isn't prepared for this—with me or anyone else—makes me feel better. "I can run out and get something . . . " he suggests.

I hesitate, my need to have all of him conflicting with not wanting to break from the moment. "Not now."

"All right," he acquiesces, not pressing, willing to take what is offered. For a minute I wonder if our encounter has gone as far as it will, but then he lifts up on one elbow, pushing me back to the bed and lowering his head, lips trailing down my torso as his hands travel farther. I close my eyes.

Afterward we lie in the darkness, not speaking. His breathing grows long and even and for a minute I think he is asleep, but when I turn toward him he is watching my face, studying me. "What?" I demand, pulling my rumpled shirt down, immediately self-conscious.

"Nothing. I was just thinking about something you said earlier, that you were betrayed by someone you trusted. Who was it?"

I swallow, realizing how very little I've told Ari about what happened. "A few people, actually. You see, there were men looking for Jared because of his research, powerful men. And Mo . . . " I am unable to hold back any longer. "She was the deputy ambassador in London. She was also my mentor at State and someone I thought I could trust. But then I found out she helped fake a letter from my best friend, Sarah, who's very sick with ALS, to get me to come to England to help draw out Jared."

"I see," he says, his expression impassive.

"There was someone else, too." Sebastian's face appears in my mind. "I worked with a man in London, a Scottish agent. We were on a task force together, but he turned out to be a traitor."

"There was no way you could have known, I'm sure." His voice is soothing.

I shrug. "Maybe, maybe not. I wasn't at my best in England—I was emotional and on edge with all of the baggage from my past there and I made a lot of mistakes because of it. I got close to Sebastian and became involved, and it clouded my instincts. My colleague

Sophie and another person were killed as a result, and my friend Sarah nearly was as well."

He is silent for several seconds and I wonder if he thinks less of me now that he knows about my error in judgment. But then he wraps his arms around me, burying his head in my neck. Our chests rise and fall in unison until I cannot tell where his breathing stops and mine begins. My body still tingles, reminding me of what just happened between us. It was not as unexpected as I would like to pretend—there has been a spark of attraction between us since we met, flamed by the adrenaline of the danger we just encountered while chasing Nicole.

I like him, I realize suddenly. Really like him. The thought is as startling as it is undeniable. This is not some fling because we happen to be together, a moment born out of convenience, or our considerable physical attraction. We understand each other in a way I haven't felt since Jared, perhaps even more so because our bond comes from our shared experiences, the deeper nuances that have made us who we are as adults. There is a connection between Ari and me, an intensity to the chemistry between us, that tells me it could be something more.

My muscles tense. This can't happen. I cannot afford to get involved in anything complicated now, while my life is so unsettled and the answers I need from Jared so close.

Not that I think Ari is looking for a relationship. I've known men like him, operatives who travel the world, picking up mercenary assignments. They have women in every country, slip in and out of liaisons as seamlessly as the James Bond–type characters they seem to play. Men like Ari do not, cannot, allow themselves to become attached.

Drowsiness washes over me then, dulling my confusion. Bury-

ing my head deeper into Ari's chest, I close my eyes and allow myself
to be carried off to sleep.

My eyes snap open. It is completely dark and for a moment I
cannot remember where I am. The hotel, I think groggily. What
time is it? My arm begins to throb and I recall the confrontation
when I went to see Nicole, my encounter with Ari. I reach beside
me, feeling for him, but the bed is cold and empty.

I sit up. "Ari?" I call. Silence. I reach for the lamp. Where is he?
I check the pad of paper on the nightstand, but this time there is no
note.

I lie back down, replaying our earlier encounter in my mind, the
pleasure we had given each other that, while short of everything,
was intense. Did I do something wrong? Perhaps he was angered by
the fact that I had stopped things. But I had made that mistake once
before. I see it now, an impulsive moment in my college room one
spring morning a lifetime ago, Jared rising above me, passion overcoming common sense.

The scene clears as quickly as it had come, replaced by the darker
vision of the doctor's office. I had taken the home pregnancy test as
soon as I missed my period, shortly after returning from England,
my heart dropping as the second pink line appeared, confirming my
fears. So I was not more than a few weeks pregnant when I called the
clinic that I had found in the phone book, located in northern Vir-
ginia just beyond the Beltway, begging for the earliest appointment
possible. The receptionist's response was perfunctory, our exchange
routine, as if we were scheduling a hair appointment or dental
checkup.

I called in sick to my State Department orientation class that
late summer morning and drove to the clinic, drowning out the
shouts of the few protesters that stood by the entrance to the park-

ing lot. Yes, I lied as I filled out the preadmission paperwork, there was someone coming to pick me up afterward. I did not listen to the nurse's presentation as she explained the procedure, the other options that were available to me. I had always been staunchly pro-choice, had marched in the demonstrations as an undergraduate to keep *Roe v. Wade* legal, even before I was old enough to vote. Anyway, what else was I going to do? I was twenty-two years old and on my own, about to embark on a career that would take me to places around the globe. Jared was dead. There was no place in my life for a baby.

I do not remember the procedure itself. Afterward, I lay on a recliner in a room with a half dozen other women, nibbling on graham crackers, sipping orange juice, and listening to someone weep. Just a few months earlier I had been at Cambridge, drinking Pimm's at garden parties, basking in the sunshine. How had I come to be here? It seemed as if my happiness had been so wrong that I was now being forced to atone for it.

In the intervening years, I never told anyone, not even Sarah. I had buried the memory so deep that it sometimes seemed a figment of my imagination, a nightmare that hadn't actually happened. Even as I returned to England, chasing the ghosts of my past, I had not allowed myself to think about it. But since learning that Jared is alive, the images have begun to creep into my consciousness again, a persistent shadow reminding me of what I had done.

Now for the first time, lying in this strange hotel room, the memories and remorse come flooding back unchecked. Assuming that Jared was gone forever, I had taken his baby. Would my decision have been any different if I had known? I want to say no, to shroud myself with the certainty that I would have had the abortion anyway, gone ahead with my solo life and career. But in truth I know that I would have returned to England and told him the news. Together we would have made the decision, I am sure, to take the leap into the chaos of an unplanned child and have a family. If only I had known. It would have been different. Everything would have been different.

I understand now for the first time that it is not just my memories of Jared that have kept me from getting close to another man all of these years, but my guilt over what I had done. I didn't believe I deserved pleasure after all that had happened, could not separate in my soul the passion I had enjoyed with Jared from the consequences that would be with me for a lifetime.

Feeling the walls start to crumble in on myself, I push the memories from my mind. Sarah, I think. Despite the years and thousands of miles that have separated us, she's always been my best friend, therapist, and confessional, all rolled into one. Now I find myself wishing she were here, that I could speak to her and try to make sense of it all.

I fish my cell phone from my bag. I hesitate. It is the middle of the night. But that's never mattered before. I dial her number.

"Hello?" Sarah answers sleepily.

"It's Jordan, Sar," I say.

She is instantly awake. "Jordie, what is it? Is everything okay?"

"Fine," I reply quickly, feeling guilty and foolish at having woken her. "I'm sorry for calling so late. I just wanted to say hello."

"I'm glad to hear from you. How are you?"

"Fine . . . " I falter, unsure how much to say. "My initial lead didn't pan out, so we—"

"We?"

I swipe my hair from my forehead. I'd nearly forgotten how much has happened in the few days since I last spoke with her. "I'm traveling with a man named Aaron, who is looking for Nic—" I take a deep breath, realizing that I need to back up and explain, trying to figure out where to begin. "Jared's married," I blurt out.

"Oh." She is not, I can tell, that surprised. "Are you okay?"

I falter, uncertain how to answer. Since learning about Jared's marriage, I've focused on the fact of it, what it meant for my search. But it is the emotions beneath the discovery that hit me—for years, Jared's death was something determined by fates larger than us. It wasn't personal. Now, speaking with Sarah, the reality sinks in: Jared had chosen a course other than coming back to me. It was rejection, as surely as if he had broken up with me before our time at college had ended. "I don't know. Anyway," I swallow, brushing away the subject, "Aaron, the man I mentioned, is trying to find Jared's wife, Nicole. So we've teamed up—"

"You're still going after Jared," Sarah interrupts.

"I am. I still want answers." And to see him again. "And Ari thinks—"

"Ari," she repeats, her tone observant, noncritical. "What's he like?"

"Israeli. Handsome. 'Fit,' as our British friends would say." I cringe, hoping she cannot sense me blushing. "Very stubborn."

"Sounds like someone else." She laughs, then her voice turns serious. "But Jordie . . . " Though she does not finish the sentence, I can hear the conflict in her voice, mirroring my own internal debate, worrying that I will misplace my trust again so soon after Sebastian, but not wanting to discourage me from opening up if there is finally a chance of finding something real.

"I know. The timing is all wrong and I still have to find Jared."

"I don't care about Jared," she snaps. Her tone, sharper than I remember hearing her speak, startles me. "You don't owe him anything. You mourned him for ten years—needlessly, I might add. You put your life on the line to make sure his research got into the right hands and now you're traveling around the world trying to find him." And he's married, I finish silently for her, knowing that she will not. "I just don't want you to get hurt again," she finishes.

"I won't. I'm being careful, I promise. But enough of this. How are you?"

"Great." Her voice brightens. "I haven't started my treatments; they're still running tests. But it's beautiful here and lovely having Ryan with me. In fact, we're taking a drive out to the lake tomorrow. So whatever happens . . ." I can tell that she is trying not to get her hopes up, to be content with Geneva, whether the treatments can help or whether these turn out to be her last days.

"Don't say that, Sar. Don't even think it. You're in the best place in the world and the protocol is going to work." It has to work. "Now you go get some sleep, okay? I'll talk to you soon."

As I lower the phone, there is a clicking noise and the door opens. "Hello?" I call the way I might have as a child when I heard my parents come up the stairs.

"It's me," Ari says, the use of the pronoun in lieu of his name as intimate as anything that has transpired between us. "Sorry to wake you."

"I was already up. Is everything all right?"

"Yes, I didn't mean for you to worry. I went to get some water. Oh, and here . . ." Then he reaches into his jacket and pulls out his pistol, aiming it at the floor and checking the chamber to make sure it is empty. I stare at the gun, surprised. "You said you needed one," he explains.

"I do, but . . ."

One side of his mouth lifts in a half smile. "I think I can trust you with it." Then his face turns serious. "And I'd feel better knowing you have it." There is a protectiveness in his voice that tells me more than I have known about his feelings for me. It is not just physical for him, either. "In case we get separated," he adds.

"Separated?" I repeat. In that moment I realize how accustomed I have gotten to having Ari at my side in the very short time since we met, of thinking of us as a team. "Why would that happen?"

"No reason." But a strange look flashes across his face, making me wonder what he isn't telling me. "You know how to use it, right?"

I smile inwardly, remembering the surprise of my male colleagues when I outscored them all at the range. "Sure." I wrap my hand around the grip, feeling the weight of the pistol, trying it on for size. "But what about you?"

He shrugs. "I can use the one I pulled off Heigler's body."

"I can take that one, if you want."

"No, take mine. It's better, more reliable. Be careful, though. Kicks a little to the right."

Longing rises within me as I picture my own Glock, left back at the embassy in London. One does not part with one's own gun easily and it means a great deal that Ari is trusting me with his. "Thanks." I put the gun in my bag.

"I should have given that to you before. Of course I didn't realize . . . " His voice trails off. Despite all that has transpired between us, he is still stung by my earlier betrayal, the fact that I had gone after Nicole on my own. Then his face brightens. "And I also got these." He holds up a box of condoms.

"Oh." I pause, not sure what the appropriate response might be, whether to thank him or make a joke.

"Not presuming," he adds quickly. "But just in case."

"Just in case," I repeat slowly. Desire rises up in me again and I reach for him, pulling him down to the bed beside me.

As I draw him close, I feel a vibrating sensation, his phone against my leg. He continues kissing me and for a minute it seems he will ignore it. But then he groans and rolls away. "Hello?" I hear a man's voice speaking rapidly on the other end of the line.

A moment later Ari closes the phone. "Who was that?" I ask.

"Someone who might have the answers we need." He lingers close to me for a second before jumping to his feet.

I sit up reluctantly, pulling down my shirt. "Where are we going?"

"There's no time. I'll explain on the way. And bring everything with you." I cock my head. "If we are able to get the information I'm hoping for, we won't be coming back."

chapter TEN

I OPEN MY EYES and peer across the car in the semidarkness. "Hey."

Ari does not look away from the road, but shifts gears, navigating around a sharp mountain curve with ease. The low purring of the engine breaks the night stillness. "Get some rest?"

"Mmph," I mumble, rubbing my eyes and sitting up. "Where are we?"

"Close to the border."

We left the hotel a few hours earlier. Ari didn't check us out, and though he did not say so, I knew that he had done this in case we were being watched, not because he really expected that we would return. Then he led me to the car we are in now, a small black Fiat that had been parked in a garage around the corner from the hotel. I wondered if the car was his or, if not, how he had gotten it, but I didn't ask and he didn't offer an explanation. We drove out of the city in silence, the neighborhoods growing more residential as we passed through the outskirts, houses dark and shuttered for the night.

"Where are we going?" I asked, once we reached the autobahn.

"Northern Italy. There's a winemaker there who might be able to help us find Nicole."

"Italy," I repeated, surprised by the distance we were traveling, as well as the fact that we seemed to be doubling back toward the Mediterranean region we'd left so recently. "Wouldn't it have been faster to fly?"

He shook his head. "The vineyard is a good distance northwest of Trieste, the closest city, and by the time you factor in waiting for flights, then renting a car at the airport, it would have taken just as long."

"Oh." Though his explanation made sense, I could not help but wonder if this was his real reason for driving, or if he wanted to keep our travels beneath the radar so as not to be detected by Santini's men.

South of Vienna, the landscape grew rugged. Ari drove skillfully, anticipating curves and avoiding bumps with the confidence of someone who had traveled the roads before. He did not speak further but turned the radio to a station playing jazz and, lulled by the music and the motion of the car, I soon became sleepy.

I sit up now, peering out the window and trying to get my bearings. The terrain is less dramatic than it had been a few hours earlier, the topography more hills than peaks. The road, now a single lane in each direction, is deserted as far as I can see.

"How are you feeling?" Ari asks and I cannot tell if he is referring to my stitched arm or our earlier intimacy.

I decide to assume the former. "Fine. My wrist is just a bit sore. I could do with some coffee and a bathroom, though."

"Me, too, but there's nothing around here. It makes me miss those American rest stops with their Howard Johnsons."

I smile. "More like Starbucks these days."

"It's been a while," he concedes. "Anyway, no lattes here. If you

need to use the toilet, I can pull over once we clear the checkpoint."
He glances up at the sky, which has begun to fade to pale gray, and
I can tell he is anxious to cross the border before dawn.

"I'm okay," I say, eyeing the thick, ominous brush that lines either side of the road. I open the window. The crisp night air is
earthy, perfumed by a mixture of burned leaves and manure. "Are
we going much farther?"

He pulls a bottle of water from his bag and hands it to me. I take
a sip, enough to moisten my mouth but not worsen my bladder.
"Not too far." Trieste, I recall, scanning the map in my head, is on
that little bit of Italy over by the Balkans.

Ari takes the bottle from me and gulps several mouthfuls of
water. Watching his throat move in the moonlight, I am reminded
of our earlier tryst. Despite my eagerness to find Nicole, part of me
wishes we were back in the hotel, able to finish what we started.

We travel farther along the desolate road and a few minutes later
reach the border crossing. It is little more than a shed, and through
the cracked, dirty window I see two guards, one napping, the other
watching a black-and-white movie on a small television. There is no
gate or checkpoint, nothing to stop us from passing by undetected
into Italy. It seems a sharp contrast to my memories of backpacking
as a student, border guards knocking on the door of our train com-
partment two or three times each night, turning on the glaring overhead lights to scrutinize our passports.

Ari pulls close to the shed, raps lightly on the door. The guard
sticks his head out and scans our passports idly before nodding us
on. "I miss the days with all of the stamps," I remark when the door
has closed again.

"This borderless European Union has its advantages but that
isn't one of them," he agrees.

I notice then that the radio program has changed from music to some sort of discussion in German. "What are you listening to?"

"It's a news and commentary program." He grimaces. "They're talking about Israel and the Gaza situation."

I nod. The latest round of Israeli attacks against Hezbollah had been all over the British press before I left London, the coverage of Israel's actions and the repercussions for the Palestinians scathing. "I've been out of touch for a few days. What happened?"

"Israel went after a Hezbollah stronghold and some civilians were killed. The U.N. is demanding a cease-fire."

"That's terrible."

"The collateral damage is awful," he agrees. "But unavoidable."

Hearing his cold, detached tone, I feel myself growing annoyed. Did he regard his own family's deaths as collateral damage as well? "But if your country—"

"Which one?" he interrupts, stiffening.

I falter. With his accent and bronzed skin, it's easy to forget that he is also American. "Israel," I say.

His face reddens. "We have to be able to defend ourselves. No one else is going to make sure that there's a Jewish homeland. I remember the stories my father told growing up, of his parents being turned away from a dozen countries as they tried to flee Europe. Don't get me wrong; I love America, believe in it. But there was a time when it turned its back on the Jewish people, along with the rest of the world."

"And you think it could happen again?"

"Yes. That's why I will always choose Israel. If forced to choose," he adds.

My anger grows. "Then perhaps you shouldn't be an American citizen."

"Since when does citizenship mean blind loyalty? Don't you ever question the government?"

"I do. And I'm not saying that I don't support Israel. I understand why we need a Jewish state. But we use the Holocaust as an excuse to set ourselves apart and claim that the rules don't apply to us."

"It was genocide!" he explodes. "Six million killed."

"And what about Rwanda, Yugoslavia, Cambodia?" I demand. "Is Darfur any less horrific? Or does the world just care less because the victims aren't white and it isn't happening in Europe?" I pause but he does not respond. "Ari, I'm not saying that the Holocaust didn't give the Jews a mandate for Israel. But we've turned that into some kind of entitlement for aggression. We've taken our suffering and made it a sword instead of a shield, using it to tread on others, the same way that our rights were trampled."

He slams his hand on the dashboard. "You haven't lived as we do, surrounded by enemies. I mean, imagine it, the very people who want you dead just a few miles away. The entire trip to the border was a shorter distance from our home than the average commute in Washington."

I stare at him, surprised how heated our discussion has grown in such a short time. Then I swallow, take a step back. "I'm not saying Israel shouldn't defend itself. But some sense of proportionality, a responsibility toward the innocent civilians . . . "

"You haven't been there," he protests again. "It's almost impossible to fight an enemy that wages guerrilla warfare, uses civilians as shields, without some casualties. We do what we have to do to survive."

Frustration rises in me. Ari is a smart man—why is he so blind to the foibles of his government? "One could say the same about the

United States," he adds, before I can say anything further. "You go into Iraq and overthrow the government with little justification. Yet you ignore conflicts where the suffering is far more egregious, like the Congo and Sudan."

I bite my lip. I've encountered such opinions about the United States many times in recent years and, now as then, a knee-jerk reaction not unlike Ari's rises up in me to defend my government. But he's right. We're guilty of the same kind of aggression as Israel, maybe worse, and we don't even have the geographic proximity of our enemies as an imminent threat to justify our actions. "I don't disagree," I concede at last. "I think both countries have taken some actions that are hard, if not impossible, to justify."

He shakes his head slightly. "And I think that in Israel's case, the ends justify the means."

My shoulders slump. Ari is in a place I was not long ago, still unable to acknowledge the weaknesses of his government without allowing his whole framework to fall apart. I push down my instinct to press my point, my insistence upon prevailing. I am not going to convince him now. "Maybe we should just lay off the politics, agree to disagree."

He does not answer but stares straight ahead at the road, rebuking my peace offering. A minute later we turn off onto a narrower, winding road. In the pale, predawn light I can see that the hills on either side are covered in fields, broken only by the occasional farmhouse. Workers disembark from trucks, beginning their day.

Soon we turn again, this time onto an unmarked gravel driveway. It ends at a stone farmhouse, indiscernible from a dozen others we have passed.

Ari slows the car and just then the sun begins to break over the horizon. Beyond the house the land drops off sharply, revealing a valley, plants bathed in golden yellow light, rows of trellises stretching endlessly below us.

"This is the Conti vineyard," Ari explains as we get out of the car. "The Contis are one of the foremost winemaking families in the region. Signor Conti is also world renowned for his palate and an expert on authentication. With his connections in the industry, I thought he might be able to help us find Nicole."

Might, I repeat silently. Have we traveled all night for a possible lead? I want to ask whether he really thinks this man will be able to help, why we could not have ascertained that by phone without leaving the place we had last seen Nicole. But Ari is striding down the path toward the house. I follow, still gazing out across the vineyard at an eagle sweeping low above the plants.

As we near the porch, I study the farmhouse, wondering whether we will be waking them. But drawing closer, I notice a light burning brightly in the front window. A pane of glass in the door is broken, its jagged edges seemingly out of place in the otherwise well-tended exterior.

The door opens a crack and an older woman peers out nervously. Then, recognizing Ari, her face breaks into a smile and she flings the door wide.

"Aaron!" she cries, coming out of the house and kissing him on both cheeks.

"*Buongiorno*, Signora."

Signora Conti has to be close to eighty, I guess, with an ample figure and multiple chins. But beneath the padding she has the sculpted bone structure of a once stunning woman. She speaks to Ari in a rapid Italian, pausing to shoot me an appraising glance before saying something to him in a chiding tone. I watch, amazed, as he begins answering smoothly. How many languages does he know?

She ushers us inside. The farmhouse is simple, wide planked wood floors, a fireplace hewn from the stone walls. Behind the large oak dining table that takes up most of the room, there is a kitchen with a window overlooking the valley.

Ari nods toward a small washroom off the rear of the kitchen and I duck into it gratefully. When I return, the older woman leads us to a cellar door at the rear of the room, then steps aside. "The Contis have a fascinating history," Ari says to me in a low voice as I follow him down the stairs. "Ella Conti is actually a French Jew and comes from a well-known winemaking family. During the war, her family's vineyards were expropriated by the Nazis and she was sent to a concentration camp not far from here. Franco Conti isn't Jewish, but he was arrested as a teenager for working with the Resistance. They met in the camp. After the war, they settled here and picked up the winemaking tradition."

I follow Ari into the dim light below. The cellar is surprisingly large, running twice the length of the house above. The walls are lined with floor-to-ceiling racks filled with bottles of wine.

From a crude wood desk at the far end of the room, an older man lifts his head. He has wild, untamed hair that is equal parts black and gray, an olive complexion beneath his bushy beard. He is large like his wife, I notice as he rises. But as we near I can see that he is solidly built, thick arms flanking a broad, barreled chest. He waits for us to approach, kissing Ari on both cheeks as his wife had done. Then he extends his hand to me. I reach out to shake it, but he sweeps my hand upward to his lips, whiskers grazing my fingers.

He gestures for us to sit, turning to the wall of wine behind him, scanning it like a librarian among the stacks. Without speaking, he ducks and disappears through a low door behind him.

Ari pulls out one of the chairs in front of the desk for me before dropping into the other. A minute later Signor Conti returns, cradling a dusty bottle like an infant. He produces three glasses from under the desk and fills them, then pushes two toward us and raises the third, as though there is nothing unusual about drinking before breakfast. My stomach, still weak from yesterday's bender, rolls. But Ari raises his glass, and I can tell from his expression that I need to do the same.

"Mmm," I say after taking a sip. Though I have never had a discerning palate, I can tell the wine is exceedingly good, with subtle hints of olive, raisins, and fig.

"Signor Conti's latest vintage," Ari says to me.

"It's excellent."

But the older man wrinkles his nose, setting down his glass. "We had, how do you say, a very dry season." His English is slow and stilted, but intelligible. He waves his hand dismissively, clucking his tongue. "No, this vintage will be good only for the cheap weekend tourists in Málaga." I look away, embarrassed to have been wrong about the quality. He turns to Ari. "But you didn't come here to discuss my wine production. How can I help you?"

Before Ari can respond there is a clattering at the top of the cellar stairs. An alarmed look crosses Signor Conti's face. Then, seeing his wife appear, he relaxes again. *"Sì, bella?"*

Signora Conti gestures for us to join her. Upstairs, the wood dining table has been covered with a white cloth and set with bright blue stoneware. Plates of cured meats and cheese and baskets overflowing with fresh bread and fruit fill the center, as though company had been expected.

Ari drops into a chair, pushing down his impatience to find out what we need to know and chase after Nicole. Accepting the Contis' hospitality is a requisite social grace, the price to be paid in exchange for the information we need. Not that it is such a hardship, I muse, as I bite into a still-warm croissant from the basket Signora Conti offers and wash it down with a sip of cappuccino. .

Signor Conti reaches to the mantel behind him and uncorks a bottle. "This, I think, you will find more to your liking," he promises as he pours. More wine for breakfast. Haven't they heard of orange juice?

Ari takes a sip of the wine, rolls it around in his mouth. "Fabulous," he says, sounding as though he means it. He tilts his head. "1992?"

"Ninety-three," Signor Conti replies, and I can tell from the glint in his eye that it is a game the men have played many times before. He turns to me. "Signora?"

Everyone is watching me expectantly now, so I taste the wine, smile, and nod. In truth I cannot tell the difference between this wine and the one we sampled in the cellar, but I do not want to appear foolish by remarking incorrectly upon it once more.

Signor Conti, apparently satisfied, turns to Ari. "Now why don't you tell me why you are here?"

Ari pauses, chewing on a piece of prosciutto, and I can see him trying to figure out the best way to explain our dilemma, how much to tell Signor Conti. "We're looking for a woman who works in the wine trade, called Nicole Martine, or Nicole Short."

The older man purses his lips, as though the bite of cheese he took has soured. "I know of her."

"Does this have to do with the Chateau Cerfberre 43?" Signora Conti asks. It is the first time I have heard her speak in English and her diction is noticeably more stilted than her husband's.

"Ella . . . " her husband cautions. An uneasy expression crosses her face, as though she has said too much.

"In a sense, yes," Ari replies.

"What's that?" I cannot help but ask.

"We shouldn't . . . " Signor Conti begins. A faint tremor comes into his hand, causing a drop of the wine he is pouring to spill onto the tablecloth.

"No, darling," Signora Conti says, reaching over and patting her husband's shoulder. "It is a wonderful story." She turns to Ari. "But it will go much quicker if I do not try to tell it in English. Perhaps you will translate for me?"

"There is a legend that says a bad grape crop heralds a year of war, and a good crop the coming of peace," Ari says as Signora Conti begins speaking rapidly in Italian. "The winemakers in France had an awful time in the years just before the war, due to weather and disease. And, having seen it before in 1914, they were terrified about what would happen to their vineyards when the Germans invaded. So they rushed to harvest their grapes and hide thousands of bottles of their best stock wherever they could, behind fake walls, in cellars and caves.

"Their fears proved to be well founded: after the invasion, the Germans installed wine barons, or Weinführers, in each region to deal with the local winemakers and procure wine for the Reich, pillaging in an organized fashion. They set draconian terms, demanding quotas of wine that were impossible to meet with the labor and equipment shortages brought on by the war."

"I remember it from my own family," Signora Conti says, speaking for herself in broken English. "We had nothing to treat the wine, no glass to do the bottles. We had to use the fields to plant food instead of growing grapes, so as not to starve."

"When enough wine could not be produced, the Germans demanded bottles from the merchants' private reserves," Ari continues translating as Signora Conti resumes speaking in Italian. "The wine-makers responded by fooling the Germans, substituting inferior wines and relabeling them, or even watering them down."

"The larger community helped, too," Signor Conti interjects. "They would siphon wine from barrels intended for Germany, even divert entire train cars of wine."

Signora Conti shoots him a look of annoyance, as though the story is hers alone to tell, then continues speaking. "So the wine-makers had a terrible time of it during the war. But there was one house in the Bordeaux, the Cerfberre house, which seemed to be . . . " Ari falters, searching for the right translation. "Immune, is the word I think, from it all. Their crops flourished and they pro-duced a vintage that was said to be the best the region had seen in a generation. Of course all of the other winemakers were jealous that this house should do so well while they struggled. And it didn't help that the Cerfberres were Jewish."

Ari clears his throat, struggling to keep up as Signora Conti picks up speed. "The Cerfberres tried to hide the existence of the 1943 vintage from the Germans. But Herr Baumgarten, the Wein-führer for the region, learned of the vintage and demanded that it be produced for him exclusively, so he could make a present of it to the SS leadership.

"Monsieur Cerfberre knew he could not refuse, but he saw an opportunity and was brave enough to negotiate a price: in exchange for the wine, he wanted his family and a dozen of his Jewish work-ers, including his plant foreman, to be let go from occupied France. Of course, he didn't dare to negotiate directly with the Nazis; the mayor of the town and his longtime friend, François Mercier, acted as intermediary.

"Baumgarten agreed and the deal was set. But at the last minute someone swapped the bottles for wine from inferior vineyards and stole the real wine . . . " Ari stops translating and exchanges uneasy looks with Signora Conti.

"What is it?" I ask.

"Nothing," he replies quickly. "Just a phrase I couldn't quite translate." I glance over at Signora Conti, who purses her lips. "Baumgarten had an educated palate and knew right away he had been duped. He had the fleeing workers stopped at the border and sent to a concentration camp."

"Did any survive?" I ask.

"Only one," Signor Conti replies in English, placing his hand over his wife's.

"You mean . . . ?"

Signora Conti nods. "Javier Cerfberre was my uncle."

"My wife worked in his vineyards as a girl, learning the craft," Signor Conti explains, taking in my surprised expression. "There was nothing to return to after the war, so we decided to renew the tradition by starting fresh here."

"And the others?" I ask, dreading the answer.

She speaks softly, her eyes growing distant as Ari translates. "They disappeared like so many others into the Nazi death machine. The irony is that Baumgarten didn't hate the Jews. He himself had Jewish relatives. But it was the deception with respect to the wine that he couldn't abide and my family, as well as those who worked for us, paid with their lives."

"And perhaps even more ironically, Baumgarten never got the wine," Ari adds, commenting for himself now. "It disappeared. Some thought it had been taken by the Nazis, others by the Resistance."

"Until now," Signora Conti interjects. "Now everyone seems to think this Nicole woman has found it."

Ari and I exchange puzzled looks. "The wine?" I ask.

"Yes, the Cerfberre 43." She pauses, turning to her husband for guidance. But he shrugs and looks away, resigned that the story has already gone too far to be retracted.

"We thought that the sale was a fraud," Ari says.

"It was," Signor Conti replies. "Some say there's more to it, though, and that the real wine is . . . " He stops midsentence. "Why are you asking about this?"

"Like I said . . . " Ari begins. "We're trying to find Nicole Martine."

Signor Conti fumbles with the cork, staring hard at the table. "I should not be talking to you about this. But there is the debt . . . " He looks across the table at his wife, communicating with her silently, debating how much to say. Signora Conti nods slightly, acquiescing. "Some men came by yesterday, well-connected men. They wanted to know if I had heard anything about the wine. I suppose they thought that I might, given my wife's connection to the house that produced it. They were quite ugly about it." So that explains the broken glass I saw by the front door of the cottage, the Contis' nervousness when we first arrived.

"Do you believe the wine has been found?" Ari asks gently.

"So many years, so much has happened. It could just as easily be on the bottom of the sea. I don't know where it is and I don't want to. But these men did, which makes it a very dangerous situation. Do you understand what I am saying?"

"I do." Ari nods. "Signor Conti, do you have any idea where we can find Nicole?"

He pauses. "I don't know . . . Cyprus perhaps." Then he presses his lips together.

Ari and I exchange silent glances, agreeing that there is nothing more to be learned here. "Thank you for your hospitality," Ari says, and I can tell from his tone that he is wrapping things up, laying the groundwork for our exit. "The food was delicious, as always." Looking over, I am surprised to see that he has finished his entire breakfast during the conversation. I take a few mouthfuls of fruit from my own plate hurriedly, as much to sate my hunger as not to appear rude and wasteful. "I hope you'll forgive our leaving so soon after such a lovely meal, but we should be getting on the road."

"But you've only just . . ." Signora Conti begins, and for a moment I expect her to try to cajole us to stay longer. I am suddenly reminded of the hospitality when I was stationed in Warsaw. "A guest in the house is like God in the house," was the proverbial Polish saying and every visit, no matter the occasion, was liable to stretch into interminable hours of food and drink.

But Signor Conti stands as Ari does, cutting off his wife. "Of course. If you'll come with me for just a moment." Ari follows him into the kitchen and I see them with their heads together, talking in low voices. Signor Conti is too much of a gentleman to whisper in front of me, but there are things he wants to say to Ari alone.

Signora Conti and I look at each other awkwardly. "Ari, he is a good boy," she offers. I smile and nod, uncertain how to respond.

When the men return, Signora Conti hands Ari two bottles of wine. "I insist."

"Thank you." Ari takes them and puts them in his bag.

"Promise me you'll stop back when all of this is over and you have more time," Signora Conti says as she accompanies us to the porch. Her husband raises his hand, bidding us farewell from a distance. She kisses Ari on both cheeks before coming to me and doing the same as though, having shared a meal, I am family now. Then she turns and walks swiftly back into the house, closing the door behind her.

"Well, that was interesting," I say as we walk away from the farmhouse. "Pointless, but interesting."

"Not at all. I got exactly what I was hoping for."

I stop and turn to look at him. "Really, and what was that?"

But he shakes his head. "Not here."

Fighting the urge to run, I follow Ari to the car in silence, then climb in. His movements, as he closes the door behind him, seem deliberate, infuriatingly slow, as if savoring these last few seconds of having a piece of information that I do not.

"What is it?" I demand, unable to hold back any longer. "What did he tell you?"

"Everything." Ari starts the engine. "He gave me the precise location where we can find Nicole."

chapter ELEVEN

N ICOLE LIVES IN Greece?" I repeat a few minutes later, as we turn onto the main road.

"Yes. Have you heard of Zakynthos?" He does not wait for me to respond. "It's one of the Ionian Islands, off of the western coast of Greece."

"I thought he said Cyprus."

"That wasn't accurate. And he said he wasn't sure, which was also untrue. I think he was just nervous talking in front of you." He pauses to navigate past some geese that have wandered into the road. "Anyway, he didn't know her exact whereabouts, but the island isn't terribly large, and with the information he had, we should be able to find her."

So he didn't give you the precise location, I want to point out. But I do not. "How could he possibly know where she lives?" I ask instead.

Ari shrugs. "Signor Conti is a well-known winemaker and he has contacts all over the world. It's likely that they have mutual acquaintances."

"Or have done business together?"

"I can't see that. He's too well respected to get involved with her kind of trade."

"You think his information is accurate?"

Ari nods as he starts the engine. "I have to confirm that with my sources. But he seemed pretty certain, and I've never known him to be unreliable."

I stare out the window as we turn onto the main road, digging my fingers into the fabric of the car seat. Jared may be in Greece. I remember how surprised I was when Mo had given me his last known whereabouts in Monaco—I'd expected to have to search in South America or one of the other distant, exotic places where he'd been on the run this past decade. But Greece is just hundreds of miles from here.

"What about the men who came to see him, do you think he gave them the information as well?"

"I tried to ask him that, delicately, of course," Ari replies. "He said no."

"Do you believe him?"

"I think so. Conti's a tough old man."

"He and his wife seemed scared, though."

"They did. But even if he couldn't refuse them outright, I'm guessing that he would have told them as little as possible, or perhaps even thrown them slightly off course. Though if they do know Nicole's whereabouts, they have a day's head start."

I turn to Ari. "The story Signora Conti told us, about the wine and the Nazis, was quite remarkable."

"Few people know how significant a role wine played during the war," he replies. "The Resistance used the wine cellars to store weapons and ammunition. Some Jews hid there as well. In at least one case, people were smuggled out of Germany in empty wine barrels.

And wine shipments could often be a source of intelligence—by detecting where the Nazis were directing large quantities of wine, say, on the eastern front or in North Africa, it was possible to surmise that troops were amassing and an offensive was planned."

"Fascinating . . . but the fact that the wine might have been found. Did you have any idea?"

"I was as surprised as you." He does not take his eyes off the road. "But if that's true, it's one of a kind and extremely valuable."

"Do you think Santini's men know?"

"I'm not sure. Let's hope Signor Conti managed not to tell them and that they're still only after Nicole for the money."

"He mentioned a debt," I recall. "What was he talking about?"

"During part of the war, my grandfather had an administrative job in one of the labor camps where Conti's father was interred. My grandfather helped him obtain papers so he could get a permanent job in a factory so as not to be sent to the death camps. Signor Conti feels that he owes me for what my grandfather did."

The sun is high in the sky now, illuminating endless acres of vineyard and other crops, birds dancing among the early summer plants. The air has grown close and warm and I can see fine moisture on Ari's upper lip. He drives with greater urgency, pushing the tiny car as quickly as possible along the narrow winding road, venturing into the opposing lane of traffic when he can in order to pass the slower vehicles.

I notice him glance over his shoulder, so quickly that I think I might have imagined it. But then he does it again. "What is it?" I demand.

"Nothing," he answers, too quickly. "Just being . . . careful."

We're nearing the city, I realize, as the signs for Trieste grow more frequent, the traffic more congested. The road curves around the side of the mountain here, white limestone cliffs rising sharply above us. The smell of salt air fills my lungs and a moment later bluish green water breaks wide into view. Ahead the city appears, a swarm of red-roofed buildings, set low around a wide arc of sea.

We pass a palatial white structure set on a rocky outpost overlooking the water. "That's the Castello di Miramare," Ari says. "Trieste is a really interesting place. A little gritty, but off the tourist track, which I like. It was a huge port city for Austria-Hungary, then Italy."

"Tito's army liberated it, right?"

"Correct, and the Allies controlled it until they turned it back over to Italy in 1954. It's still more Balkan than Italian in some ways."

At the mention of the Balkans, I am reminded of Jared and his research related to Kosovo. Where is he, I wonder? Has Nicole reached him yet and, if so, did she tell him about meeting me?

We exit the main thoroughfare onto a smaller road that curves downward toward the city. Ari navigates the narrow streets, drawing closer to the water. I turn to him, puzzled. "Is this the way to the airport?"

He shakes his head. "Trieste Harbor."

I recall then that we've passed at least a half dozen signs reading PORTO. "We're going to Greece by boat?"

"Yes. It will let us be more discreet, in case anyone is looking for us."

Gazing out at the broad expanse of sea, my stomach churns. Though I hadn't minded coxing on the calm, narrow River Cam, and had even managed the Thames with a life-vest on occasion, I've never liked being on the open water, with its strong tides and waves. My earliest impressions came from our summerhouse in Cape Cod, where the ocean was often rough and inhospitable. And now the notion of a journey by sea . . . Surely there has to be another way.

"If Nicole really is on the island, as Signor Conti said, the boat will enable us to get there more quickly," Ari adds, before I can say anything.

Resigned, I continue gazing out the window. We're in downtown Trieste proper, I note as we pass a wide piazza on the left, flanked by neoclassical buildings on three sides. To our right sits the harbor. It is much larger than the one in Monaco, a sprawling tangle of pleasure and commercial fishing boats.

Ari pulls into a private marina, parking in a lot by the entrance. I follow him out of the car and down the dock, watching in disbelief as he stops in front of a massive white yacht at least forty feet long. Is he planning to buy it or steal it?

"Wait here," he says, walking up to the boat.

I see him talk to the crewman, hand him money. Then he waves me over. "Let's go."

I stare at him, dumbfounded. I had imagined a charter or ferry, not a private yacht. "How did you . . . "

"Signor Conti arranged for it."

"He takes this debt thing seriously," I mumble under my breath.

"What?"

"Nothing."

"We could have the crewman ferry us over, but I'd rather do it myself." He climbs expertly up the ladder at the rear of the boat, then holds out a hand to me.

"Do you know how?" I ask, following.

"Yes. I grew up on the water."

I climb onto the deck. "Mind if I look around?"

He shrugs. "Make yourself at home."

I adjust my gait to the gentle rocking of the boat as I make my way inside. There is a small but elegantly designed cabin, comprised of a sitting area and granite galley kitchen. Opening the miniature refrigerator, I discover that it has been well stocked with fresh fruit and vegetables, meats and cheeses. A few narrow stairs lead downward to the stateroom and toilet.

From above comes a scraping sound and the boat rocks more forcefully as we push from the dock. I set my bag on the bed, then return to the deck. Shielding my eyes, I look up to the bridge where Ari stands behind the wheel, navigating us out of the port. I am suddenly aware of the absurdity of the situation. I'm on a private yacht, chasing after my ex-boyfriend and his wife with . . . I pause, unable to come up with a label for Ari. Lover, friend, accomplice . . . ? None of these descriptions quite fit. Who is he anyway?

I drop to one of the deck chairs and pull my phone from my bag, checking to find an unread message from Lincoln: *No record for Bruck,* it reads. Strange. I had hoped with Ari's military past there might be some intelligence on him.

Gazing up at Ari once more, I feel a twinge of guilt at checking up on him. We promised to trust each other. But my intelligence background will not let me leave it alone. If there is something about him to be learned, I want to know, and if nothing, then better to know that, too.

Several minutes later, when the coast has receded to a thin strip in the distance, Ari climbs down to the deck. "Everything all right?" he asks, gesturing to the phone still clutched in my hand.

"Fine," I say, fumbling for an excuse. "Just sending a quick text to my family." I look up at the empty bridge. "Shouldn't you be steering the boat or something?"

He laughs. "This yacht has a state-of-the-art navigation system, which can guide us now that we're in the open waters and alert me if anything is in our path. I've set the GPS, so we should be fine for a while." Ahead the horizon is empty except for a few gulls, calling to one another as they dip low to the water's surface.

"You're going to want this," he says, tossing a tube of sunscreen my way. I catch it, suddenly aware of the heat on my forehead and nose. "Hungry?" he asks, as I remove the cap from the tube. Before I can respond, he starts down to the galley and I can hear him opening drawers, pulling out groceries.

I debate whether to follow him, then decide against it. Instead, I squeeze some sunscreen onto my palm and apply the warm lotion to my face and arms, the familiar smell taking me back to sticky childhood days at the beach.

Ari returns carrying a plate and two glasses, a bottle of wine under his arm. "The crewman keeps the boat stocked for its owners, so there's plenty here, even on short notice." He spreads a towel across a box that rises from the center of the deck, setting the plate and glasses down upon it. "Come eat."

I sit down, hungry again after the few mouthfuls of breakfast I swallowed earlier this morning. Ari offers the plate he arranged, heaped with cheese and crackers, grapes, figs, and nuts. Then he pours the wine. "Courtesy of the Contis." He hands me a glass. "Cheers." Though his tone is light, I notice him glancing over his shoulder as he had in the car, scanning the horizon.

He takes off his shirt and leans back. I roll up my sleeves, wishing I had a bathing suit, or at least a pair of shorts. As he reaches for something from his bag, I notice two dark, round scars on his torso.

"You've been shot," I remark, leaning forward. Closer, I can tell by their well-defined shape that the bullets had not grazed him but had actually gone through.

"Yes. It was touch and go until they could get me back to a hospital. But they were clean shots, so I only lost the . . . what is the word, appendix?"

"You were lucky," I remark. A strange look flickers across his face, as if that is not a term he has ever associated with himself, at least not in the years since losing his wife and daughter. It's not exactly self-pity, I realize, so much as a resignation of acceptance to the hand he's been dealt, somewhere far short of happiness or luck.

He leans back, tilting his face upward to the bright sunlight. It is the most relaxed I've seen him since we met. "Let me take your picture," I say impulsively, pulling out my phone and clicking on the camera function.

A look of hesitation flashes across his face. "I don't . . . "

"Why not?" I chide, trying to sound playful. But uneasiness tugs at my stomach: Is there something he's trying to hide? "We can take it together if you prefer."

"All right," he relents. He moves across to sit next to me, his arm warm against mine as he holds the phone out in front of us and snaps the picture. He does not, I notice, remove his sunglasses. Then he hands me the phone before stretching out on the deck.

"You like being on the water," I observe.

He smiles. "I love it. I was raised by the sea. When I was fourteen I had to spend a summer at a camp in Iowa and it nearly drove me crazy being so far from the ocean. And then when I was in the army, I was stuck in the desert for months. I swore after that I'd never be far from the water if I could help it, never let another summer pass without seeing the ocean. Aviva and I used to take all of our holidays on the water, even if it was nothing more than a simple rowboat."

I think of my own childhood summers. The beach was not my

natural habitat—I'd sit on the blanket and cling to my mother as the other children played, carefree in the surf, detesting the scratchiness of the sand against my skin. Once I'd been coaxed into the water by my father, only to be taken under by a wave. I flailed in the blackness beneath the waters, unable to find ground for what seemed like an eternity until he grabbed me by the shoulders and yanked me to the surface. For years after, I'd been haunted by nightmares of a giant wave, rising from the sea like a hand and swallowing me where I stood. I'd always shied away from the ocean since then. The nightmares still came occasionally, though, the waters rising up and taking me under.

I've never told anyone about my dislike of the ocean, not Jared, not even Sarah. For a second I consider sharing this with Ari, then decide against it. "Tell me more about your wife," I say instead.

He hesitates. "We met in the army. Aviva was a military police officer out patrolling a remote border area in the desert. She came upon me during a training exercise, but she didn't believe my explanation as to why I was out there. She thought she had caught someone doing something illegal." He smiles, lost in the memory. "She was so stubborn. She insisted on bringing me in to check out my story. I could have said no, tried to get away. But she was very beautiful. I found myself wanting to follow her, even if it meant getting in trouble with my superiors. Then her jeep got stuck in a ditch and we had to wait there until morning. We spent all night talking and before the sun rose, I knew I would marry her."

"That's a wonderful story. Very romantic."

"It was more than just her beauty, of course," he adds quickly. "She was the strongest person I ever met, independent. She didn't play by anyone else's rules. I remember after Yael was born, I tried to persuade her to resign her commission and stay home. But she wouldn't give up her military career, it was too much a part of who she was. And when I came back from the fighting, told her the awful things I had . . . " His voice trails off. "Let's just say I didn't come back the same man as I had left. I was broken. She was the glue that held me together, tried to make me whole again."

Tried. There is nothing whole about Ari. How far had his wife been able to heal him before she died? I imagine a recovering Ari, stronger, more hopeful. But the second blow, the loss of his family, had simply been too much to take.

He clears his throat. "Anyway, when she and our daughter were gone, I had no one."

"What about your family?" I ask. "Parents, siblings?"

He refills our wineglasses, takes a sip. "None. I'm an only child and my parents were already dead. My mother died of a heart attack when I was fifteen. After that my father just seemed to give up. He passed about a year later."

I imagine Ari alone at such a young age. "What did you do?"

"Stayed with relatives until I finished school, then joined the army. I was on my own until I met Aviva. And then it was just us, before Yael came along."

"Your wife didn't have family, either?"

"She did. A huge one, actually, seven brothers and sisters. But her parents disowned her when she told them she was marrying me. All of her siblings stopped talking to her, except for one sister, the youngest, who would occasionally sneak out to see us around the holidays."

"I don't understand."

"Aviva was Arab."

For several seconds I am too surprised to respond. "I had no idea," I manage finally. "I always pictured her Israeli."

"She was. Her family was Druze." I tilt my head, not under-standing. "They're Israeli Arabs."

"Muslim?"

"Kind of an offshoot of Islam. The Muslim world doesn't really consider them to be a part of it, but they aren't Jewish or Christian. They keep to themselves for the most part. Very few fight in the army, and so it was a huge controversy when Aviva decided to join. And then, when she met me . . . " He looks away, scratching his head. "I don't think my family would have cared so much, if they had still been alive. I mean, they had been through so much preju-dice and hate in their lives. But who knows? Anyway, her family forbade her to see me and when she disobeyed they disowned her. It broke her heart. She gave up everything for me. They never even met Yael."

"I'm so sorry." I fumble, still trying to comprehend what he has told me. "I just assumed . . . "

"That she was Jewish? No, and her family could never accept that I was. They didn't come to her funeral, though I've seen her mother at the cemetery when she thought no one else was there."

I fight the urge to reach out and touch him. "It must have been so hard for her."

"It wasn't easy. She was rejected by her own people and was an outsider among those she was serving with. But for us the army was never ideological. It was about defending our country, doing a service."

"She sounds like an amazing woman," I say.

"She was. Not perfect, of course," he adds with a smile. "Like I said, she could be stubborn. You remind me of her," he adds abruptly.

"Oh?" I am caught off guard by the comparison.

"Yes, she challenged me, like you do, on politics and everything else. We used to have great debates, arguments, really, about the state of Israel. She was angry at how it treated non-Jews, that a country that fought so hard for the rights of one people could oppress others." He bites his lip. "And then there was the question of Yael. What religion to raise her, that is."

"Of course." Their daughter would not have been Jewish by birth when the mother was not.

"We were going to raise her with both and let her choose herself . . . when she grew up." He stares off in the distance and I can tell he is seeing the life his daughter never got to live, the dreams unfulfilled. A hand seems to wrap around my heart, squeezing it hard.

"It didn't matter, about the religion," he continues. "I mean, it bothered me a little sometimes, you know; being the child of a Holocaust survivor, there was always a lot of pressure to propagate the religion."

I nod, understanding. Even with my secular upbringing, there had always been a certain unspoken guilt that if I intermarried, I would not be doing my part to keep the faith alive. Not that marriage has been a big issue in my life.

"But in the end, we loved our child and each other. That was the thing; she stuck with me through everything I did, all that happened. Though, sometimes I think she would be ashamed of me if she were here."

"Why do you say that?"

"At least then I was fighting for principle. And now . . . " He trails off and I remain silent for several seconds, hoping that while lost in thought he will say more about his work. Instead, he clears his throat, then pulls on his shirt and stands, picking up the plate and disappearing below.

I look out across the horizon to the west where the sun has dropped behind a low raft of thick gray clouds. I shiver, gazing up at the stars that are appearing in the darkening sky.

A few minutes later Ari reappears, carrying an extra sweatshirt that he drapes around my shoulders without speaking. He sits down on the deck once more. "And you and Jared, how did you meet?"

I consider the question, wondering if he is only trying to be polite. But his expression is one of genuine curiosity. "I was studying abroad at Cambridge. We were on the same rowing team." I feel silly, as though trying to equate a college romance to his marriage. "We actually hated each other at first, fought like crazy."

"Ah yes, the best ones always do start with arguments," he says knowingly. "It's that spark that tells you something is there."

Ari and I have been fighting since we met, I realize. But despite what happened between us at the hotel in Vienna, this is not, I remind myself, a romantic situation. He's attractive, but I'm here to find Jared.

"Anyway," I say, clearing my throat, forcing myself to continue with the story. "At some point we stopped fighting and acknowledged our feelings for each other and then we were together."

"Did you have much in common?"

"Not at all, other than the rowing." It is, I realize, the first time I've admitted that to anyone, including myself. "We just kind of got each other somehow." He tilts his head, as if the phrase is unfamiliar to him. "I mean that we understood one another completely."

What had drawn Jared and I together? I wonder now. We were such different people: him brooding and serious, me energetic and outgoing, at least back then. Yet there was this strange, inexplicable connection. I remember one time, shortly before I was supposed to leave England for good, when we were away on a weeklong rowing retreat with the crew, staying at a bed-and-breakfast outside the picturesque town of Henley-on-Thames. After two days the constant presence of the seven other boys, whom I otherwise adored, became unbearable and I grew frustrated because Jared and I could not find time to be alone. Suddenly at dinner that night everything caught up with me—the fact that in a few weeks I would be leaving the place that I loved more than anywhere else on earth, that I had no control over the life events that seemed to be spinning out before me. I began sobbing, to the surprise and dismay of the boys, who had been bantering jovially. But Jared led me calmly by the hand to an empty bedroom, lay down beside me on the bed, and didn't speak, seeming to know that I needed his presence more than any words he could offer. When my tears subsided, he made love to me simply, sweetly. In the preceding weeks, I had silently prided myself on being there for him, through his black moods and the indescribable demons that were chasing him. But in that moment the roles were changed and he took care of me. And I, for the first time in my life, let myself be cared for. It was the sealing of our bond.

I look up, rousing myself from my memories. Ari is still watching me, an intrigued expression on his face. Faint warmth creeps up my neck and into my cheeks. "Anyway," I say, embarrassed to have been caught so vulnerable and exposed, "we only had a brief time together, a few months before I was supposed to move back to America. And then he was gone."

"It must have been quite a connection," Ari remarks, "to have stayed with you so long afterward."

"I suppose." But my words ring hollow, without conviction. For so long I had painted Jared and me as this great love story, ripped apart by the fates. In light of his marriage to Nicole, it seems foolish, a college fling easily forgotten. My mind rolls back over the years, to the men I had pushed away, the potential relationships I'd left untested. At the time I told myself that my unwillingness to get involved was a result of my feelings for Jared, a wound that would not heal. But now it seems that had been an excuse. Glorifying the past had been so much easier than dealing with the messiness of real interaction, and so I used Jared as an alibi to remain emotionally isolated. For years I've worn my independence as a source of pride, a kind of armor. But in fact I've been hiding behind it.

There had almost been someone once, I remember then. In Liberia, my colleague Eric and I had grown close, a bond born of spending too many hours working alone together, holed up in cars or tiny apartments, waiting. There were long looks across crowded streets that made my breath catch, tiny protective gestures that told me it might have been more than sex if I let it happen.

But I hadn't. Eric was married to a third country national, a sweet Filipino woman he'd met on an earlier assignment, who was back in Washington with their three children. "We can't do this," I told him firmly after he had leaned toward me one night in the room we'd been forced to share. My denial came minutes later than it should have, after a kiss had been tried on and considered. In a world where I could see few rules clearly, it was the one I'd always had and I could not break it, even in that moment with the tantalizing possibility of real intimacy dangled before me for the first time in years.

He tried once again, as though the kiss would be persuasive enough to override my defenses. But then I put my hand on his chest and he retreated wordlessly to his corner of the room. And less than twenty-four hours later he was gone, lying on the ground in Liberia as the helicopter pulled me to safety from a country turning inward to destroy itself.

My thoughts turn to Sarah, who was alone for so many years before finding Ryan. Here she is, staring death squarely in the face. But she isn't hiding behind her illness. Instead, she's going out and embracing love, believing against the odds that she has the same chance at happiness as anyone else.

"What do you think Jared will be like now?" Ari asks, interrupting my thoughts. He rolls over and as he does, his hand brushes my knee, taking me back to the night before, sending shivers through me.

I look up, considering the question. "I don't know." In my mind's eye, Jared remains the same as the night I last saw him. But the years have surely changed him as they have me.

"You know, it's been a long time . . ." Ari says gently. "A lot may have changed. He could be working with Nicole or . . ."

"Jared would never do that." But even as I speak, I can see where Ari is going with this, the validity of his point. How could Jared live with Nicole all of these years and not know what she has been doing? Of course, I'd been by his side at Cambridge for months and had never guessed the depths of his darkness, or the trouble that he faced.

"Didn't you ever wonder where he got the money?" he asks. "To fake his own death, change identities, live on the run all of these years?"

I start to reply that Lord Colbert, the Master, or head of our college, had helped Jared because he was one of his students. But the Master, while wealthy, did not have that kind of money. He surely assisted with the logistics of leaving, but I doubt he could, or would, have been willing to finance Jared's living expenses indefinitely.

"And what has he been doing?" Ari presses gently. "I mean, you said Jared was an academic, but there's no record of him teaching or publishing. How has he been supporting himself?"

"I don't know!" I explode, my frustration bubbling to the surface. "What are you saying?"

He shrugs. "It's just conjecture. But his low profile, his ability to move beneath the surface, combined with Nicole's activities . . . "

Would have made Jared the perfect black market accomplice, I think, finishing the thought when Ari does not. "I just can't believe it," I whisper. Jared had almost died, had given up everything for the principles he believed were right; I cannot envision him as a petty criminal. "He would never do something like that."

"Maybe it isn't true," he offers. "Like I said, it's just speculation. The sooner we find them, the sooner we'll know for sure." He lifts his head to the now star-filled sky. "It's getting late. We should get some rest."

I glance toward the galley uncertainly. The narrow bed downstairs is a fraction of the one we shared in Vienna. Does he mean for us to be together again? But he unrolls a blanket. "Help yourself to the cabin. I'm going to stretch out here."

"Okay . . . " I falter, standing up. "Good night."

I take a few steps, then look back, wondering if he will say something more or try to stop me. But he has turned away and is staring out over the water, seemingly deep in thought.

As I make my way below, my confusion swirls. What happened? I thought after last night he would surely want to pick up where we left off. Brushing my teeth in the tiny washroom, I wonder whether he has lost interest, if I had said something wrong during our conversation tonight. Perhaps it is all the talk of his wife that has made him distant. Or was it something else? There's so much I don't know about him.

I remember the photos we had taken earlier. Pulling out my phone, I open the email from Lincoln, then hit reply and attach the photo of Ari before sending. *I know you said there was nothing on Aaron Bruck*, I type. *But here is a photo, just in case.*

I put the phone back in my bag and climb into the narrow bed, still puzzling over who Ari is, how he feels about me. It doesn't matter, I tell myself, trying without success to push the image of him lying on the deck above me from my mind. Soon we'll find Jared and all of this will be over. I draw the thin blanket up around my neck, then close my eyes, lulled by the gentle rocking of the sea.

chapter TWELVE

I AWAKEN TO THE sounds of pots banging. Bright sunlight fills the tiny cabin and the savory smell of grilled meat tickles my nose. Swinging my feet to the ground, I pad toward the kitchen where Ari stands, open boxes of salt, flour, and other ingredients strewn across the countertop, spilling onto the floor.

"Good morning . . . ?" I say, as much question as greeting. He does not answer but continues staring into a frying pan, perplexed. "Everything okay?"

"I wanted . . . " he begins then stops again, gesturing to the mess on the stove top. "The eggs are all right, but the pancakes . . . " He holds up a bowl of what was supposed to have been batter but is instead a thin gray water.

I suppress a smile. He is trying to make me an American breakfast, I realize, touched. "Why don't I finish up here?" In truth, I've never been much of a cook. My father grew up in the restaurant business, a skilled but unwilling disciple of the culinary trade. Then he met my mother who, as the child of bohemian artists, had never cooked a meal in her life, and he taught her the basics before permanently abdicating all kitchen duties. She never quite caught on, though, instead relying on premade mixes and packaged foods. But once, when I was six and my mother was away for the weekend, my father made pancakes, teaching me his secret recipe for the batter, how to heat the griddle just enough. After that, I subjected all houseguests, regardless of the meal or time of day, to my breakfast specialty.

Ari gives me the spatula, then raises his hands in a gesture of surrender. "What time is it?" I ask.

"Nearly eleven." I blink at him, surprised. I had no idea I'd slept so late. "It's the sea air," he explains. "Good sleep, no?" I nod. I cannot remember the last time I felt so well rested.

He disappears up the stairs. Fifteen minutes later, I climb to the deck, balancing two plates. Ari is shirtless and barefoot, working on a coil of rope at the bow of the boat. Watching him, I feel a tug in my stomach.

"Breakfast," I call.

He turns toward me. "Good news. I've done some checking with one of my contacts, and he confirmed that Nicole has been seen on the eastern side of Zakynthos in the main town Zante. He didn't have an exact address, but he told me of a restaurant there, Café Nikolai, where I can ask for her."

I look at him evenly. "You have some impressive contacts for a private investigator."

"You know how it is," he replies, seemingly unruffled. "Some of my army pals are now in government, and we trade favors every so often."

Thinking of Lincoln, I decide that the explanation is a plausible one and that pressing further would be fruitless. I scan the horizon. "Where are we, anyway?"

"Just off Croatia, north of the Albanian coast. We should reach the island by midmorning tomorrow, all being well."

The island where Jared may be living. "What is it?" Ari asks, noticing my expression.

"The fact that we're so close, that I might see . . . " I trail off, suddenly self-conscious talking about Jared with Ari. "It's just that for so many years, I thought he was dead."

"You know, you never really told me about that. I mean, about what happened when you went back to England, how you found out that Jared was alive."

I study his face, wondering if he is trying to get information from me for his own purposes. But he appears to be genuinely concerned. I know him now, I think. I can trust him. "Like I told you, last month when I was in Washington, I got a letter from my friend Sarah, who is very sick with ALS, asking me to come to England. Or so I thought—the letter turned out later to be a fake. It was actually sent from someone who needed me to come to London to find Jared and lure him out of hiding."

He scoops a forkful of eggs from his plate. "Why?"

I pause uncertainly. The instinct to bury the past in order to protect Jared is so ingrained in me it is hard to overcome. "Jared had found information during the course of his doctoral research that was damaging to some powerful people." I still cannot bring myself to share what Jared found, the extent of its implications. "And those people wanted to see what he had learned buried forever. Fortunately, we were able to stop them and get the information to the authorities before it was too late. But the betrayal included some of my closest friends and coworkers."

He whistles long and low. "That's wild. But it doesn't explain how you found out Jared was alive."

He's right, I realize, swallowing a mouthful of pancake. What happened in England has so many pieces, it's hard to put them in a logical order. I need to back up. "When I first got to England, an old college friend, Chris, contacted me with a hunch that Jared didn't drown, as we were told, and he asked for my help figuring out the truth. We started digging and found out about Jared's research and the fact that people wanted him dead. And at the same time I was working on the government investigation. There were some strange coincidences—I had to speak to another classmate, Duncan Lauder, about my work investigation and he wound up telling me about Jared's research. Then Duncan disappeared and when I went to talk to his significant other, Vance, about the research Duncan had done with Jared, he mentioned something that connected it to my investigation.

"But it wasn't until later, after I figured out someone had faked Sarah's letter and confronted my boss, Mo, about it, that I learned Jared wasn't really dead and that they had brought me to England to help find him." I watch Ari's face as he tries to put it all together. "Sounds crazy, I know."

"Actually, it explains a lot. I mean the things you did, that you had to go through . . . " He clears his throat. "You're an impressive woman, Jordan."

I drop my eyes, feeling the heat rise from my neck to my cheeks. Then I start to gather the breakfast dishes.

"I can do that," he says as I reach for his plate. His hand brushes mine.

Neither of us moves for several seconds. Our hands remain close, still touching. I look up and am caught off guard by the nakedness of the desire in his eyes. He turns away, then carries the dishes from the deck.

A few minutes later Ari returns, his expression serious. "What is it?" I ask.

He hesitates, and I can tell from the conflicted expression on his face that he's debating how much to say. "I just got a message from the boatman at the Trieste harbor, who I paid off well, saying that another yacht set out shortly after we did on the same course."

"Is that unusual?"

"Maybe, maybe not. But they were asking questions that seemed to suggest they were looking for someone."

"You're thinking it could be Santini's men?"

"It's a possibility. They could have been following us since Vienna, or perhaps they saw us leave the Contis and are trailing us to see if we will lead them to Nicole. I'd like to pull in to shore until they pass by, just to be safe. There's a cove not too far from here where we can wait without being seen."

My heart sinks. Stopping will slow us down, worsen our chances of getting to Nicole. "We made good time overnight," Ari says, seeming to read my thoughts.

"But we need to get to Nicole as soon as possible," I protest, strains of our disagreement in Vienna returning.

"Better to lose some time now rather than not make it at all. We can make up time on the water. Trust me, okay?" He seems to be talking about something larger than our travel schedule.

I hesitate, considering. "Okay."

Ninety minutes later we near a rocky cove, surrounded on three sides by tall, rugged cliffs. Ari pulls us in along a jetty that juts out from one side of the enclave. He drops anchor, then pulls out a pair of binoculars, scanning the still-clear skyline behind us.

"Do you see anything?"

"No." He takes off his shirt. Watching his body, desire rises up in me anew.

"What are you doing?" I ask as he opens a wooden box on the deck and pulls out a mask and snorkel.

"Just a quick dip while we wait." He dives into the water, moves with sure, easy strokes. I start to protest that the last thing we have time for is a swim. But he's right; there's nothing to do but wait. "Are you coming in? The water's perfect." His voice is easy, giving no indication of our conversation a moment earlier.

"I don't have a bathing suit," I reply, hearing the weakness in my own excuse.

"There's no one around for miles and I promise I won't look." He turns away, as if to prove his point. "There's another mask in the chest."

I pull out the snorkel, strip down to my underwear and bra, grateful that they are the newer set I purchased after leaving London. Walking to the edge of the boat, I peer down uncertainly at the calm, transparent blue. Then I climb over the side and slip into the water, still clinging to the ladder. Something flutters beneath the surface a few feet away. Flailing, I try to recall the nature programs I've seen to determine whether this is a shark-prone area.

Hands, warm and strong, envelop my waist from behind. "Easy," Ari says, steadying me. He lowers his face beneath the water, turning in the direction of the splash, then lifts his head and removes the mask. "It's just fish. Sharks aren't prevalent in this area at this time of year. Of course, you shouldn't panic in that situation; it just makes things worse."

"Sorry," I say when we have drifted in silence for several minutes. "I've never liked the ocean. In fact, it terrifies me." I look away. "It's kind of embarrassing."

"Not at all. We all have our fears. I can't stand heights." I study his face to see if he is making a joke, mocking me. It seems hard to believe he is afraid of anything. Then, remembering his discomfort when the plane took off the other morning, I know that he is serious.

Ari reaches around and lifts the chain from my neck that holds the ring. "Are you going to give it back?"

I pause, considering the question for the first time. "I don't know. I suppose."

"It's all very *Lord of the Rings*," he remarks. Puzzled, I turn to look at him. "You've read it, yes?"

"Sort of." My mind reels back to a night at college shortly before Jared and I first kissed. We were sitting in the college bar, talking with some of the other members of our crew, when Jared began animatedly describing a Tolkien retrospective he had seen when visiting Oxford the previous year.

"You like Tolkien?" I asked, surprised that someone as serious as Jared could be so passionate about a fantasy tale.

"Adore. The epic hero's journey, the creation of a whole other world . . . and, well, it's just a great story," he concluded somewhat sheepishly. "Have you read it?" I shook my head. "Really?" His expression was incredulous.

The next day a dog-eared paperback copy of *The Hobbit* appeared in my college mailbox. Reading the story, I was swept away. Later when we were together, Jared began reading to me almost every night a chapter from *The Lord of the Rings*, beneath the small pool of light cast by his desk lamp. Remembering now, I can almost hear the scratch of his finger on the pages and smell the musty paper. Even in those final dark days the worry would melt from his face and his eyes would begin to dance as he recounted the elves and dwarves of Middle-earth, bringing that strange world to life for me as I drifted off to sleep.

Our reading pace slowed as his late nights of research intensified, and we knew we would not have time to finish before it was time for me to move back to America. So we talked of reading the remaining chapters simultaneously from a distance, an act of transatlantic communion. We made it almost halfway through the second book together before he disappeared.

What had happened to the books? I wonder now. They had not been in the trunk of belongings Chris had taken from Jared's mother's house in our search for clues.

"Anyway," Ari says, interrupting my thoughts. "I just meant your quest to find Jared, coupled with the ring. It's like you're carrying it back to Mordor to drop it in the Cracks of Doom like that hobbit."

"Frodo." Did he ever make it, I wonder, to destroy the ring and complete his quest? Unable to bear the pain, I stopped reading the day Jared disappeared. I never finished the books, avoiding the movies in more recent years and leaving the tale as incomplete as my own.

I relax slightly, leaning back against Ari and allowing him to carry me away from the boat in the gentle current. Looking up at the cloudless blue sky, I can almost forget why we are here. A feeling rises in me, warm and unfamiliar. It is more than just attraction, I realize. With Ari I feel safe, understood.

I stiffen. What am I doing? I don't know him, what his motives are, whether or not I can trust him. I started to open up with Sebastian when I was in London and it almost got me killed. Anyway, I'm here for Jared, I remind myself. He's alive and even if he is married, this is no time to go falling for someone else. I need to concentrate, finish what I set out to do.

"What is it?" Ari asks, noticing.

I pull away. "This," I say, gesturing between us. "I don't know, it's just the timing . . . this business with Jared."

"Jared." He frowns. "Yes, of course."

"I just can't get involved, not until I find him, get the answers I'm searching for."

"Even though he has a wife?"

"Even then. I didn't plan on this." A hurt look crosses his face. "Ari . . . " I reach for his hand but he pulls it away.

"Forget it," he says, his voice gruff. "Let's just go find Nicole."

"I'm sorry."

"Don't be." He turns away. "It's for the best, you know?"

Now it is my turn to be confused. "I don't understand."

He stares hard at the water, moving his hands beneath the surface in circles. "You shouldn't get close to me. Everyone who does winds up hurt, or dead."

I am taken aback by the familiarity of his words. I thought the same thing about myself not long ago. My colleague Eric had been killed when our mission in Liberia went wrong. Jared was dead, or so I thought. And then in England people around me started dying: Sophie, Vance, and nearly Chris and Sarah as well. Now looking back, I know that it had nothing to do with me. Jared is alive and Eric died in the line of duty, an unfortunate consequence of the coup. The attacks on the others were beyond my control. No, I understand now that these tragic events were not my fault, but Ari still believes it about himself.

"That's not true," I say finally.

"Actually, it is." His tone is matter-of-fact, but his eyes are hollow. "The day Yael and Avi were killed, they were coming to see me at the base. It was my birthday and they wanted to see me, but I told them I was too busy and that I couldn't get leave to come home . . . " His voice cracks slightly. "They were on their way to surprise me when they drove over the ordnance."

"It wasn't your fault."

But he continues, seeming not to hear me. "It isn't just them. My partner was killed during a raid that should have been straightforward. And then . . . " His breath catches.

I watch him expectantly. "Then what?"

"When I was in the army, we were ordered to shell a facility in a small town near Beirut. It was an ammunition depot, or so we were told. But the intelligence was bad, and it wound up being a makeshift school. Dozens of children were killed—" He breaks off.

I raise a dripping hand from the water and place it on his shoulder. "You couldn't have known."

"My gut told me something wasn't right. I should have tried to stop it. And afterward, we could have helped, but we were ordered to retreat." His eyes grow haunted as he remembers the children, not much older than his own daughter.

I understand now his earlier defensiveness about the collateral damage of war. "Have you ever told anyone about this?"

"No. I would have told my wife, but I was too ashamed. And not long after I came back she was gone. She and Yael being killed so soon after—it seemed like punishment for what I had done." His face is haggard, a man aged in a moment by his memories.

"It's a horrible thing, but it wasn't your fault. You aren't cursed and—"

Suddenly Ari grabs me around the waist. "Shhh!" he says, cutting me off, his voice urgent. He pulls me close to the boat, jerking his head in the other direction. In the distance, beyond the entrance to the cove, I see a yacht about a half mile to the east. It is the first craft we have seen since clearing the Italian coastline yesterday.

Ari drops low in the water so that only his nose and eyes are exposed, a human crocodile. I follow his lead silently, trying to breathe and not panic against the sense of submersion that has always terrified me so.

Beneath the surface, Ari squeezes my hand. Minutes later, when the other boat has disappeared past the entrance to the cove, he rises in the water again. "They're gone." He releases me.

I take deep gulps of air through my mouth, my heart pounding. "Were those Santini's men?"

"Maybe. Hard to tell from this distance."

A chill runs down my spine. "Do you think they saw us?"

"If they had, we wouldn't be sitting here talking about it." His eyes shift back and forth, calculating. "We should go." Still holding me, he starts swimming toward the boat.

I start up the ladder of the boat, feeling his eyes on me. The brisk air hits my wet skin, making me shiver. Ari steps onto the deck, then picks up a towel and wraps it around me. I clutch the edges, grateful for the soft cloth, warmed by the sun. "You okay?"

"Yes," I reply, trying not to let my teeth chatter.

"Good. Why don't you go wash up? I'm going to go reset our course."

I make my way toward the bathroom, rinse off in the tiny shower. The boat begins to sway more roughly, telling me we have left the cove and reentered the open water. A few minutes later I step out and dry myself, dressing in the soft white T-shirt Ari left for me and my jeans, which are still warm from lying on the deck. I pick up the necklace chain bearing the engagement ring from the sink and start to put it around my neck. Then, remembering my conversation with Ari, I stop again—it seems wrong somehow, out of place here. Running my finger over the engraving one more time, I take it off and tuck it carefully into my bag.

Back on deck, I see Ari on the bridge, plotting our new course. "May I?" I ask, climbing the stairs to the bridge, taking in the impressive array of gauges on the display before him.

"Sure." He does not look up. "There's no sign of the boat, so I think we should be in the clear. But we've got other problems." He points to a computer screen projecting a map, with a mass of brightly colored reds and purples just to the left of us. "There's a storm coming in from the west." He looks up and I follow his gaze beyond the stern of the yacht, but the sky is a cloudless blue.

"What should we do? Can we go back to the cove?"

He shakes his head. "We could get stuck there for hours and you were right, we need to get to Nicole before Santini's men." The concession, I can tell, is not easy for him to give. "We've got no choice but to try to outrun the storm."

Try. My stomach clenches.

"You should go back downstairs, do whatever you need to do before things get rough." He turns abruptly to the controls once more.

I climb down to the deck and stare out across the horizon, wondering how far ahead Santini's men have gotten, whether or not we will beat the storm.

Then from behind me comes a loud clicking sound. I look up. Ari is checking the chamber of his pistol, making sure it is fully loaded, and I know then that it's not just the storm he's worried about. Despite his bravado and reassurances, the prospect of encountering Santini's men scares him as much as it does me.

chapter THIRTEEN

HOW'S IT LOOKING?" I ask Ari as he comes into the stateroom. I stand up, starting toward him. Two hours earlier we left the cove, setting out again on the open sea. At first the weather seemed unchanged, other than a strong breeze that blew the ocean into whitecaps all around us like a frothy meringue. But the sky blackened swiftly and as thick raindrops began to fall, I took cover below.

Before he can answer, the boat sharply jerks to the left and I lurch in that direction. Then it rolls to the right, sending me flailing backward. "Easy." Ari is at my side immediately, moving across the rocking cabin with experienced, certain feet and catching me by the elbow to steady me. "It's all right. Just the sea kicking up ahead of the storm."

But his serious expression says otherwise. "You mean it's going to get worse?" I ask.

He nods grimly. "I've checked on the radio and the storm is a lot stronger than forecasted when we left Trieste." I wonder now if he regrets our decision to travel by boat, whether he would have chosen another means, had he known.

As if on cue, the boat pitches to the right again. "It's getting close," Ari says, looking upward. He puts both hands on my shoulders and pushes me down to the bed. "Stay here," he instructs. "Don't get up, no matter what." He races across the cabin and charges up the stairs.

Above, I hear heavy footsteps, followed by a creaking sound as the entire boat seems to groan. Then there is silence for what seems like an eternity, broken only by the fierce howling of the wind. What's happening?

Waves lap up against the tiny cabin windows. Instantly, it is as if I am submerged, my childhood nightmares about the ocean come to life. Breathe, I command myself, forcing the panic down. Ari knows what he is doing. Everything will be fine.

But the storm is growing more violent, tossing the boat in all directions. Ari's bag flies from the shelf onto the floor, contents scattering. In the kitchen a jar slams against something and shatters. I cling to the headboard, trying in vain not to think of the scary lost-at-sea-in-a-storm movies I've seen. My stomach rolls.

From the deck comes a loud banging sound, followed by a scream. Ari! Heedless of his earlier warning, I let go of the bed and cross the cabin, holding on to the wall and trying not to fall as the boat lurches to and fro.

As I reach the deck, I am thrown backward by a wall of wind. Frantically, I grasp at the railing and fight my way up. "Ari!" I call, scanning the bridge and not seeing him. The sky is as dark as night and great waves of rain lash the deck.

I run to the side of the boat, clinging to the rail. "Ari!" I cry again, my voice lost in the roar of the wind. There is no sign of him in the wild surf.

"Jordan!" Ari's voice comes unseen from above. Struggling to maintain my balance, I make my way to the ladder, climb to the bridge in time to see Ari pulling himself into the chair.

In the distance, lightning shoots straight downward, breaking the surface.

"Are you all right?"

"Fine. I slipped, bumped my head." His expression is suddenly angry. "I told you to stay downstairs. Couldn't you have trusted me enough to listen for once?"

"But I thought—"

Another bolt of lightning crackles, closer this time. "We need to get inside." He climbs down first, then reaches back to help me. The wind is stronger now, every step a struggle as we fight our way to the cabin.

Inside, we collapse to the floor, soaked and exhausted. "Are you okay?" I ask. He does not reply but clings to me tightly, still gasping for breath. We lie wrapped around each other for several minutes. I look down at him, flooded with relief. He pulls me to him, bringing my lips to his. Then, seeming to find strength, he rises and carries me to the bed. I peel off his shirt. He falls onto the bed, drawing me on top of him.

This time there is no question of turning back. I remove my own wet clothes, breaking from him only long enough to lift my shirt over my head. Revived, he rises, pushing me back against the bed.

"The condoms . . . " I remember as his lips trail my neck.

He pulls away and I fear the moment will be lost again. But he sits up and reaches for his bag, now on the floor. Then he presses against me again, the intensity of our movements fueled by the rocking of the sea.

Later we lay silent, limbs still entangled. The wind has dropped to a whistle and the boat moves more gently as the storm recedes. "How are you?" he asks, his voice softer than I have heard before.

"I'm fine," I reply. "But I'm not the one who fell."

"I wasn't talking about that. I mean, what you said earlier about not getting involved because of Jared . . . "

"It's okay," I say quickly, cutting him off. For the first time in over a decade, sex was not about running from memories or erasing or avoiding them. I do not want to think about Jared now.

"Good." He smiles. "Because I've been wanting to do that since Monaco."

"Really? But last night, when you stayed up on the deck, I thought . . . "

"I like to sleep on deck sometimes. And I didn't want to presume that just because we were alone here together, that things would pick up where they left off. I wanted it to be right."

"Like now?"

"Like now," he repeats, then kisses me.

A few seconds later I pull away. "Seriously, though, you took a huge spill. Are you hurt?"

He sits up slowly. "A wave caught me off guard. I'm usually pretty good on my sea legs. But I never saw it coming . . . " I can tell he is shaken by the experience. I put my arm around his shoulder and draw him tight. There is something in the way he clings to me, vulnerable as a boy, that reminds me of Jared. I stiffen.

"What is it?" he asks warily, sensing the change in my demeanor.

"N-nothing," I manage, not wanting to ruin the moment.

But he pulls away, recalling our earlier conversation, my reticence to become involved. Then he stands up. "I'll be right back."

I sprawl across the narrow bed, still tingling. My mind reels. A day ago, I would have thought of this only as a fling. But my feelings when I thought Ari was in danger belie something more.

I sit up as he reappears. "The worst of it has passed," he reports. "We've sustained some damage, though, and we need to get to a port for repairs."

"Isn't that going to slow us down from finding Nicole?"

"It is, but we have no other choice. Hopefully the boat can be fixed quickly. If not, we'll leave it and find another."

I hate the idea of losing more time. "So what now?"

"I've set the GPS for Argostoli. That's on Kefalonia, the island just north of Zakynthos. I'm fairly certain we can have the work we need done at the port. We'll get there sometime in the middle of the night. We should get some rest while we can."

He stretches out beside me on the bed and I expect him to close his eyes, but he does not, instead turning to me. "Jordan is such an interesting name. Why were you named that?"

"I don't know," I admit. "I had a great-grandmother named Jenny and I assume that my parents wanted to use the *J* to honor her memory. But I'm not certain how they got to Jordan. They've never been to Israel or the Middle East."

"In Hebrew, it means to descend or flow down, like the river. It suits you." I pause, considering the irony. I wish that I flowed and was easygoing. "And my name, Aaron, means mountain. They go rather well together, then, don't they, your name and mine?"

"I think that's what we just did," I joke. "Flow down from the mountain." He doesn't respond, but rolls away from me. "What is it? What's on your mind?"

"My wife." I am unprepared for his response. "Sorry, I know that's the wrong thing to say right now. It's just hard for me. There have been others, of course, since Aviva. But this . . . "

"Seems like a betrayal?" I finish for him. He nods. I understand what he is feeling, recall it from the first time I was with someone else after college. Even though it was nearly a year after Jared was gone, it felt like putting something between us, a break in the bond that time was already stretching thin, and I hated it.

But Ari said he had been with other people. So why was this bothering him so? Because he has feelings for me, I realize, as much as I do for him. I shiver, then draw the blanket tighter.

I feel Ari's breath grow long and even behind me. Looking over my shoulder, I can see that he is sleeping soundly, exhausted from his earlier ordeal. I turn and wrap my arms around him as my eyes grow heavy.

Sometime later I awaken. I'm on the boat, I remember, as waves of pleasure nibble at my body. I lie with my eyes closed, trying to summon the sexy dream I must have been having. Hands, I realize with a start, running down my body, probing. It isn't a dream. Ari is inside me and I am half on top of him as if drawn by a force outside myself.

Did he start it? Did I? The questions fade as heat rises within me. He moves slowly, unlike any man I've ever known, allowing me to feel every inch against me, bringing me close, then stopping. When at last I can take it no longer, he grows stronger, more deliberate, taking me over the edge, and I explode, crying out in a stupor from my half sleep.

"Well, that was different," he remarks after I have pulled away.

"I'll say." As my desire ebbs, the confusion returns. "What happened?"

"I don't know," he replies and I can tell from his voice that he is sincere. "One minute I was asleep and the next . . . "

A vague recollection shoots through my mind of reaching for

him, rousing him from sleep. "It may have been me," I admit. "I'm not sure."

"It's okay. Though I think being asleep prevented us from being as cautious as we would have."

Panic grips me as I remember the night that Jared and I had forgotten to be careful, the price paid afterward.

"You should know I've been tested," he adds awkwardly. "Recently, as part of a physical."

But my heart pounds, anxiety unabated. I do the math quickly, decide that the risk of pregnancy now is low. Forcing myself to breathe, I listen to the rhythmic sound of water lapping gently against the hull. Beneath it comes another noise, wood scraping. "Are we docked?"

"Yes. I had to get up and navigate us into port. I tried not to wake you. We'll see about fixing the boat at first light."

Neither of us speaks for several minutes. "Did you think, before you knew about Nicole, that you might reunite with Jared?" he asks abruptly.

I bite my lip. It feels strange, lying here with the man I've just slept with, talking about an ex-boyfriend. "I don't know." But the question reverberates in my mind. For so many years, I thought Jared was dead. There were clearly times in the past week, since learning he might be alive, that I had allowed myself to dream of a reunion, seeing if we still felt the same, contemplating a life together. But that is out of the question now.

I could turn around. Just give up. Jared is alive, and he's married. Why am I still searching for him? Because even knowing all that I have learned, there are still so many questions: Why did he leave me and why didn't he come back?

"He's married," I say finally.

"And if he wasn't?"

Ari is asking whether I would still be here with him if Jared were single. "Nothing would change," I reply quickly, taking his hand.

But inside, my stomach flips. It is not a question that I've allowed myself to consider: If Jared was not married to Nicole, would I have become involved with Ari? Or would I have stopped this before it started, plunging headlong forward with my quest to find Jared? I want to believe that I still would have chosen Ari—we are so much more alike than Jared and I, and despite our quarrels he seems to understand me better than anyone has. But my image of Jared is so laden with memories, ten years of nostalgia that until last week had been rose-colored, untainted with the flaws and imperfections that time together would have brought. It is impossible to undo those trappings, to fairly compare the man I have dreamed of for a decade with the one who lies beside me.

"Anyhow," I say. "It's a moot point. Jared is with Nicole. And I'm here with you, where I want to be." And if your wife were alive, I want to add, you wouldn't be here with me. But that would be unfair to say. I cannot compete with a ghost.

He does not speak further but rolls slightly away, still holding my hand. Why did he have to bring these questions up now, when we are so happy and content? That need to dig beneath the surface, scratch away the shiny exterior, and search for imperfections, is one I recognize in myself. It comes from a deeply rooted belief that we are undeserving of good, that the gift given to us must be somehow secretly flawed.

"I'm just looking for answers," I add, as though there is still a question pending. "So I can put things to rest and move on with my life."

"A reckoning." He reaches down and squeezes my hand. "Is that why you never married?"

"I don't know," I reply honestly. There's never, I realize, been anyone remotely in contention for the job. "I'm just a loner, I guess."

"We're all loners until the right person comes along. But it's hard, moving on after losing someone." He rolls over, stretching. His hand comes to my neck and begins to knead the muscles there, and I close my eyes, melting under his touch. He presses my arms to my sides like a swaddled infant, in a way I didn't know until this very moment I needed to be held.

He begins to breathe evenly again and I lie awake in the darkness as the sea rocks gently beneath us. My thoughts turn to Jared. It is hard to believe that tomorrow I might find him, that we might have our reunion at long last.

Restless, I slip from beneath Ari's warm, heavy arm and sit up. I stand up and climb to the deck of the boat. The unfamiliar harbor is silent except for the sound of muffled voices from another boat. In the distance a few lights twinkle on the shoreline.

I consider his question about marriage, why I never wed. Will I wind up alone? The question has always been an uncomfortable one. The single woman—forty-something, no kids, and a couple of cats—is a Foreign Service cliché, kind of like Mo, only less successful and without Katie and Kyle, the gorgeous twins she adopted from Vietnam two decades ago. Despite the advances that women have made in the profession, it's still not as easy for a female diplomat to find a partner who is willing to forego his own career to follow her around the world as it is for her male counterparts.

Not that I've never been the type of woman who felt she needed a husband. There are worse things than winding up alone, such as being stuck in an unhappy marriage like some of my coworkers, staying with the status quo because of children or because getting out was simply too hard.

Tired now, I make my way down once more to the cabin, which is still a mess from the earlier storm. I go to the kitchen, clean up the jar of olive oil that had cracked in the sink and straighten the dishes quietly so as not to wake Ari. Then I tiptoe back to the stateroom where the air is thick with sleep.

I walk to my bag in the corner, rummaging for my toothbrush. A red light flashes from the side pocket. My phone. I pull it out.

I press the button and the phone comes out of power save mode, the screen glowing in the darkness. A message from Lincoln, responding to our earlier string. *Found Nicole Short,* the message reads. So she was using Jared's last name after all. *Last reported residence is somewhere near a small fishing village on the southwestern coast of Zakynthos called Keri. No exact address but you should be able to find her there.*

I study the message, my heart pounding. Zakynthos again. But Ari had said Nicole could be found in Zante town in the east, a different part of the island entirely.

Why, I wonder, had Mo's file said nothing about Greece? Was it because the address somehow was only linked to Nicole? I don't think Mo would have given me all that information but held back that one piece if she had known about it. More likely Lincoln had access to information that Mo did not.

I start toward the bed to wake Ari and tell him what I've found. But there's more, I notice, looking at Lincoln's message again. I scroll down: *Ran profiles with photo. Actual name Aaron Borenstein. He's Mosaad. No intelligence on his present mission.*

I take a step backward, nearly tripping over a shoe that lies in the middle of the floor. Across the room, Ari moves, stirred by the noise.

I freeze, thinking that he will awake, but he snorts and rolls over. I reread the message, recoiling. Ari lied to me about who he is. What is he really doing here? Is he after Jared?

Mosaad. The word ricochets in my head. Though the possibility had crossed my mind when I first met Ari, I am still surprised to learn that it is true. Suddenly it all makes sense—his caginess about his clients, the sources of his information, and his resources.

I sink to the floor, disbelieving. Ari has been lying to me the whole time. Nausea rises in me as I remember what just happened between us. Was that part of the act, too?

I start across the room, seized with the urge to confront him with the information and demand the truth. But even if I could get him to talk, what's the point? He's just going to deny my allegations unless I show him proof, and I can't do that without exposing Lincoln and the fact that he has helped me. No, there's nothing to be gained from confronting Ari.

I walk to Ari's bag, which still lies open, contents strewn across the floor. I reach for his wallet, looking for . . . what, exactly? It's not as if a covert agent will carry a Mosaad business card. Still, I thumb through it, searching for something that will confirm the information Lincoln conveyed.

Suddenly there is a rustling noise from the bed. Ari rolls over once more and his eyes open, seeming to stare straight at me.

Startled, I drop the wallet back into the bag. My mind races, trying to come up with an explanation as to what I was doing. Then his eyes close again. He is still asleep, I realize, flooded with relief. But I do not dare continue looking.

What to do now? I can't continue on with him as though nothing is wrong. I need to get as far away from him as possible, get to Nicole ahead of him. I am flooded with doubt. Can I find her on my own? I have the new information on Nicole's whereabouts that Lincoln provided, the name of the village. Press forward, a voice inside me, not quite my own, seems to say. Suddenly I am leaving the embassy again, setting out in the taxi on my quest. Alone.

Which is the way you like it, the voice reminds. I've never relied upon anyone else before. I can do this myself.

I tiptoe across the cabin, still clutching the piece of paper with the address. As I pass the bed, the sight of Ari sleeping makes me stop. Anger and longing collide. I wish I could step back in time an hour ago to the moment when I was lying in his arms, allowing myself to hope. But I cannot. I have played the fool, again.

My doubts rise again, stronger. I don't know if I can find Nicole, or whether I will encounter Santini's men on my own. But I am back to that place, that fundamental truth that the only person who is sticking around, the one person who can be trusted, is me. So I will keep going.

To get to the one place I always needed to go. To find Jared.

I pick up my bag and take a long last look back at Ari, then climb to the deck. The harbor lights seem to shine more brightly now, beckoning me, urging me forward in my quest. I step over the edge of the boat onto the dock. Then I walk from the yacht, leaving my heart behind on the ground.

chapter **FOURTEEN**

I STEP FROM THE rear of the battered car, closing the door. Before me, a cluster of rectangular buildings, blindingly white in the morning sunshine, wind their way up the hillside. Men unload the early catch from the few dozen boats that bobble in the calm blue waters of the harbor below. The air is thick with the smell of salt and dead fish.

I crept from the yacht in Argostoli before dawn while Ari still slept, making my way down the dock to the larger marina where tourists were embarking upon ferries for various islands. There I boarded a midsized boat headed for Zakynthos and as we set out on the water, I hovered along the rail, observing the other travelers revel in a carefree manner so unfamiliar to me. When was the last time I had been on vacation like that? I could not remember.

A few feet away a young couple, newlyweds perhaps, nuzzled each other, oblivious to the other passengers. Watching them, I could not help but think of Ari, the passion we shared just a few hours earlier. It had all been a lie. How could I have been so wrong about him? I leaned on the railing, dropping my head to my hands. First Sebastian and now Ari. Even Jared, in his own way, had deceived me. For years I wanted to believe that he was the one man who would never do that. But what was the difference, really? He had lied about his death and disappeared. No, he was just like the others, maybe worse.

At least with Sebastian, I discovered the truth before things went too far. But with Ari . . . I pushed the memories of the previous night from my mind, distracting myself by studying the other passengers once more. I noticed a forty-something man, dressed in golf shorts and a collared shirt that screamed American. He was standing alone, looking in my direction across the bow of the ship. My skin prickled. Another government agent, sent to persuade me to come back in? But the man turned away and a second later was joined by a brunette woman several years younger. Enough, I thought as they strolled away. Paranoia would not help on top of everything else. Anyway, the Director had tried once; I felt certain that he would respect my decision and not bother me again.

When the ferry arrived in the port town of Agios Nikolaos on the northern edge of Zakynthos, I set out in search of a driver who could take me south to the village of Keri. Just outside the harbor, I was pointed in the direction of a car by a man selling fruit on the curbside. The driver and I had eyed one another warily—he was reluctant to travel so far, and I had my reservations about getting in an unmarked car with the stranger, who could not have been more than sixteen years old. But that was as close to a taxi as I was likely to get in these parts, I concluded, and when I pulled out cash to pay him in advance, his enthusiasm grew considerably.

The driver made no attempt to speak but put in a cassette of music and lowered the window to dangle a hand-rolled cigarette outside. We drove south, jostling along a series of roads in various states of disrepair in a car that had seemingly lost its shock absorbers long ago. For some time, the landscape on either side of the road was shrouded in thick brush and trees, olive groves covering the rugged hillsides. But then there was a sudden break to the right, and as the breathtaking coastline of bright blue sea burst into view, I was reminded of the Côte d'Azur as I had first glimpsed it on the train ride from Milan to Monaco. But the landscape was more pristine here, the lush terrain broken only by the occasional cubed white house, bright beneath the midday sun.

I sank back against the seat, overwhelmed. I had no idea how to find Nicole once I reached the village, or whether she would tell me where Jared was if I did find her. Not to mention the dangerous criminals who were also after her who I might encounter along the way. And for what—a conversation with an ex-boyfriend who hadn't cared enough all of these years to tell me he was alive? Perhaps I should give up, I thought yet again. I could catch a flight from Athens to Geneva, check in on Sarah, figure out what to do with my life.

My hand closed around something in my pocket. The ring. I pulled it out, holding it up to the light. A promise unfulfilled. And I knew then that I had to keep going. To give up would be to admit defeat and make all that I'd gone through in London and since worthless. I needed to see this through, find Nicole, get to Jared. Only then could I move on.

I wrapped my arms around myself, shivering despite the heat, then gazed out the window once more. The road had grown less paved and the car moved with greater effort through the thick, fresh mud as it climbed. We rounded a bend and a fishing village came into view. The driver stopped before a cluster of dilapidated buildings, gesturing with his head, and I realized he was telling me we had arrived.

As he drives away now, I study the village, then start up the dirt road that runs from the harbor into the hills. The streets are strangely quiet at midday, the rundown storefronts deserted. Outside a small grocery store, a group of mostly shirtless men lounge on two benches, clustered around a game of cards. They look up, eyeing me as I approach. Despite the close proximity of a resort just down the beach, this is clearly not a part of the island that sees many tourists. How can Nicole and Jared possibly live here without standing out?

The men are staring at me expectantly. I clear my throat. "English?"

There are several seconds of silence. A man who had been sitting with his eyes half-closed, head tilted back toward the sky, looks up at me. "A little."

I hesitate, wondering whether Nicole is known here by name. "I'm looking for a woman called Nicole." I gesture to my hair. "Blond?" I remember then the picture of Nicole and Jared from Maureen's file. I take it out, show it to the man.

Alert now, his eyes light up and he turns to the others, speaking rapidly in Greek. One of the men points to the hills in the distance.

He is telling me that Nicole lives in that direction. But the craggy hills seem uninhabited, ominous. I gesture, as though steering a car. "I need to go there."

The man shakes his head. "Not possible. The road . . . " He pauses, searching for the right words. "Too much rain." As he translates my request, the other men cluck in agreement.

"What can I do?" I press, anxiety rising. "Is there another way?"

"Only wait," he replies before tilting his head back up toward the sun.

Wait. My heart sinks. Even in this heat, it could take days for the road to dry. I don't have that kind of time. Deflated, I turn away, starting back toward the harbor. Then I stop again. "How long has the road been out?" I ask.

"Week," the man says, opening just one eye this time.

My breath catches. Perhaps Nicole has not been able to make it any farther, either. But where would she be?

I turn away, shielding my eyes with my hand as I scan the horizon. Down the coast, I glimpse a tourist resort, hotels and sunbathers dotting the shoreline. Would Nicole have waited there until the road home was passable again? It's a long shot, but the only lead I have at the moment.

I turn to thank the men, but they have already returned to their card game. Without speaking, I start down the road, which soon ends at a narrow strip of pebbled beach. As I make my way along the water's edge, my doubts grow. I don't know that Nicole made it back, or even that she and Jared really live here. But what other choice do I have? I can try to find Nicole in hopes that she will lead me to Jared or else give up and go home.

A few minutes later I reach the edge of the resort. The beach is more sand than pebble here, dotted with straw umbrellas. A handful of small hotels sit just above the bay. I walk into the first one, a peach-colored, two-story villa. "Yes?" a young woman behind the desk asks.

"I'm looking for a guest called Nicole Martine, or Nicole Short," I hasten to add.

The woman hesitates and I wait for her to tell me that she cannot share guests' private information. But she scans the ledger. "No one by that name."

Is she using an alias, I wonder? I pull out the photo and show it to the woman, but she only shakes her head.

"Thank you." I move on to the next hotel down the beach, a

slightly larger, white stucco building, and repeat the same exercise with an older male clerk, who is similarly unfamiliar with Nicole.

Twenty minutes later I reach the last of the hotels. As I approach the front porch, my shoulders slump at what is quickly proving to be an exercise in futility. Villa Kyrianos is smaller than the others, more of a guesthouse than a hotel, with a handful of tiny bungalows scattered behind it. There is no desk in the lobby, just a sofa and low table bearing a vase of wildflowers. A boy of no more than fifteen polishes the windows.

"Hello," I say. "I wonder if you can help me. I am looking for a woman . . . " He does not speak English, I realize, as confusion floods his eyes.

I reach for the photo but before I can show it to him, a fiftyish woman appears and shoos the boy away. "You want a room?" she asks brusquely.

I show her the photograph. "Have you seen this woman?"

I hold my breath as she studies the photograph, biting her lip. "Maybe," she says, pronouncing the answer with more certainty than it warrants. "She isn't a guest here, but perhaps on the beach. So many visitors to our resort, it's hard to say. Now, do you want a room?"

I hesitate. The last thing I want is to be stuck here. I have to find Jared. But without Nicole, it seems I have no other choice than to wait until the road is passable again and try to make it to their house on my own. "Please." I fill out the card she gives me, then hand it back.

"The room is being cleaned," she says. "If you come back in an hour, it should be ready. There's a café just down the beach, if you're hungry."

"Thank you." I walk out of the guesthouse and start down the beach in the direction the woman indicated, away from the other hotels. Nestled in a cove by a small harbor at the far end of the bay, the café is nothing more than a hut with a few wooden tables. The tantalizing aroma of fresh fish cooking over an open fire wafts through the air.

I walk to the grill, point to a plate of fish and vegetables. After I've paid, I carry the plate and a beer to one of the tables. My stomach grumbles as I stab a bite of the flaky whitefish. I study the harbor, a few small sailboats and other pleasure craft bobbing around the docks.

My thoughts turn to Ari once more. He must have woken up by now and discovered me missing. Would he understand why I left or try to find me? He will go after Nicole, not me, I remind myself with a mixture of relief and regret, to the address in Zante town that his contact provided. It has always been about finding her.

Why hadn't he told me that he was Mosaad? Because he couldn't, any more than I could have told those closest to me about my investigation in London or any of my other classified assignments. It's the nature of the job or, as one of the other men tells Michael Corleone in *The Godfather Part II,* "the business we have chosen." It was one of my dad's favorite movie quotes and rather ironic, in light of the mobsters we've encountered.

I remember my first meeting with Ari in Monaco, the confrontation in Nicole's apartment. At the time I'd been too preoccupied with finding Jared to focus on the unlikelihood of the coincidence that we were both searching for Nicole at the same time. Now it seems so improbable. Perhaps he had been following me all along, hoping that I would somehow lead him to Nicole.

I should have known, I berate myself silently. This isn't like Sebastian, where I had no clue. With Ari, part of me had always suspected that something wasn't right, that there was more to the situation than met the eye. Yet I had still gone with him. Why? Was it the adrenaline rush, the thrill of the unknown? Or was I simply drawn to men who would ultimately betray me?

And I still don't know why Ari wants to find Nicole. His earlier explanation, the rubric of being a private investigator, was clearly a lie. What if his true purpose is to harm Nicole, or even Jared? Suddenly it seems as if by searching for Jared, I might be inadvertently leading others to him, putting him in harm's way. Would he have been better off if I hadn't come looking for him?

I pick up the beer, taking a large swig and surveying the harbor once more. I can see Jared living somewhere like this. But how did he come to be here? One of the sailboats shifts slightly in the breeze, revealing a small boat behind it. My hand stops, beer bottle suspended midair. Standing in the dinghy, fussing with the motor, is a woman with blond hair.

"Nicole!" I call, jumping up and pushing back from the table, spilling the food from my plate. What is she doing? A boat, I realize as the motor begins to purr, to take her home to Jared when the road cannot.

I start down the beach, running as fast as my sandals will allow. She looks up, jaw dropping as she sees me. "Wait!" Suddenly it feels as if we are back at the airport in Nice, her contemplating the quickest means of escape. "I just want to talk to you, please."

I sprint down the dock, waving my arms. As I reach the end, my foot slips on a wet spot. "Ahh!" I cry frantically as my legs fly out from under me. Unable to stop, I careen over the edge, landing rear end first in the surprisingly icy sea.

I plunge beneath the surface, water quickly covering my head, filling my open mouth and nose. Instantly I am a child again, helpless against the waves. I flail my arms, trying in vain to bring myself to the surface but instead sinking farther as I panic.

Hands grab my shoulders and pull me up hard. I break the surface, choking and gasping for air. Nicole is leaning over the side of the boat, holding on to me. "Easy," she says, barely containing her disdain. "You're all right."

"Barely. I thought for a moment you might let me go," I add with a laugh.

"I considered it." She does not smile.

"I'm a terrible swimmer," I confess as she helps me over the side of the boat.

She pulls the boat back into the dock. "It's barely six feet deep. You were hardly likely to drown." We eye each other icily for several seconds, neither speaking.

"Thanks," I say, embarrassed, as she throws me a tattered rag to use as a towel. I take in her crisp khaki pants and white blouse, the flat canvas shoes that are so much more practical for the terrain here than my own wet sandals, yet still elegant. Remembering her panicked, bloodstained appearance in Vienna, I wonder where she has been in the days since I saw her last.

"You should be more careful around water if you can't swim." Her voice is terse. She hands me my bag, which thankfully landed on the dock and not in the water as I fell.

"Well, I appreciate your helping me." I wipe the water from my face. "This time, anyway," I add pointedly, recalling how she fled in Vienna.

I wait for her to apologize but she does not. Her expression is harrowed, dark circles ringing her eyes. Despite her polished appearance, I can tell that whatever is going on has taken its toll on her.

"What are you doing here?" she asks wearily.

"Like I told you at the airport, I'm looking for Jared."

She runs her hand through her hair, exhales sharply. "And I told you it was better if you left him alone."

"I need to see him."

"Why do you want to find him so badly? I know, you said you need answers," she says. "But this is quite a long way to travel, really, for a conversation."

Why do I want to find Jared? I consider the question. To touch him and confirm the unbelievable, that he is alive, that he wasn't killed that night in the cold waters of the River Cam. To tell him that I'd learned the truth, delivered the secret that nearly cost him his life to the right hands. But beyond that there is something more. I need answers: Why did he disappear without saying good-bye? Didn't he trust me enough to share his plan of escape? How could he leave me alone all of these years to grieve?

"He doesn't need saving, Jordan," she adds, before I can answer.

I look up, surprised. "That's not it." But my words ring hollowly.

"Jared had to run for a lot of years," she continues, ignoring my denial. "But he's safe, at least as safe as can be expected. He has a home, with me."

And the only thing I can do is stir that up, bring back painful memories of the past, I think, echoing the silent implication of her words.

She runs her hand along the edge of the boat, eyes me levelly. "I'm his wife, you know."

For whatever he might have done and whoever he might really be, I am grateful to Ari in that moment for telling me about Jared and Nicole. Hearing now for the first time, from her, would have been unimaginably stunning and painful. "I know." I force my voice to remain even, taking satisfaction in the flicker of disappointment that flashes across her face at my lack of surprise. "I don't want to cause him problems. I just want to talk to him."

"You must hate me, Jordan," she says. Her voice is neutral, as though observing the weather or discussing a newspaper article.

I am disarmed by her candor, unprepared for the conversation I never expected to have. "I don't . . . " I begin. Her face is skeptical. "That is, it's all been such a whirlwind. You have to understand: until about a week ago, I still thought Jared was dead. Finding out he was alive was the shock of my life. And then, to learn about you . . . But no, I don't hate you."

Because I haven't had time to get there yet, I want to add. I am not sure if I ever will. It seems silly, when there are so many other people I have better reasons to blame for the way things turned out: Mo for betraying me. Sebastian for making me believe he liked me. The others for setting it all in motion. Without them, Jared would have never disappeared and he and I might be together, living a quiet country life somewhere on the southern coast of England. Instead, I am standing here, talking to his wife.

No, there are at least a half dozen people I hate more than Nicole. The white hot ball of anger that I've buried deep in my stomach these past few days begins to burn and glow. I swallow, pushing it down. There's a fine line between needing to deal with the past and being consumed by all of the rage and regret. And despite the dance I've done with my ghosts and demons all of these years, I've managed to keep the latter at bay. I saw Chris cross that line with his obsession to learn the truth about Jared's supposed death, and it nearly destroyed him. Something tells me if I give way to all of the anger, let it see the light of day and the oxygen it needs, it is going to feed on me until there is simply nothing left.

"Well, I hate you," she announces abruptly, jarring me from my thoughts.

Stunned, I look up at her. I don't know Nicole really, shouldn't care at all what she thinks, but the words still sting. She stares out across the water. "It must seem silly to you, I know." Bitterness roughs the edges of her words. "I have Jared. I go to bed beside him almost every night and wake up beside him in the morning. Why should I care about a college girlfriend, one who he dated for a few months?" She turns toward me. "Because it is your name he calls out when he cries in his sleep. You're the one who keeps the shadow over his eyes, and there's a part of him tucked away that I will never be able to get to because it belongs to you."

The weight of her words crashes into me. I understand now the fear in her eyes when I came to her flat in Monaco that morning and she realized who I was, the trepidation that remained even after I told her that I had not come to do Jared harm. It was more than a need to protect him from the forces that had been chasing him all of these years. She was terrified that I had come to take him from her, that she was going to lose the man that she loved.

A hint of smugness jabs at me. He still loves me. He still wants me.

Am I trying to take him? I turn the question over in my mind, considering. I suppose when I first set out from London to find him, that was the fantasy: I would find Jared, alone and waiting for me, and we would be reunited, pick up again as though nothing had changed. But even then, some piece of me knew that it was impossible.

Still, as I made my way to find him, part of me stubbornly thought that we could start over, get to know each other again, this time as the adults we had become. After I had seen Nicole, learned who she was, the dream still persisted. She was just a placeholder, a warm body that could be easily removed. But even if I was the kind of woman who would break up a marriage for my own selfish happiness, I knew Jared would always be loyal.

And then I understand why I am here. "You asked me why I came. You asked me that same question a few days ago when we first met in Monaco, too. I didn't know how to answer you, but I do now: I'm here for closure. I came to say good-bye."

"Good," she says, but her voice is flat. There is little satisfaction in having me decide not to pursue Jared. His choice is the vindication, the one that matters. I want to tell her that he would never become involved with me while married to her. But my presuming to tell her about her own husband would be more offensive than reassuring.

"And the man you're traveling with?"

I did not realize she had seen Ari. "Was traveling with. We aren't together anymore."

"Aaron." I stare at her, surprised. How does she know his name? "He is searching for me, no?" I nod. "Aaron is Mosaad, you know." She delivers the pronouncement matter-of-factly.

"I know," I say, again glad not to be hearing news from her for the first time. But the revelation is still hard to accept.

She brushes her hair from her face. "I hope he doesn't think that just because we're related . . . "

"Related?" I interrupt and for a second the boat seems to slide sideways beneath me.

"Yes. Aaron Bruck is my cousin."

chapter FIFTEEN

I STARE AT HER, dumbfounded. "Or maybe 'cousin' isn't quite the right word," Nicole adds. "My grandmother Leah was married to Aaron's grandfather. She was his first wife." I remember then Ari telling me of his grandfather's family before the war. She continues, "My grandmother died in Belzec, but their daughter survived, was adopted by a gentile couple after the war. Of course, my grandfather had no idea; he thought his family was gone and he moved on and married again, had a son, Aaron's father. It wasn't until years later that my mother made the connection, and reached out to her half brother.

"I've seen Aaron a handful of times over the years. He was always trying to persuade me to give up my business, do some honest work." She laughs cynically. "As if Mosaad is honest work. You know about his wife and child, yes?" Nicole asks. I nod. "After they were killed and he came home from the army, Aaron had nothing, so he was an easy recruit for the agency and his skills made him very desirable to them. He told me a year or so ago that he was getting out, but I guess he didn't go through with it. People like him can never really walk away."

I let the information Nicole has shared sink in: she and Ari are related. "Do you know why he's looking for me?" she asks.

"Yes. I mean no, not really. Something to do with the wine, at least I think so." Hearing myself fumble over the words, I instantly regret not bluffing better, sounding more confident.

"The wine." Her mouth twists. "How much do you know about that?"

"Not much. Only that there was a transaction you handled, some wine sold on the black market that wasn't what it was supposed to be."

"You must think very little of me, a criminal married to your Jared."

"I didn't say . . . "

"You didn't have to. Let's not waste time being insincere." She gazes out across the water. "I was born and raised in Beirut during the civil war. My father was dead and my mother preoccupied with raising my brothers and sisters. So it fell to me to help support my family. The black market was huge then, people turning to it for what they needed. And there was a demand for supplying those that had money with luxury goods that couldn't be gotten elsewhere. I worked for a man from the time I was twelve, running cigarettes and alcohol and other items for pay.

"I knew, though, that I didn't want to spend my life working for someone else. It's like having a pimp, you know?" There is a harshness to her voice that I have not heard before. Has Jared seen this side of her? "So when I was sixteen, I made my way to Paris. I was able to set myself up independently there and make a lot more profit, get an apartment.

"Of course, it wasn't like I wanted to do this kind of work forever. I finished school, studied art history at the university. It was there that I learned of a much more profitable kind of trading: rare antiques and documents. It was a funny sort of market, more gray than black really, existing just below the surface of legitimacy. I'd procure items and sell them to contacts from some of the most prestigious antiques houses in Europe. Using my background in art history, I could identify the really special pieces, the hidden gems that were overlooked. I once handled a transaction involving a very well-known museum curator in Britain for what became a major piece in a national exhibition. No one looked too closely if the item was desirable enough or the price was right.

"I was still at university when a friend of a friend approached me, a Bulgarian man I'd met once at a party. He told me he had a client who was interested in selling certain rare vintages of wine, ones that could not be found on the commercial market. I put him in touch with some wealthy individuals I knew from my antiques work and made a healthy commission on the sale. That was how I became involved with wine trading for the first time. I quickly saw how much money there was to be made, how great the demand. So I learned the business." She gives a slight toss of her hair. "And I became the best at it."

She runs her hands down her knees. "After we settled here on the island, that same man contacted me and said he'd come into possession of a valuable case of Bordeaux, the Chateau Cerfberre 43. He was very vague about its origins, which is not unusual in my line of work, but the price he claimed it could fetch was astronomical. I was skeptical at first, but the wine appeared to be authentic, and still packed in the original wooden case. I told Jared about it and we quickly figured out that wine was so valuable not only because of its vintage but its unique historical significance—it was one of the last wines produced by the Cerfberre house."

Before the Cerfberre family was destroyed by the Nazis, I think, remembering the story Signora Conti had told us. Nicole continues, "Finding the right buyer for such a valuable shipment wasn't easy, so I contacted one of my associates, Friedrich Heigler, to broker the transaction. I'd worked with him a half-dozen times before and saw no reason to distrust him. He arranged the deal with the investment fund, of which Marcos Santini is a principle investor. You know who he is, yes?" she asks, but does not wait for my response. "Without telling me, Heigler moved up the transaction date, sold them another wine that he passed off as the Cerfberre Bordeaux and hid the money in an offshore account."

"You had no idea?"

"No," she retorts, visibly annoyed. "In fact, after I found out, I went to Vienna to see Heigler to try to talk him out of it before he could disappear. His plan was to sell the real wine to someone else, and he offered me a cut of the profits to go along with the scam. But when Santini's man showed up, things got ugly and he killed Heigler." Her face sags. "So now Santini thinks I tricked him out of his money and murdered one of his men."

"Yeah," I say. "And they're still following you." I tell her of the yacht we saw at sea. "I think we lost them, though."

A look of terror crosses her face, replaced quickly by one of re-crimination. "Did you ever consider that by coming to find Jared, you've led this danger right to him?"

"I . . ." I start to protest. Faltering, my anger rises. How dare she blame me for the situation she created?

"It's all right," she says, raising her hand before I can continue. Her shoulders slump in resignation. "There's no hiding from these people. They would have found me sooner or later."

"But you could just explain things to Santini and repay him the money he lost, or give him the real wine." Even as I say this, the notion of dealing with the criminals makes me cringe. I recall the Albanian investigation I worked on in London, the way that the mob exploited and trafficked in women. Surely Santini would use the money to generate such other enterprises further as well.

"It's not that simple. I'm afraid it gets worse. You see, when I was first approached about the wine, I knew it was the opportunity of a lifetime. But I didn't have the kind of cash needed to buy it. So I contracted with Maria Ivankov for a loan."

"Who?"

"She's a French-Russian financier, based in Marseilles." She, I repeat inwardly, remembering what Ari had told me about Lucia Santini. Is organized crime the new black?

Nicole continues, "She fronted the money for the transaction. It happens more often than you can imagine in my line of work. Private interests will often loan money without looking too closely or asking the kind of questions a bank might, and then after the transaction is complete I repay them with healthy interest. It's never been a problem."

Until now, I think. Nicole is in debt to two bosses and can't repay both because Heigler stole the money.

"When you saw me in Monaco, I'd just been to see Ivankov to explain what happened, ask for forbearance or at least some time. She was not, let's say, understanding." She looks helpless then, more girl than woman. "You have to believe that I didn't know this would happen. I thought it was just a legitimate transaction. Jared had been begging me to get out of the business and I thought with the commission on this trade that I would finally have enough to stop working these deals. It was never supposed to be like this," she insists again, and beneath her cold, proud voice I hear a plea for understanding. "I would never intentionally jeopardize my family."

That's exactly what your line of work does, I want to say, though I do not. "The wine shipment was the deal of a lifetime," she adds defensively. "The chance to make a profit that would enable me to quit for good."

Stop running, get out of the game. I want to believe that Nicole is telling the truth. But there is something in her that I recognize in myself—the game itself is the thing that keeps us going. She said as much about Ari, his inability to leave Mosaad. Could any of us really be content without the thrill of the chase?

"So what now?" I ask. "Can you go to the authorities?"

She shakes her head emphatically. "Not without admitting my role in the affair." Ari had said the same thing. "No, the only thing to do is get rid of the wine, sell it for a high enough price to pay back both of them. That's what I was doing after I left Vienna, trying to broker a deal. I've got a potential buyer, but they want me to produce one of the bottles so it can be authenticated."

"But why is Ari chasing you?" I ask. "I mean, what does he want with the wine?"

She shrugs. "I have no idea. The last time he contacted me a few weeks ago, he was acting strange, asking specific questions about the Cerfberre wine. And then I saw him, lurking around the café instead of approaching me directly. I knew he was up to something, and that's why I left Monaco so quickly to find Heigler."

"I thought . . . "

"That I left because of you?" She waves her hand dismissively, as if the notion of being scared off by me is inconceivable.

"But one minute you were bringing in groceries and the next, after speaking with me, you were gone."

"Coincidence. I was restocking the kitchen as a courtesy to my grandmother. It really is her flat."

"And you're assuming Ari's looking for the wine as part of his job, not out of personal interest?"

"Yes. Aaron hasn't had any personal interests since his family was killed. He loved to sail but he doesn't even do that anymore." In my mind, I see Ari yesterday as we traveled to Greece by yacht. He seemed so happy on the water, as though a part of him, long buried, had been set free. "Wine was never his thing anyway," she adds.

I remember then our visit to the Contis, how Ari discussed the various vintages we sampled so knowledgeably. Was that a side of him that Nicole did not know, or just an act? "But what would the Israeli government want with a case of wine?"

"I don't know. The wine is an extraordinarily rare World War II vintage, and there's been a lot of interest in it from historians as well as collectors. That still doesn't explain why the government would care, though, or why they would go to such lengths. But whatever Aaron wants, it isn't to help me sell it." Her voice is cold now, businesslike. "I need to get rid of the wine and pay off my debts in order to keep my family safe."

"But Ari said—"

"Ari," she repeats, cutting me off, raising an eyebrow at my use of his nickname. "What is going on between you two anyway?"

"Nothing," I reply, too quickly. "We just met in Monaco a few days ago. We were both trying to find you. That is, I was looking for Jared through you," I correct, fumbling. "So we agreed to work together."

Her skeptical expression does not change. "I know my cousin— he's a very independent man. He wouldn't accept help, nor would he let someone else come along, unless he had good reason." Squirming,

I look away. "And you?" she asks bluntly when her previous comments do not yield the desired response. "You have feelings for him?"

None of your business, I want to say. But antagonizing Nicole will not serve me well now. I pause, unsure how to answer. "I don't know," I say finally. "I mean, I like him, or I thought I did anyway." I watch her face as it relaxes slightly. My interest in Aaron seems to give her comfort that I am not trying to recapture Jared. "But he lied to me," I add.

"We all have our secrets," she replies, and I guess that she is thinking of Jared, the things she has not told him about her work. "Where is Aaron now?"

"I left him in Argostoli. Our boat was damaged during a storm so we had to pull in, but I don't know if he was going to wait for it to be repaired or find another way to Zakynthos. We had a lead that we might be able to find you at an address in Zante town, a café called Nicholas."

"Nikolai," she corrects.

"That's it. So that's likely where he's headed."

"What on earth . . . ?" Her brow furrows with concern. "No, that isn't right. I mean, I've heard of that place, but I've never been there."

"Maybe his source was just misinformed."

Nicole raises an eyebrow. "That's rather specific for bad information, don't you think?"

She's right. Had someone fed Ari the wrong location in order to throw him off course? Or worse, is it some sort of trap? Alarmed, I pull my cell phone from the bag as well as the card Ari gave me the night we met. I dial the number on the card. It does not ring but goes right to a prerecorded message, telling me that the owner is not in range. "Damn," I swear. "Out of service."

"How long ago did you leave him?" she asks.

"Just before dawn." I glance at my watch. "He was going to sail out again after the boat was fixed. But I had to take the ferry and then a car, which slowed me down. I think he was planning to sail directly into Zante town."

"You need to get to him, warn him that the information is bad," Nicole says.

I look at Nicole, considering. She is right, of course. "But . . . " I peer down the beach over her shoulder, wondering how far I am from Jared. I imagine him looking up, his face breaking as he sees me approach. I have waited so many years for this. The notion of further delaying our reunion and the answers to the questions I've had all these years is unbearable.

"So what are you going to do? Are you going to go after Ari and try to reach him before he gets there?" It is both a real question and at the same time a test. If I really care about Ari, I will choose to help him before going to talk to Jared.

"If I go to help Ari, can I come back and see Jared after? I mean, will he still be here . . . ?"

She shrugs. "I don't know. This has been our home." Home. Will I ever get used to the status quo as it now exists? She smiles faintly. "And Jared won't leave without me." Her face grows serious once more. "But with all that has happened . . . my first priority is our safety."

So saving Ari might mean losing Jared, perhaps this time to somewhere I cannot find him. I don't have to do it, I remind myself. Ari lied to me about who he was and what he was doing. I don't owe him anything and this isn't my fight.

Ari's face appears in my mind. I remember how it felt on the ship during the storm, and I thought I might have lost him for good. How he saved my life in Vienna, the pact we made to be there for each other always. And I know then that, despite everything that happened, the fact that he deceived me, I have no choice.

"All right, I'll go find Ari," I say at last.

"No," she replies abruptly. "I will."

I stare at her, dumbfounded. "I don't understand. Why would you help me?"

"I'm not doing it for you. Aaron's my family and I need to warn him that there might be danger. I owe him that much."

Then why had she asked me to go? It was a test, I realize. She wanted to see which man I would choose, whether my feelings for Ari or Jared would prevail. Apparently I passed. "I can go with you," I offer.

"No." She bites her lip. "You go to my husband."

Surprised, I hesitate. "Really?"

She nods. "I can find Aaron while you have the conversation you need to have with Jared."

"But the man in the village said the road is out."

"It is. Take the boat." Nicole points down the coast past the village. "Follow the shoreline around the ridge and dock at the next inlet. Our cottage is on the bluff overlooking the sea. Can you manage it?" I nod. "Good."

I am flooded with disbelief. She is not only giving me permission to go to Jared, but telling me where he is and giving me the means to get there. "Why are you doing this?"

"We all need things resolved, Jordan. Me with the wine. You with Jared. Otherwise we'll never be able to stop running. The thought of you seeing him again terrifies me," she adds, with surprising candor. "But I don't think it will change anything and if it does, so be it. It would be far worse to keep living as a prisoner of my fears. So go to Jared, get your answers if you can. And then we can all move on with our lives."

"What are you going to do?"

"Go after Aaron and find out why he is interested in the wine. Try and stop him before he runs into any trouble. Don't worry," she adds, seeing my expression. "My cousin is the strongest person I know."

Her words are no comfort. The possibility that something might happen to Ari fills me with a terror and sadness that I have not felt in a decade. In that moment, despite everything that has happened, I understand exactly what he has become to me in the very short time we have known each other. I cannot lose him.

I should go with Nicole, I think suddenly. Ari and I made a pact to protect each other. As badly as I want to see Jared, I am even more desperate to make sure Ari is all right.

"Go to Jared," Nicole says, seeming to read my thoughts. "There's nothing you can do for Aaron. And the sooner you get your closure," she pronounces this last word with all but a roll of the eyes, "the sooner we can all move on."

She's right, of course. But still I linger uncertainly. "If you find Ari, I mean, when you find him, please tell him . . . " I falter. Tell him what, exactly? I'm not sure how to explain my feelings for Ari to myself, much less to him through this near-stranger.

"Tell him yourself," she says, "when you see him."

Without speaking further, she steps from the boat onto the dock. I start to call after her to thank her, but she is already walking away. I watch as she recedes in the distance. Then I climb into the boat to begin the end of my journey.

chapter SIXTEEN

I FOLLOW THE COASTLINE as Nicole instructed, my discomfort with the water muted by anticipation. Seconds stretch to minutes and minutes to hours as I navigate the small boat through the gentle surf. Finally, I round the curve and a white cottage, set back from the beach on a rocky hilltop, comes into view.

And then I see him, a figure crouched low by the water's edge, untangling something in the surf. My breath catches and my eyes begin to burn.

As if he senses my approach, Jared straightens, face breaking into a smile. But it is not me he is searching for, I realize, as his eyes widen with anticipation. He is waiting for Nicole. Confusion clouds his eyes as I dock the boat, a ghost from the past instead of his wife, the woman he never thought he would see again in the last place he expected. I know now that Nicole had not told him about our meeting or the fact that I have been looking for him, either purposefully or because she never had the chance.

I guide the boat in alongside the narrow dock and climb out. Then I start cautiously toward Jared. He does not move, but blinks twice, his mouth slightly agape, expression helpless. "Jordan?" he says, hoarse and disbelieving.

"Hello, Jared." And at this moment I have waited for so long, my voice is calm, my breath even.

I step forward, close to him now, expecting the questions to spill forth, but they do not. It does not matter how we have come to be here, what has happened in the years in between. He reaches out and touches my face like a blind man, reacquainting himself with the familiar topography, making sure I am really there. I close my eyes.

His fingers stop in the deep space just below my lips and I can feel his gaze burning through me, measuring the changes brought by time. I am suddenly mindful of my damp clothes, hair pasted flat from my earlier fall into the water. This is not how I anticipated appearing for our reunion. But then I open my eyes and, seeing his rapt expression, I know that he has not noticed or does not care.

"Jo," he says, more breath than voice, using the name I have not heard for so long. He opens his arms and wordlessly I fold myself into them, wrapping myself hard around his midsection, not caring if it is right or wrong or awkward—I need to touch him and be this close, to know that this is real. I bury my nose in his white T-shirt, inhaling deeply, and as his scent envelops me, I feel the years melt away. Suddenly, I am twenty-two again, stripped of all pain and fear.

"I don't understand," he whispers, his words muffled in my hair. Reluctantly, I pull back. "How did you . . . I mean, what are you doing here? And why do you have Nicole's boat?"

I try to figure out how to answer, then decide to take the last question first. "Nicole had to take care of an errand related to the wine shipment and she sent me here to see you."

"Bloody hell!" he swears, pulling back. His face is instantly fearful, as though he had expected something bad to happen, rehearsed for this moment a thousand times in his mind. "I asked her not to do this. Is she all right?"

I'm jealous at his concern for Nicole and annoyed at its intrusion upon our reunion. "She's fine."

"How do you know each other anyway?"

"We met in Monaco a few days ago," I reply. "I was there trying to find you."

"And you know that she is my . . . "

"Yes." There are several seconds of silence. I study his face. From a distance he seemed timeless, the same boy I saw on the deck of the boathouse the day we met. Closer now, I notice the passage of time, the receding hairline not quite hidden by his longer locks, the fine lines of worry etched at the corners of his mouth. They do not, I decide instantly, detract from his looks. His eyes are the same emerald green as they had been and though less haunted than in those final desperate months before his disappearance, they seem to carry a heaviness of years, of memories that he cannot outrun or erase.

How do I appear to him, I wonder? In my mind I am the same girl I was a decade ago but surely the differences are palpable. Do I seem more mature, enigmatic? Or simply worn down by the care and burdens that time and age have brought?

"Maybe we could go sit down and talk somewhere?" I suggest.

"Sure," he replies, his voice matter-of-fact. He leads me from the beach, up a steep pebbled path to the white cottage. Inside there is a modest-sized room with a table and chairs, a sofa with overstuffed cushions set close to a fireplace. A bright orange rug covers much of the crude wood floor. "Coffee?"

"Please." There is something surreal about the mundane nature of the exchange, as though I had simply stopped by his college room on the way home from the library.

As he busies himself in the kitchen nook at the rear of the cottage, I glance around once more, taking in the large bowl of flowers on the table, the bright linen curtains framing a breathtaking view of the sea. There are intimate touches: a basket of clothes waiting to be folded by the door, a note hastily scrawled on the pad by the table. Little signs of Nicole and Jared's life together. I feel like an intruder.

"It's like something out of a movie, I know," Jared concedes with a laugh as he fills the kettle. "No television. We catch fish, buy rice and vegetables from the village market."

"So tell me," he says, sitting down at the table a few minutes later with a glass coffee press and two cups. "How did you find me?"

I hesitate; I had not expected to be the one answering questions. "I came back to London on assignment for my job, State Department, you know." He nods in a way that confirms my suspicion that he'd been keeping up on me over the years. "Sarah is sick with ALS and I thought she needed me. After I arrived, Chris contacted me almost immediately and told me that he didn't think you really drowned." Quickly I recap for him our trip to the coroner, the subsequent developments that led us to the answers. "It wasn't until later that I learned the truth—that they had brought me to London to try and find your research."

"To find me," Jared corrects, his jaw tightening.

"Right. Anyway, when I realized that someone had faked Sarah's letter to get me to England, I confronted my boss, Mo. She confessed everything, including the fact that you were alive. She gave me the information she had on you and I went to your last known address in Monaco. That's where I met Nicole. She didn't want to admit that she knew you or tell me where you were but I followed her."

He smiles faintly. "She's protective like that."

Jealousy rises in me again, followed quickly by anger. I didn't come here to exchange pleasantries about his wife; I came for answers.

Seeing my expression, his face grows serious. "Sorry, Jo."

Jo again. At the sound of the nickname only he called me, my insides crumble. "Why?" I ask simply, knowing that he will understand the question.

"I was desperate," he says, his voice cracking. "We had to get the information we'd found into the right hands." I know he is referring to himself and Duncan, his partner in the research. "But we were shut down at the Madrid conference, not allowed to present our findings." I listen as he recounts the now-familiar details, seeing the events unfold from his eyes for the first time. He stands and begins pacing. "Then the threats started coming. And after Duncan caved in and agreed to give up on publishing our report, they focused the pressure on me."

He stops in front of me. "I could handle it when they were just threatening my life. But then one day I came into your room before you got home and they'd left a photograph on your pillow—it was a man standing behind you in the library as you read, totally unaware. They were trying to send me a message, that they could get to us anytime, anywhere, that the people I loved were not safe."

I shiver. I always felt so protected at Cambridge—how could I not have known? He continues, "The government had turned its back on me when I asked for help and the police would be useless, even if they did believe me. So I bought those plane tickets to Rio. I figured I would surprise you after the last day of the race, maybe plan it as a vacation and then see if you would keep running with me once we were safely away. But they found out, even before I'd left the travel agency." His eyes grow fearful as he relives the events. "I knew then that there was nowhere we could run that they couldn't get to us. The only way I could keep you safe was to get as far away from you as possible. So I made plans to fake my death and disappear."

"But the timing . . . " I rub my eyes, overwhelmed by all that I've learned. "I mean, it was the night of the May Ball. And the race . . . another day and we would have finished the Bumps, taken the Head of the River."

"I felt horrible about it," he admits ruefully. "You know the race never meant to me what it did to some of the guys." I nod. The May Bumps were the pinnacle of the rowing calendar and for other boys, like Chris, the chance to finally win them and reclaim the title, which the college hadn't held in a generation, meant everything. But to Jared, the race had been just a game. "Ironic, isn't it? I was brought to college to help us win the headship. And we almost did. We would have done it the next day, barring a broken blade or some other misfortune. But because of me, my disappearance, we didn't. I was the one person who was supposed to make it happen and I was the reason why it couldn't."

"Then why?"

"It wasn't my choice. I didn't even know I was leaving that night. I'd gone to the Master a few days earlier, asking for help, and was waiting to hear back from him. Then, the night of the May Ball, I received word, just hours before I was to go. It was only then that he told me how he planned it, the fact that everyone would think I had drowned. I tried to come back and give you a sign, some clue of what was happening, but . . . "

His voice trails off. I see the moment in my mind. Jared coming back to speak with me after our fight and finding Chris and me behind the marquee in that stupid, meaningless kiss. How might things have been different if he had been able to talk to me and explain what was going on?

He sits down again before continuing, "I decided then that my initial impulse was correct." He sounds so unapologetic now, so certain that the course of action he had taken was the right one. So Jared. I feel a faint tug of irritation, a familiar feeling forgotten through the years. "That by not telling you I would be setting you free, leaving you to move on."

Except that I hadn't. The exact opposite had, in fact, happened.

"But if you meant to tell me yourself, why did you leave the ring?" I ask.

"I had done that a few weeks earlier, before the Master agreed to help me. I was terrified by the threats and I thought that I might be killed. So I wanted to leave you a message to help you find my research, just in case. I meant to move the safe deposit box key to a better location," he adds. "One where you were certain to find it if I was gone. But I never got the chance."

And so it had lain taped to the underside of that student desk for a decade, I think. If the furniture had been moved to another room, if someone else had found it, I might never have known. If he had only told me. So many things left to chance.

My hand travels to my pocket, circles around the ring. For a minute I consider offering to give it back. It doesn't belong with me anymore. But I'm not ready for that. "How did you manage it?" I ask instead. "Being on the run for so many years?"

He folds his hands behind his head, stretching out in the chair and gazing out the window toward the sea. "It wasn't easy at first. When I left that night, I was scared and alone. I had nothing. But the Master proved to be as good as his word—better in fact. He provided everything I needed, put me in touch with the people who could help me keep moving. It turns out there's a secret society of some sort, Jo. You and I never would have heard of it, but it's comprised of well-placed Cambridge alumni all over the world, people in high places who can be trusted. He called on them to help me."

Sarah and I had always joked about such a conspiracy. I smile inwardly, imagining her reaction to learning it actually exists. "Why would he do it?" I ask. "I mean, I know the Master liked you, but to call in those favors and take such a risk . . . "

"I wondered that myself any number of times," he admits. "In the beginning, I think it was simply out of concern—one of his students came to him in serious trouble and he did what he could to help. But then, about a year later, he came to me with a request—a professor he knew at one of the other colleges was struggling with some research that was close to my area of expertise; would I be willing to help? I said yes, of course; after what he had done for me, how could I say otherwise? I worked on a paper for the professor and he was able to finish his research."

"And publish it, without giving you credit," I add.

He shrugs. "Does it really matter? He needed help that I was able to give. And it isn't as if I could publish under my own name anymore. Over the years, the Master came to me with other such requests, always acting as the intermediary to protect my identity and whereabouts. In a funny way, my situation actually worked in my favor—I could travel to the places that the academics needed primary research done, slip in and out easily. The arrangement worked.

"Of course, I don't travel much anymore." He gestures around the cottage. "But we're settled now. Nicole's work, combined with some of my consulting projects, has brought in enough income to support ourselves. It's not as if we need a lot of money to live here. And I make donations to the college, anonymously, to continue to show my appreciation. Without the Master's help, I would have been killed years ago."

"Why didn't you let me know you were all right? Afterward, I mean."

"I wanted to. But it still wasn't safe. As long as I had the information, they would always be looking for me. So I kept moving, South America, Africa."

"I expected to find you in one of those places," I remark. "I never imagined Greece."

"I was a little surprised myself," he replies, half laughing. "When Nikki suggested it . . . " he stops, a faint blush creeping into his cheeks. So he has a nickname for her, too. There is an intimacy to the way he says it that tells me now that despite whatever feelings he ever had for me, or may still have, his marriage to her is real. "But it's turned out to be the perfect hiding spot," he adds.

He still has not explained why he chose a life with her instead of me. "So how did you and Nicole meet?" I ask, posing a question just shy of my real one, forcing myself to use her name without changing my inflection.

"It was the spring of 1999 when we ran into each other again and—"

"Again?" I interrupt.

He pauses, looking away uncomfortably. "Yes. Nicole and I had met once at an archive in France when I was doing some research for my dissertation."

"But . . . " The words stick in my throat, and I am unable to speak. Jared had known Nicole before his disappearance. When he was with me.

"It was nothing, Jo." His voice has an urgency now, a need for me to believe him. "We had a cup of coffee in the library canteen, talked about our work. That was all. We didn't even exchange contact information. I was completely wrapped up in my research . . . and you."

I believe him, of course. For all of the questions that have arisen, there has never been a doubt in my mind that Jared was faithful. But the notion that he could have been interested in Nicole back then, even if he didn't act on it, still makes me nauseous. Why her? I want to ask.

"It wasn't until the following year that we met again, when our paths crossed in a bar in Belize one evening," he says. "I had been alone on the run for months. It was good to see a familiar face, talk to someone who knew me back when I could still be myself." I imagine it: a beautiful woman, a shared interest in research. Now I understand. She had been there when I could not. I curse the fates that brought them to the same place and reunited them that night.

"It was almost a year after I'd been gone," he says gently. I nod, but inside I am screaming. A year was a heartbeat in the lexicon of my grief; the pain then as fresh as the day he had left. "We were both in Belize for several weeks, Nicole taking a holiday after completing a business transaction and me doing research. We got along really well and when she was ready to move on, I was, too. It happened very quickly," he adds. "Like us."

I fight the urge to reach across the table and shake him. Not like us. I believed that the immediacy of our bond was special, unique.

Now he just seems like one of those men who falls in love easily, clings to each woman like a life raft.

I remember the chess set Jared used to keep in the corner of his college room. Chess was too long and slow for me and I grew impatient with the endless waiting, the tiny advances that each turn seemed to bring. But for Jared it was always chess. Sometimes he would play with a lone opponent, someone else from college who shared his intrigue with the game. Other times, there would be a game in progress, Jared on one side and the opposing side played by various students, whoever came into his room and wanted to take a turn. Those were the ones he really loved. In addition to the normal challenge of thinking several moves ahead, he had the chance to face off against different opponents, each with his or her own strategy. It kept him on his toes, he said, forced him to change plans midgame. That's how he lives his life, I understand now. When circumstance had made his plans impossible, he changed strategy seamlessly, trading me for Nicole, one life for the other.

"We traveled together for several years before settling down and getting married. And we've had a nice life here, until this." His smile fades and for a second I think he is angry about my finding him. Then I realize he is talking about the jeopardy that has resulted from Nicole's work on the wine deal. "I warned her that this last transaction was too much, that she was in over her head. But she wouldn't listen. She's stubborn, like you."

Ari said I reminded him of his wife in that way, too, I recall. As if stubbornness was a highly sought virtue in a woman. Why do men seem to have this need for comparison, to legitimize one relationship to the next? I want to tell Jared that Nicole is nothing like me. I served my country, did what I thought was right. Nicole is a petty criminal. But I bite my lip, knowing he is too blind to Nicole's flaws to understand the difference, and that he means this as a compliment.

"I kept tabs on you," he admits. "I was glad to see that you left England without looking back, that you had moved on." I want to laugh out loud, to tell him how untrue that is. "I wanted to stop running, too, and have a life. I needed to put the whole thing to rest."

"And that's why you sent Chris the article," I interject, realizing.

"Yes. When I heard that the British government was investigating, I knew this was my chance to get my research into the right hands once and for all. As a reporter, Chris had the investigative skills, and he was the one person I knew who was determined enough to try to see this through. But I never counted on you coming back to England or on him dragging you into this."

"It pretty much ruined him, you know," I say, more reproach in my voice than I intended. "Chris became obsessed with finding you. His marriage and his career fell apart."

"I know." Jared's shoulders sag. "Have you told him that I'm alive?"

I shake my head. "When I left England, I wasn't sure if it was true and I couldn't bear to get his hopes up after all he had been through. And later, well, I didn't know if it was safe for you. It's your secret to share." I watch his eyes working as he imagines reaching out to Chris and telling him the truth.

"What about Duncan?" he asks, running down the litany of friends who paid the price for his actions. I can tell from his voice that he heard about the death of Duncan's partner, Vance. "Do you know where he is?"

"I don't know," I reply. "When I came back and started asking questions, he got nervous and ran. I tried to reach him several times after he left London, but he was gone. And then once Vance was killed, there was no way Duncan was coming back."

Jared lowers his head, running his hands through his hair. "Duncan never understood that even though he agreed to keep quiet and stop pursuing our research, he couldn't really be free because he knew too much."

"He might have been," I reply remorsefully. "If I hadn't stirred things up."

"Jordan, don't." He reaches out, puts his hand atop mine. "Even if you hadn't spoken to Duncan, it was inevitable that those skeletons were going to get unearthed at some time." Hearing the comforting, take-charge Jared of old, I am reminded of a time when I could let him take care for me and make me feel safe. "I tried to help him," he adds.

"You did?"

"Not directly, of course. But last month, when I caught wind of what was going on in London, I got in touch with Lord Colbert to ask if he would help Duncan."

Duncan had attended a different Cambridge college; he wasn't one of our own, but the Master would not have refused Jared's request for assistance. "The Master found Duncan for me. He wouldn't tell me where Duncan was, but he said that he was safe. I got the impression that Duncan was trying to persuade Vance to join him, and that it was somewhere they could have perhaps gotten married, or at least had their union recognized legally."

Would Vance have gone? I remember his haggard, haunted face the night I had followed him to the club to ask about Duncan's whereabouts. As an actor, the decision to leave the place where he was known for a life of anonymity in a foreign country would not have been an easy one, but I believe he ultimately would have done it for the man he loved.

"I can't believe it's over," I remark. "So many years, looking for answers." Jared bites the inside of his cheek and I can tell that he is unconvinced, galled by the fact that some of those implicated by the information he found have not been brought to justice. "It's over, Jared," I repeat. "Your research got into the right hands and the government is finally taking care of everything."

"How did you get to Greece, anyway?" he asks finally, changing the subject.

"I traveled here by boat from Trieste with Ari but . . . "

"Nicole's cousin Aaron?" he interrupts, grimacing as though he has a bad taste in his mouth.

I nod. "He was coming to see her. Something about the wine."

"How much do you know about that?" he asks, echoing Nicole's earlier question.

"Enough."

A strange look flickers across his face and I can tell that he is aware of the kind of people Nicole deals with in her work, the danger it has brought. I want to ask him how he can bring himself to compromise his principles to be with someone like her. But I refrain, unsure if I really want to know the answer.

Jared clears his throat. "What on earth does Ari want with the wine?"

"I don't know. But the address in Zante town where he thought he could find Nicole turned out to be bad, and Nicole is going to warn him before he gets into trouble. Then she's going to get rid of the wine."

"I don't like this . . . " His brow furrows as he contemplates the danger his wife might face. "Damn Ari, he's always been trouble for her." I want to point out to Jared that it was Nicole who got herself into this mess. But it isn't my place to defend Ari anymore. "How do you know him anyway?" he asks.

"Um, we met in Monaco. I was searching for you and he was trying to find Nicole, so we traveled together."

He looks out the window, not speaking for several minutes. "Where are you headed from here?" he asks finally.

For a second I am hurt by his brusqueness. Am I being dismissed? But that's just Jared, I remember, practical and to the point. "I don't know," I admit. I had been so focused on getting here to find Jared, I hadn't really thought about what I would do once I was finished, how I would get back now that Ari and I are no longer traveling together. Or where, for that matter, I would be going back to—the States or somewhere else? "I need to make my way to Athens, I guess. Book a flight home." Wherever that is.

"It will be impossible to get off the island by ferry tonight," he informs me.

"I booked a room at the resort . . ."

"It's too dangerous to get back there by boat now that the tides have changed." He shakes his head. "No way. I'm afraid you're stuck here until morning."

A mixture of dread and relief washes over me. I've waited a decade for this moment with Jared and I'm not eager to see it end. At the same time, the notion of spending the night here, in this house he shares with Nicole, is not a comfortable one.

"There's a spare futon," he adds, setting the terms of my stay for himself as much as me. This pronouncement, more than anything else, serves to drive home the state of things, the distance we've come since being together.

I shift awkwardly. "Great, thanks."

"Are you hungry?" he asks, as if there is nothing unusual about the situation.

I shrug. "You know me, I can always eat."

He goes into the kitchen alcove. I stand up and walk to a low bookshelf by the fireplace and kneel down. It seems to hold mostly copies of the classics that I wonder if anyone has ever actually cracked open. I scan the spines, then stop. Wedged between *The Canterbury Tales* and the edge of the shelf is a worn paperback.

"Oh," I say aloud as I pull it out. It is *The Two Towers,* the second of the Tolkien trilogy. I run my fingers over the familiar cover, recognizing the coffee stain as my own.

Jared walks over to me. "I took it with me. I guess I thought that since we were reading it . . . " He does not finish the sentence. I imagine him now, scared and alone, taking the book from the shelf. He could bring virtually nothing with him in order to fake his death and yet he had dared to take the book.

"Did you . . . ?"

"Keep reading? No. I must have read it a dozen times as a kid, but I haven't picked it up since college." Somehow the thought gives me comfort. At least in one respect he had not gone on without me.

He returns to the kitchen and I replace the book, then straighten. I glance around the cabin once more, noticing several framed photographs on the mantelpiece. Curious, I get up and move toward them. There is one of Nicole and Jared beside the cottage, another of Nicole in front of a mountain somewhere, smiling at the photographer, presumably Jared. The two of them, I realize as I scan the pictures, always together. I reach the second to last photograph from the right, then stop. It is different from the rest, an image of Nicole lying in a hospital bed, holding a small bundle of white cloth. Jared stands behind her, gazing down adoringly.

"Oh!" I say aloud, bringing my hand to my mouth. Hearing me, Jared comes out of the kitchen, wiping his hands on a towel. He walks over.

"That's Noah," he says, taking the photo from me. "That's our son."

chapter SEVENTEEN

T HAT'S OUR SON."

Jared's words seem to reverberate off the cottage walls, echoing in my head. A scream rises within me, sticks somewhere between my bowels and my throat.

"You said you knew about Nicole, so I thought you knew about Noah, too."

Jared pulls the final photograph from the mantel, smiling as he runs his finger over the image. It is a picture of him and Nicole, clutching a toddler between them. "He's three years old."

Jared has a child. I digest the news slowly, letting it sink in. Instantly the portrait of his life since he disappeared is complete. When it was simply a wife, it was easy to imagine her as a stand-in, another woman who filled the empty space in the years that he could not be with me. But faced now with the somber child, with his exquisite dimpled cheeks and blue eyes, the reality is unavoidable. Jared has gone on these many years, lived his life, learned to love again, and created a family. He has the life that I do not, that I could not have while I was eternally grieving for him. I feel angry and foolish at the same time.

Why hadn't Nicole told me about their child yesterday? The fact that she bore Jared's son would have been the ultimate trump card. Because as much as she hates me and needs to claim Jared as her own, she is not willing to use her child as a game piece. Whatever else I think of her, I have to grudgingly respect her for that.

I study the photograph once more. Looking at the little boy, embraced in his parents' arms, I cannot help but remember the baby that I decided not to have years ago. Jared's baby. He or she would be here now, if I had chosen differently.

"He's a wonderful boy," Jared says, not seeming to notice my reaction.

"He's beautiful," I manage, taking in the image of the child, a miniature version of Jared, only with Nicole's warm coloring and blond hair.

"He's staying with friends of ours on the northern side of the island for a few days while Nicole is gone. He loves to go there because they have twin girls about his age. It can get a little boring for him here with just us." He replaces the photograph and returns to the kitchen. "You don't have children, I take it?" he asks over his shoulder.

I might have, I think, if you had only told me you were alive. If only I had known. I consider telling Jared about the baby that I had given up, believing that he had died. Part of me wants to share the burden of guilt, to make him carry some of the pain. But even though I made the decision based on bad information, the choice was still mine—and the consequences, too. There is nothing to be gained by telling him, nothing I can say that will change the past.

"No," I say with effort. "I never married. It's the job, you know. Just too hard with all of the moving around." I hold my breath, wondering if he will see through my explanation, realize that my solitude has more to do with the feelings I've harbored for him all these years.

But he seems to accept what I've said at face value. "I caught this earlier," he says, returning with two plates of steamed whitefish, rice, and green leafy vegetables heaped on either side. He carries a bottle of wine to the table and opens it.

"Smells delicious." I sit down. "Does anyone know that you're here?"

He takes a bite of the fish. "Just you, the Master, and Nicole. No one else back home, not even my mum. I hate her living alone, thinking I'm dead. But if she knew, she would want to see me and meet Noah and of course that's impossible. It's better this way."

"Is it?" I hear the bite in my own voice, angry as much at what he had done to me as to his mother.

"I don't know." He sets down his fork and drops his head to his hands, the armor of certainty he's worn all these years cracking. "I did what I thought was best. I've always tried to do that. But I've hurt so many people, Jo. My mum, Chris, Duncan, you. I'm so sorry."

It's okay, I want to say, but I cannot. I take a sip of the wine. The taste is simple, less sophisticated than the bottles Ari and I received from the Contis, but good and crisp, with hints of dates and nuts. Ari. I cannot help but wonder where he is, if he is all right. Whether he misses me. I stop, glass still at my lips, caught off guard by the thought. Here I am with Jared, the man I've been longing for all of these years, yet I cannot stop thinking about Ari.

We eat the remainder of the meal in silence, slipping back to that easy place from years ago where we could enjoy each other's company without speaking. Jared clears the dishes, waving away my offer to help.

I walk to the window. Outside, the sun has set and the water sparkles in the moonlight, a sea of jewels. Jared always wanted a place like this, somewhere quiet and beautiful and away. Nicole was right: he's at peace here, or as close to it as any of us will get.

"It's getting late," Jared says, after he has finished cleaning up. He moves toward the room at the back of the cottage. There is a large futon close to the wall on the left, a narrow bed opposite it. "You can sleep here," he says, gesturing toward the futon. "It's more comfortable."

"No," I blurt out. It's bad enough I have to sleep in this room that Nicole and Jared share, but sleeping in their bed would be really too much. "I mean, the other one will be great."

Jared shrugs and hands me a set of simple white cotton sheets, then walks from the room. I make up the bed before sprawling across it. This must be Noah's, I realize, taking in the faint odor of sour milk.

A moment later Jared returns, having changed into a T-shirt and sweatpants, his face still damp from washing. He tosses something to me. "Here."

A sweatshirt. My mind reels back to a certain night at college. It was during the Lent term, sometime after the December boat club dinner when Jared and I realized we did not hate each other, but well before the night in London that spring when we first kissed. We had been drinking with the rest of the rowing crew and as the college bar closed and the loitering crowd outside dissipated, Jared and I found ourselves alone. "Would you like to come around for coffee?" he asked as we stood in the shadows of Chapel Court, our breath smoky against the wind.

I hesitated. Coffee or tea was, in some cases, a euphemism for something more, an invitation to hook up. Studying Jared's face, though, I knew there was no such pretense. It was simply a proposal of conversation, an alternative to the night ending. But I shook my head. "I should be going."

He shrugged as if to say "Suit yourself," then turned and started across the courtyard. After he disappeared through the college gate, I started through the back field toward my own house on Lower Park Street. Suddenly an unfamiliar sense of loneliness swept over me. I did not want to go back to my cold, solitary room. I walked quickly out of the college and onto the street, following Jared home and knocking on his door.

If he was surprised by my change of heart, he gave no indication. "Coffee?" he asked again.

"No. I mean, yes," I stammered. "That is, I just didn't want to be alone." I felt my face turn red.

Without speaking further, he led me into his room, but instead of putting on the kettle, he made up the sofa with sheets and handed me a sweatshirt. I returned from the bathroom wearing it and slipped under the blanket. Then he bent over and I closed my eyes, thinking that he might kiss me. There was a momentary pause and then his lips pressed against my forehead, a parent checking a child for a fever. When I looked up again, he had retreated to his own bed across the room and turned out the light. The next morning I slipped out before dawn, and even months later after we were together and it would not have been awkward, we never spoke of that night again.

"Jo?" he says now, tearing me from my thoughts. I look up. "Where were you?"

"Nowhere," I reply. The memory seems overly sentimental to share. He might not even remember.

"Happy belated birthday, by the way," Jared says.

"Thanks," I reply, surprised that he remembered. My thirty-second birthday, May 3, had passed in London nearly two weeks earlier, sandwiched in between my confrontation with Sebastian at Embankment, at which he took his own life, and Mo's revelation about the scheme to get me to London a few days later. I spent the day at Chris's hospital bedside as he struggled to recover from the gunshot wound I'd inflicted upon him, reminded only by an unanswered call from my parents offering birthday wishes and a card from Sarah.

I walk across the cottage to the washroom to change and when I return, Jared is on the larger futon sprawling, as he used to, on his side, one arm propped beneath his head. I lie down on the other bed.

"Sleepy?" he asks. I shake my head. "Me either. I could read to you if you want."

I cannot tell if he is joking. "That's okay, thanks." Somehow bringing that here, as if the years had not passed and nothing had changed, seems a mockery. And where would we begin, where we left off a decade ago or at the beginning of the book? Or would we read something else entirely? I am suddenly mindful of the short distance across the tiny room. I don't know which part is more surreal, the fact that I am sitting here talking to Jared, or that we are alone and cannot be together.

"It's strange, isn't it, Jo?" he asks, reading my mind as he used to. "Us being here, I mean?"

I draw my knees into my chest. "It's like that game we played as kids, Spend A Day With Anyone."

He stares at me blankly. "Never heard of it."

Of course not. There are differences, I realize, always have been.

Despite the bond that once existed between us, there were certain things that never quite synced up, things that I could not write off as simply cultural. Once, at college, I had run to him, devastated by a call I'd received from my parents with the news that my beloved childhood collie, Ranger, had died. Jared tried to be sympathetic, but to him pets were just animals and in the end he could not comprehend the depth of my grief for a dog that had been my closest companion in the absence of a sibling. No, he does not totally understand me, never did—nor I him. How, for example, can he allow his own mother to believe that he is dead?

Of course, it's impossible for anyone to be completely understood. In the end, no matter how many people we surround ourselves with, each of us stands alone. I learned that years ago after I thought Jared had died: no one was sticking around but me. And so I simply stopped trying.

Jared is still staring at me across the room, waiting for an explanation. "It was a game we played as children. We would ask one another, 'If you could spend a day with any person in the history of the world, living or dead, who would it be?' and sometimes we would talk about what we would do with the person, how we would spend the day."

"Who did you pick?"

I laugh. "Oh, I don't remember, really. Sometimes it would be some movie star I had a crush on, or a historical figure I was reading about. Or my gran, after she died. The point is, tonight reminds me of that game." I swallow. "Because all of these years, if someone had asked me the question, the person I would have wanted to spend the day with would have been you."

He smiles and for a second I wonder if he thinks I am foolish. "I get it. I've imagined so many times since I've been gone what it would be like to go home just for a day. I'm not sure that this is how I would choose to spend it, though."

A knife twists in my stomach. "No?"

"There are lots of things I'd like to do again, of course, hug my mum, kick a football with Chris and the boys. But if I only got one choice, I would want to spend the day with you." Is he just being nice, I wonder? No, Jared never did anything just to be nice. He means it, I decide, the wound ebbing slightly. "But we wouldn't spend it lying on opposite sides of the room," he adds.

I swallow hard over the lump that has formed in my throat. An awkward silence passes between us and I can tell he is thinking of the nights spent in our college beds, bodies pressed close. Until now, I'd been so caught up in the emotion of seeing Jared again that I'd been ignoring the magnetic attraction that still exists between us. But it is here again, as real and raw as a decade ago. I shiver.

"Are you cold?" he asks. I shake my head, but he stands and pulls something from a wicker trunk then crosses the room to me. "Here," he says, laying the blanket at the foot of the bed. "I've gotten so used to the weather here that I can sometimes forget how the temperatures shift. It can really drop at night." He covers me with the blanket, then sits on the edge of the bed. His brow furrows. "You're flushed." He brings his hand to my brow and I close my eyes, trying not to tremble at his cool, familiar touch.

"I got too much sun today, that's all." I look up. Jared's face is just inches from mine. What would happen if I kissed him right now? Would he respond or refuse? I close my eyes again, not leaning toward him or away, unwilling to move things in either direction, but letting the moment carry me.

Another second passes. He clears his throat and when I open my eyes, he has pulled back, a tortured expression on his face. He stands and walks quickly from the room and I wonder if he is angry, whether he will sleep elsewhere.

But a minute later he returns and hands me a jar. "It's a cream that the locals swear by. Nicole puts it on Noah when he's had too much sun."

Nicole. Noah. Suddenly they are in the room with us and the moment of intimacy has passed. Struggling to breathe normally, I put some of the lotion on my nose and cheeks, feeling the coolness soothe my burn as Jared lies down again on his own bed, his shadow long in the dim light.

"I wanted to kiss you just then," he says finally, a man giving his confession. "More than almost anything in my life."

I wanted it, too, I think, but I do not say this. Part of me desperately wishes that he had given in and we lived this one and only moment of reunion time had given us. That I was the kind of woman who could let go of her principles long enough to be in the moment and seize this opportunity of fate. Surely it could have been forgiven, understood. But another part is glad we had not. Despite the passage of the years, the fact that he has gone on and married, my memories of Jared are intact, pure. An illicit kiss, maybe more, stolen in his wife's absence, would just taint what we once had, a tidal wave of regret that would surely dwarf the brief satisfaction of once again having him. And no matter how magical the moment might be, the sun would come up and Nicole would return, claiming him for her own. Nicole. What does it say about his feelings for her that he wanted to kiss me? What does it mean that he did not?

He clears his throat. "You and Aaron, is it serious?"

I turn to look at him. I had not said anything about becoming involved with Ari. But I shouldn't be surprised—Jared had always been able to see right through me. Suddenly I am indignant—this is none of his concern, not now. "I'd rather not talk about it."

He rolls away, not speaking further. Is he angry? As I curl up on the mattress, I consider apologizing. I never handled our disagreements at college well and would often say that I was sorry, even when I wasn't sure I was wrong. But I'm not that girl anymore and I can't bring myself to apologize simply to avoid a fight.

"Jared . . . " I say. But there is no response. He's asleep, or pretending to be anyway, I think, remembering the way he used to prowl Cambridge restlessly long after the streets had gone silent and dark. As I listen to the sound of his long, even breathing just feet away, a cold emptiness opens inside me, threatening to swallow me whole. I'm lonely, I realize. But not for Jared. I miss Ari.

Confused, I push the thoughts from my mind and gaze at Jared once more. Part of me wants to watch him all night, savoring these last few hours before morning comes and I have to leave him again. At last my eyelids grow heavy until I can fight closing them no longer, drifting off to a dreamless sleep.

Sometime later I open my eyes slowly, blinking against the sunlight that bounces blindingly off the white walls. For a second I cannot remember where I am. Jared and Nicole's cottage, I think, as the events of the night before come rushing back: my long conversation with Jared, our almost kiss. The fact that he and Nicole have a son.

I glance across the room, expecting to see Jared asleep. But the larger futon is empty, the sheets neatly made. He is gone, up and out before I awake, just like he always was at college.

A clattering sound comes from the other room. I stand and change quickly from Jared's sweatshirt back to my own clothes. As I walk from the bedroom, I smooth my hair.

Jared is by the stove. "Good morning," he says brightly, as though there is nothing unusual about my waking here. "Sleep well?"

"Very." I drop to a chair at the kitchen table, accepting the cup of coffee he offers. I did sleep soundly, atypical for me in a strange place. "It's the salt air," he says, echoing Ari's comment on the boat. But I know it was more than that. Jared's presence, his slow, even breathing, was like a protective blanket that comforted me in a way that few things in life ever had—even from across the room after all of these years.

As he turns back to the stove, a phone I had not noticed hanging in the corner rings. I am surprised; I had not expected the remote cottage to have a land line. Jared goes to it. "Hello? No, she isn't." His eyes dart back and forth as he listens to the voice on the other end. "What?" His voice rises. "Now, you wait . . . " He pulls the phone away from his ear and stares at it in disbelief, his face paling. A second later the receiver drops from his hand, clattering to the floor.

"What is it?" I ask. "What's wrong?"

"They've taken Noah," he says, his voice barely a whisper.

"I don't understand." But even as I say this, my heart sinks. "Who?"

"It's the men who bought the wine from Nicole. They have our son. And if we don't give them what they want, they're going to kill him."

chapter EIGHTEEN

I AM UNABLE TO breathe over the rock that has formed in my throat. "Are you sure?" I manage. "Maybe it's a bluff."

He shakes his head. "I could hear Noah in the background. I recognized his voice." There are tears in his eyes, something I have never seen before.

"How did they get him?"

"I don't know, I don't know." He paces frantically back and forth in front of me, a tiger caged. "We sent him to stay with friends because we thought he'd be safe there. They're good people and we'd trust them with our lives, but why wouldn't they have called if . . . ?" He stops, then picks up the phone again, punches the buttons hurriedly. "No answer," he says after several seconds, hanging it up. "Oh God, they're probably dead." He is close to hysterical now. "Dammit, I told Nicole—"

"But Nicole is selling the wine so she can repay them."

"The man said they aren't interested in money. They want the wine."

"It doesn't make sense," I say, my mind racing. "Why wouldn't they just take the money?"

"It doesn't matter why." He stops and turns squarely to face me. "We have to find Noah."

We. I am suddenly in much deeper than I anticipated. I don't have to help, I realize. I found Jared, accomplished what I set out to do. I could say no, head back to Ari. But a child is in danger and I cannot walk away. And it's not just any child—this is Jared's son.

I look up at Jared, who is watching me with the same desperate expression he wore a decade ago. Only this time I can do something. "All right," I say, forcing strength into my voice. I put my hand on his arm, soothing him as I would have back then. It is my turn to be strong again for both of us. "We need to stay calm and think about this clearly. Who was on the phone?"

"I don't know. It wasn't a voice I've ever heard before, but then again, Nicole doesn't include me in all of her business dealings. He had an accent of some kind."

"Tell me everything he said."

Jared resumes his pacing. "He said that Nicole is to get the wine and bring it to Keri harbor in two hours. If not, they're going to . . ." He does not finish the sentence.

"Can you call her?" I ask.

He runs his hands through his hair. "Maybe." He picks up the phone again and dials. "Dammit, Nicole," he swears under his breath in a way that suggests he's been unable to reach her before. "I don't know if she could make it back in time anyway."

"Do you know where the wine is?"

He nods. "In a cave by the water."

"Is it far from here?"

"Not very. We can't drive there, though, and it's about a forty-five-minute walk."

"What about the boat?"

"Quicker, but the waters around the cave get too choppy at high tide for a dinghy like that. No, the only way is on foot."

"Then we should get started."

"But the man said it had to be Nicole and that she has to come alone."

My mind races. "Has Santini ever met Nicole?"

"I don't think so. Her dealings with him have all been by phone."

Except in Vienna, I think, remembering Santini's man who fled the apartment there, Nicole bloodstained and holding the knife. Of course Jared doesn't know about that, either. "So I can be Nicole," I say. "If they've never met her before, they won't be able to tell the difference." I do not mention the Vienna encounter to Jared, knowing it will feed his doubts about our best—and only—option. "I don't suppose there's anywhere to get a blond wig?"

Through his panic, he shoots me his most exasperated look, the one he always saved for times when he thought I was being truly ridiculous. "What do you think?"

"Maybe a bottle of peroxide, then." Jared's expression remains unconvinced. "I know, I look nothing like Nicole. But if I get there and give them the wine, perhaps they won't check too closely, or care. Anyway, what other choice do we have?"

I watch him searching for a better plan and finding none. "Fine," he says at last. "There's peroxide in the medicine cabinet. But hurry. We don't have a lot of time."

Ten minutes later I emerge from the bathroom, combing my freshly bleached hair. Jared stands at the kitchen sink, filling a canteen with water. "I always wondered what I'd look like as a blonde," I quip, trying to ease his terror, but he stares at me blankly, not responding.

I walk to him. "You're scared, and nothing I say is going to

change that. But it's going to be okay. I'm trained for this, Jared."
His eyes widen as I pull my gun from my bag and tuck it into my
waistband, reminding me that I am not the same girl he knew a
decade ago. "This is what I do." Even as I say this, though, doubts
creep into my mind. I have no idea what I am walking into, how
many will be waiting for me. Going in alone is foolish, but I don't
have a choice. If only Ari was here. "Just tell me how to get to the
caves."

"We'll go together. I'm taking you there and then to the harbor."

"But they said Nicole had to come alone."

"I can hide out of sight," he presses, unrelenting.

"No good, Jared. I've seen this sort of thing before. They could
have someone watching me to make sure I'm not followed. You
need to let me go by myself."

"No," he insists. "I have to—"

"What you have to do is trust me," I say, cutting him off. "Let
me do this for you. Let me help." The way I couldn't years ago, I
finish silently. "We're wasting time," I add.

I can see him wrestling with what I have said, realizing I am
right but not wanting to admit it. "All right," he relents. "I'll get you
close enough, then let you go the rest of the way on your own."

I hesitate, wanting him to wait here but knowing he will concede no further. "Okay."

I follow him outside to a path that leads farther up the rocky
hillside behind the cottage, ascending away from the sea. "I thought
the cave was by the water," I remark.

"It is. But it's a good distance down the coast from here and
Nicole said the quickest way is over the hills."

"You've never been there?"

"No, like I said, Nicole didn't involve me in her work. But she described the location, pointed to it from a distance once when we were sailing. I can find it." There is a slight waver in his voice. "Goddammit, how could I . . . " He does not finish the sentence but curses himself silently for letting Noah out of his sight, for not being able to keep him safe.

"Tell me about the caves," I say as we walk, trying to distract him from his terror.

I can tell by his face that he is not fooled. "These particular caves were used by the locals as bomb shelters during the early years of the war," he says, playing along. "Later, by the Resistance. They used the caves as hiding places and to store munitions—and wine." I nod, remembering that Ari had said the same thing about the cellars in France. "Not just the Cerfberre Bordeaux. They hid lots of wine from the Nazis and used it to trade for things that they needed."

We continue up the hill, neither speaking for several minutes. We pass the ruins of an old church, crumbling stone walls rising to a nonexistent roof, steeple still rising defiantly against the clear blue sky.

I brush my hair back from my eyes for the hundredth time. The midmorning sun beats down, hardening the recently muddy earth into craggy fossil. Jared moves quickly in front of me and I struggle to match his long-legged strides and keep up. Sweat runs down my neck, pooling beneath my T-shirt. "Here." He hands the canteen of water back to me, not stopping. I wonder if he has noticed how hard I am breathing, but he stares straight ahead, fixated only on finding his son.

I gulp several mouthfuls of water, then pass the canteen back to him as we reach the top of a bluff. On the far side, the ocean comes into view once more. The rugged coastline forms a wide curving inlet, a thin strip of sand giving way to blue sea. The water is rougher here, waves crashing against the shoals.

I reach out and grab his arm. "How much further?" I ask, concerned that if I do not stop him, he will take me all the way to the caves. We are exposed now, atop the ridge, and I do not want anyone to see him approaching with me.

"There it is," Jared says, a note of reluctance in his voice. He points downward to the deepest part of the cove, where a massive expanse of sheer cliff face gives way to a wide opening, partially obscured by a huge freestanding rock.

"All right, then this is the end of the line for you."

"But—"

I cut him off. "It's too risky for you to be here, Jared. I shouldn't have even let you bring me this far. Someone could see you. Once I have the wine, I'll head toward the harbor."

"Do you know the way?"

I nod. "I can find it. But what am I supposed to do once I'm there?"

"The man didn't say. I assume he'll find you. The case is probably heavy, though. How are you going to get it there alone?"

It is a question I had not considered. "I'll manage. I want you to go back to the cottage and wait in case the men call again. I'll let you know as soon as I have Noah."

I expect him to argue further, but he does not. "The entrance is only passable for about another forty minutes," he informs me instead. "After that, the water will rise and the cave will be flooded." I notice then that the tide is high, the water lapping against the rocks.

"What about the wine? Don't the waters jeopardize it?"

He shakes his head. "When you enter the cave, the path you'll take rises to what Nicole called the upper chamber. She said it doesn't flood, so the wine remains safe and dry. Here." He pulls a flashlight from his pocket and hands it to me. "I'm not sure exactly where you go once you're inside, but Nicole said she followed the writing on the wall."

"What kind of writing?"

"I don't know. Something left by the partisans, maybe, though the caves are ancient, so it could be much older than that." He looks at his watch. "We'd better hurry."

"Not we," I correct. "Me. You're going back."

"I can't let you do this alone. It's too dangerous, and you need my help."

"Jared, we've been over this already. If they see you, they might not show . . . or things could get very ugly. You could be endangering Noah even further." I watch as he processes what I've said. "Go straight back to the cottage and wait for my call. If you don't hear from me in two hours . . . " I do not finish the sentence.

He nods, understanding. "Jordan," he says as I start to walk away. I turn back once more. He opens his mouth helplessly but no words come out. It is a plea, a prayer to save his son.

I reach out and put my arm on his shoulder. I failed him once; I will not do it again. "Don't worry. I'll bring him home."

I make my way down the narrow path toward the beach, struggling to keep my footing on the rocks, which grow damp and slippery as I near the water. A few minutes later I look over my shoulder, expecting to see Jared still standing there, but he is gone. I am surprised—he has always been so stubborn. Did he really return home, as I told him to do, or is he somewhere nearby, hiding out of sight? Suddenly the magnitude of what I am doing crashes down upon me. Jared is trusting me, counting on me to save his son.

What am I doing here anyway? I found Jared, finished what I set out to do. This wine business was never my fight. But I have the chance to help Jared as I could not a decade ago and save his child as I could not save ours. This child, who a day ago I did not know existed, suddenly means everything.

If I can do it, I think, reaching down and wrapping my hand around Ari's gun. Hostage situations are a unique area of expertise and I've never handled one, had only the most cursory training. Despite the confidence I tried to portray to Jared, I'm pretty sure I'm in over my head. But I have to try.

I hurry down the path toward the entrance to the cave. The water is higher now, swallowing the thin swatch of sand. I bend down and take off my sandals, carrying them as I wade through the surf, cool water licking at my ankles.

Inside the entrance to the cave, the water ebbs, giving way to damp sand. Daylight quickly disappears and I stop, trying without success to adjust my eyes, then reaching for the flashlight. The pale yellow beam illuminates the ground just a few feet ahead of me before being swallowed by the darkness. I point it around, trying to acclimate myself. The cave is enormous, passages off the main chamber leading in several directions.

I put my sandals back on, then shine the flashlight along the walls, searching for the writing Jared described. About twenty feet inside the cave on the left wall are markings etched in the stone. I move closer. Names, I realize, of those who have been here before, written in a single lengthy scroll that runs for several feet. I follow the writing deeper into the cave, wondering who had carved the artful, flowing script, whether he or she made it out alive. It must have taken forever. I take a deep breath, inhaling the cool, moist air.

The writing ends as abruptly as it began, a final flourish fading into a crevice. I look up. The path has narrowed to a tunnel less than a foot across and just tall enough for me to stand, inclining sharply upward and bordered by high rock walls on either side.

A few feet farther, the tunnel ends as the wall to my left disappears, giving way to open space. My heart pounds. The path is no more than a ledge here, dropping off sharply into the abyss. I shine my flashlight down. It is a gorge, so deep I cannot see the bottom. Water trickles, unseen, far below.

I stop, panicking. I am alone in this cave with no means of contacting anyone if I fall and get injured, or worse. I think of Ari, his fear of heights. Though I know he would hate this, I cannot help but wish he were here with me now. Steeling myself, I continue along the narrow path, forcing myself not to look down. I clutch the rocky wall to my right, concentrating on each step to keep myself from falling into the unforgiving abyss below.

Then there is a break and the rock beneath my hand seems to move. Something flies out of the wall, fluttering against my face. I raise my hands to ward it off, dropping the flashlight.

"No!" I cry as it falls to the ledge and goes out. My voice echoes through the cavern.

I bend over, trying not to lose my balance as I feel for the flashlight. My fingers brush the handle but it rolls away, clattering close to the edge. I reach for it again and begin to wobble, my arms flailing dangerously. Steadying myself, I run my hand along the ground, finally touching the flashlight and picking it up.

I grab the wall again, straightening. It was a bat, I recognize, regaining my balance, forcing myself to breathe. Disgusting, but relatively benign under the circumstances.

Trembling, I continue forward until the emptiness beside my left hand ends. Ahead, the flashlight dimly reveals two steps leading to a doorway. I step up through it into some sort of room. There is a different smell here, musty and man-made, of dirt and wood that is somehow familiar.

I shine the light around the room, revealing wooden racks that line the walls from floor to ceiling, reminding me of the Contis' wine cellar. This must be the upper chamber.

I walk toward one of the racks, hope rising in me. If only I can find the wine. Suddenly, as if by magic, the chamber is illuminated. I start to turn to see where the light has come from, but then there is a clicking sound and someone grabs me from behind.

"Hello, Nicole," a man's voice says behind me, his breath warm and foul against my ear.

My heart stops. An accent—Russian, I think, surprised. Does Santini have Russians working for him? The man could also be affiliated with the financier, Ivankov, but it seems a stretch. He must have been following me, but for how long? Had he seen Jared?

"Y-yes," I manage, trying to mimic Nicole's accent. "But you said to come to the harbor—"

He presses a gun into my ribs. "The wine."

I swallow. "Where's my son?"

He smashes me against the wall, knocking the wind out of me. "First the wine."

I struggle to catch my breath. "No good. I need proof that Noah is safe."

The man calls out something in Russian and out of the corner of my eye, I see a second man appear, holding a small child. I fight the urge to cry out at the sight of the tiny version of Jared. He looks tired and dirty, but otherwise unharmed.

"Darling." I pull back from the wall. The child looks bewildered, and for a moment I fear that he will say something to give away the fact that I am not his mother, but he continues to stare at me, wide-eyed.

"Enough," the man says, grabbing me once more. "The wine."

I move slowly, getting a good look at him for the first time, noting his black ponytail and dark eyes, the scar that runs from his right temple to his chin. The man who holds Noah is shorter and stockier, with sandy hair and an unkempt mustache. Details, I realize through my panic, that will be important in case they get away.

But whether or not these men are apprehended is the least of my worries right now. I need to give them the wine, then get Noah and get out. I start toward the racks, eyeing the dusty crates and boxes. They are mostly unmarked and the few that have labels are faded and illegible, one indiscernible from the next. How am I ever going to figure out which one contains the Cerfberre Bordeaux?

Suddenly there is a clattering sound behind me. I turn in time to see another man appear. There, pushed before him with arms behind her back, is Nicole.

chapter NINETEEN

PANIC FLOODS MY brain. What is Nicole doing here? She's sup-posed to be in Zante, warning Ari.

"I've found her, Ivan," the man holding Nicole says in English, gesturing with his head. He must not be Russian like the other two. Turkish, I think, processing his accent and swarthy complexion.

The man he called Ivan looks at him blankly. "Who?"

"Nicole."

Ivan's eyes widen. "That's Nicole?" He turns back in my direc-tion. "Then who the hell are you?"

For a minute I consider continuing to insist that I am Nicole, that this other woman is an impostor. But then Noah reaches out in Nicole's direction. "Mama!" he cries, and I know the charade is over.

"I'm Nicole's cousin," I manage, trying to come up with a plau-sible explanation. "I was at her house when you called and said we had to give you the wine in two hours and I didn't think she could make it so I came instead."

But Ivan is not fooled. "Police," he hisses, his expression turning from surprise to anger.

"I'm not . . . " I begin, but he slams me up against the wall again, harder this time. My jaw bangs into the rocks, sending pain shooting upward through my head. Before I can recover, he twists my arms behind my back with one hand in a single fluid motion. Holding my arms in a vicelike grip, he uses his other hand to frisk me, plucking my gun from my waist and flinging it away.

Then he walks to Nicole. "I told you, alone," he says, hitting her across the mouth so hard that she breaks from the Turk's grip. Noah begins to cry.

"Darling . . . " Ignoring her now bleeding lip, Nicole starts for the child, but the Turk grabs her once more and pulls her back roughly, throwing her to the ground. Noah's cry rises to a wail, his face growing beet red. The sandy-haired man clamps a hand over Noah's mouth, but he begins flails wildly, unwilling to be contained.

Anger flashes white hot through me, and I start toward Noah, heedless of any danger. But Ivan steps between us, leveling his gun at me and cocking it. Now that he has the real Nicole, I am just a liability. He does not have any reason to keep me alive.

"Wait . . . " I step back, raising my hands. I need to buy time, to come up with a reason for him not to kill me this very moment. I glance from my gun, which lies on the ground several feet away, to the man holding the now-limp Noah. I cannot risk his safety by diving for it, and reaching it and using it would be virtually impossible.

"You," Ivan waves the gun in Nicole's direction. "Get the wine."

"But I don't understand," Nicole replies, her voice trembling. She gestures toward the man who brought her in. "Like I told him, I'll give you the money and—"

"Now!" Ivan cuts her off, then raises the gun menacingly.

Cowering, Nicole goes to a lantern that hangs from the wall. She takes it down and lights the wick inside with a match. She looks at the wine racks hesitantly, seeming to stall for time.

"Enough," Ivan growls. He walks to Noah, shaking the child until he squeals. "The wine. And no games."

A mixture of horror and rage crosses Nicole's face as she struggles not to lunge for her child. "Do it," I urge her in a low voice. I don't think the men are bluffing and we can't take a chance.

Defeated, she hurries to one of the wine racks, the bottles dancing green in the light as she nears. She pushes aside the rack with surprising ease. It's a decoy, I realize, surprised. The bottles are empty. Behind it is a rusty gate, held in place by a padlock. Nicole produces a key and struggles with the lock for several seconds until there is a loud popping sound. She pushes the gate open to reveal a deep closet. I wonder what she is doing, if she is somehow trying to mislead the men, but I know that she would not jeopardize her son.

With great effort, Nicole drags a wooden crate out into the chamber. Ivan nods and the Turk moves quickly to the box, kneeling before it and producing a metal tool from his jacket pocket. He pries open the crate, then pulls a bottle from the straw lining and lifts it to the light, running his hand over the label and appraising it with a knowing eye.

As the other men watch intently, I glance toward the door. Now that they have what they've come for, it's only a matter of time before they dispose of us. We have to get out of here.

"Come on," I say, stalling for time. "You've got the wine. Why don't you let us go? Or at least let Nicole take the child out of here. You can keep me, if you're worried about getting away."

There is no response. The Turk stands, still holding the wine bottle. "It's good," he says to Ivan. Then, without warning, he lets go of the bottle. It drops to the dirt, breaking loudly. Liquid seeps into the earth, begins to disappear.

I search Ivan's face, expecting to see dismay. Surely he will have to answer to Santini for losing the priceless bottle. But his face remains nonplussed as the Turk lifts a second bottle from the case and holds it out, ready to break that one, too. Nicole and I exchange stunned looks.

"Wait," I call, surprise overcoming fear. All three men turn to me. "What are you doing?"

"Destroying the wine," the Turk replies, as though it should be obvious. He drops the bottle to the ground.

"But it's so valuable." My mind whirls. Why would Santini order his men to destroy the wine he'd gone to such lengths to get? "Surely the people you work for . . . "

He lifts three more bottles, dropping them in unison, adding to the pile of broken glass at his feet. "Wait," I say again, but he ignores me and picks up another bottle, this time hurling it so it smashes against the wall. Noah yelps, alarmed by the sound.

The Turk picks up speed, breaking four more bottles in rapid succession. His movements are almost festive now, as if smashing plates at a Greek celebration. Only two more bottles left. Then the wine will be completely gone—and the men will have no reason to keep us alive any longer.

"You know, you really should save those last two bottles of wine," I say, "as an insurance policy."

Ivan walks toward me, brandishing his gun impatiently. "This one talks too much."

But the Turk takes a step forward, a bottle of wine still suspended in his hand. "Insurance policy?"

I swallow. "To make sure that the people you are working for give you everything you've been promised—and that they don't finger you if something goes wrong."

"We can't," Ivan replies. But the Turk's eyes dart back and forth as he considers my idea.

"If the wine is all gone, you have no leverage. But as long as you have a few of the bottles, they'll do anything you want. You could even ask for more money," I add, gaining steam.

"And the wine is worth a fortune," Nicole chimes in, following my lead. "You could sell those bottles on the black market for a great deal."

The Turk tucks the last two under his arm. "Let's go."

"We can't take those," Ivan protests again. "We were hired to destroy all of the bottles." Nicole and I exchange glances, trying to figure out how to use the dissent to our advantage or at least prolong the debate. But then the sandy-haired man who has been holding Noah says something in Russian to Ivan. It is, I realize, the first time I have heard him speak.

Seemingly outvoted, Ivan shrugs. "Take them." He points his gun in our direction, gesturing toward the chamber exit. "Move."

I blink with surprise as Ivan starts for the door. I was certain that they were going to kill us here. Surely they do not intend to let us go. Something isn't right. I try to catch Nicole's gaze to signal to her, but she has hurried to the man holding Noah, who releases him into her arms. Not looking back, she scampers for the exit, clutching the child tightly.

Following Nicole from the chamber, my mind races. The men are about to get away with the last of the wine. Let them, I decide. Get Nicole and Noah to safety first, then figure out what to do.

I step through the doorway down onto the ledge that runs along the gorge. Halfway down the narrow path, Ivan stops and turns back toward the Turk, who is behind me. "Here?" The Turk asks. Ivan nods.

My stomach drops. They mean to kill us after all, throw our bodies over the edge. Nicole turns to me, not understanding. Then, as she takes in my expression, her eyes grow wide with terror.

The Turk pulls a pistol from his jacket. Nicole screams, turning away as if to shield Noah from a bullet. The man pauses, seeming to have second thoughts about killing two unarmed women and a child. Seizing upon his hesitation, I knock one of the bottles of wine from his arm, expecting it to break. But it clatters to the ledge, rolls forward.

The Turk's eyes dart to the bottle and as he lunges for it, I dive for his gun. I stumble and fall to my knees on the ledge, reaching the bottle of wine before he can. I grasp the neck of the bottle with one hand, fighting to keep it out of his hands. As he struggles for it, I am pushed closer to the edge.

Desperately, I claw at the rocks, digging my feet into the earth and trying without success to gain some traction, something to keep me from falling. Then my hand involuntarily releases the bottle, which flies over the edge. The Turk dives for it again, this time over-reaching.

"Ahhh!" The Turk flails, waving his arms wildly, wobbling. He grabs me by the shirt and before I can react, pulls me with him as he falls backward over the ledge.

I am too surprised to scream. I guess this is it, a calm voice in my head says as we careen through the darkness. I did what I set out to do, found Jared, got the answers I was seeking. There is a seeming hesitation in time, then a sense of weightlessness as we fall, and I wonder how far down it is to the bottom, how long until we reach it.

Suddenly I crash into something hard, pain radiating through my body. I've landed on another ledge that juts out from the cave wall several feet below in the gorge, unseen from above. I grunt as the Turk lands on top of me a second later, his full weight crushing me against the ground. His hesitation is gone now, hands instantly at my throat, squeezing my windpipe.

I reach down blindly for his gun. Sensing my motion, he releases my throat and his fingers close over mine as I struggle to turn the gun toward him. A shot rings out between us.

He's hit, I realize as he rolls off of me. Taking a deep breath, I kick hard against his chest, sending him over the edge. His scream fades as he falls into the gorge below. Seconds later there is a loud thump, then silence.

"Jordan!" Nicole cries out. Above, the sandy-haired man pushes Nicole close to the edge as she struggles unsuccessfully to hold her footing while clutching tightly to Noah. I look around. I am more than ten feet below the precipice, with nothing to grab on to to get back up. And I cannot get a clear shot at the man without risking hitting Nicole or Noah.

"Hold on," I call. She does not respond, but stands paralyzed as she clutches the child, eyes closed, mouth moving in silent prayer.

From the doorway, there is a sudden roar and another figure appears. Ari! At the sight of him, my heart flips. How did he find us?

In one fell swoop, Ari pushes Nicole and Noah to safety, then leaps at the sandy-haired man, knocking him down. But the man, much larger and heavier than Ari, rolls on top of him, pinning him to the ground.

The two men grapple for what seems like an eternity. With a mighty shove, Ari pushes the man over the edge. I jump back, hugging the wall as he flies past, joining his accomplice in the abyss.

"Jordan?" Ari calls from above, his panicked voice echoing through the cavern.

"Down here."

He straightens and his eyes widen, relief flooding his face. He leaps over the edge, bending his knees to soften his landing beside me. "Are you okay?"

"F-fine," I manage, trying to catch my breath. "But how did you . . ."

"Nicole found me in Zante before I reached the address, told me that the information was bad." His words come out in a breathless rush. "We figured out a way that she could give me the wine and I could get her the money she needed to pay off her debts. But when I went to arrange the fund transfer, Nicole disappeared. At first I thought maybe she'd gotten cold feet about our arrangement, but when I got ahold of Jared, he told me about Noah being taken and I figured that Santini's men grabbed Nicole, too. So I—"

"Ari!" Nicole cries out from above. Ivan stands in the doorway to the wine chamber, kneeling over something. Dynamite, I realize, as he lights the charge. Blowing up the cave must have been their contingency plan. Ivan stands and picks up the last bottle of wine where the Turk dropped it. Then he runs past Nicole and out of the cave.

"Nicole, go!" I cry. With a last desperate look back, she disappears through the entrance with the child.

"Here," Ari says. He lifts me up over his head, pushing me back up to the top ledge. I scramble to my feet and turn to help him, but he waves me off, climbing with stunning agility, gaining traction by finding notches and crevices in the sheer rock face that I hadn't known existed.

I start toward the entrance of the cave. I look back, expecting to see Ari following close behind. Instead, he has run to the far end of the ledge and is reaching for the still smoldering dynamite. "Ari, no . . . "

"Get out!" he orders as he picks up the dynamite and starts to fling it into the gorge. "Now!"

Desperately I run toward the entrance of the cave. As I reach the archway to the main chamber, there is a deafening bang. I am thrown forward to the ground and everything goes black.

chapter TWENTY

Ⅰ LIE IN THE darkness for several seconds, unable to move. Am I dead?

Pain shoots through my shoulder then, reviving me. Sensing daylight, I open my eyes. I am lying on the soggy ground in the entrance chamber to the cave. Nicole is standing over me, still holding Noah, trying to pull me to my feet. Bright sky fills the space behind her.

She tugs at my arm. "Get up!" she says, as though talking to a lazy child. But her voice is urgent.

I inhale, filling my lungs with dirt and smoke. The last thing I remember is Ari flinging the dynamite over the gorge. Where is he? I leap to my feet, start back into the cave.

"Jordan, no." Nicole holds me back. There is a rumbling sound from farther inside, low and deep. "The walls have collapsed. It isn't safe."

"But I have to . . . " I break from her grasp and run deeper into the cave.

"Come back," Nicole calls from the entrance. "He's gone. The whole thing could go at any second. It's suicide to go back in there."

Her protestations fade behind me as I reach the tunnel that leads to the ledge, struggling to see through the darkness and dust. "Ari?" I call blindly. There is no response. "Ari?" I repeat, shouting now, my words echoing off the walls. From the far side of the gorge comes a scratching sound. "Is that you?"

An indiscernible mumble is the only response. "He's alive!" I call over my shoulder.

"Then wait, let me get help," Nicole replies, her voice faint in the distance. But there's no time—the rest of the cave could collapse at any second.

I feel along the wall, extending one foot before me. Then I stop. The ledge that once connected the entrance and wine chamber has collapsed with the explosion. Already narrow, it is now half its original size, no more than a few inches of rock hovering precariously over the vast chasm below.

Taking a deep breath, I step gingerly out on the ledge, inching forward. Dirt crumbles beneath my feet. I grasp at the wall beside me for support, moving as quickly as the precarious walkway will allow. As I near the far end, I see a figure lying beneath a pile of rubble. "Ari!" I kneel beside him.

He stares at me, dazed. "Jordan?"

"Are you all right?"

"Fine. But my leg . . . " He gestures to where his limb is caught between two rocks.

I start toward them. "Is it broken?"

"No, but wait." He points to the larger boulder, which is wedged against what remains of the doorway to the wine chamber. "That rock is supporting the frame. If you move it, you'll destabilize the whole cavern."

"We have to get you out," I insist.

He shakes his head. "You could be killed." He grasps my wrist. "I'm not letting you do this."

"Well, I'm not leaving without you."

We glare at each other, another battle of wills. "Look," I say, trying again, "we have to hurry. If we sit here the whole cave is going to collapse and then we'll both die."

"Then go now."

"Not a chance. I'm going to move the larger boulder on the count of three and then we run for it." I see him glance over my shoulder, hesitating at the narrow ledge over the gorge. Fear of heights, I remember; his one weakness. "You can do this. We can do this together."

A flicker crosses Ari's face, as though he wants to believe me. But another rumbling sound comes from farther inside the cave, closer now, more ominous. "All right," he concedes.

"Ready? On three: one . . . two . . . three . . . " Leaning all my weight into the rock, I press against it. There is no movement.

Ari reaches up. "It's okay. You've done everything you can."

"No . . . " I say, unwilling to give up. Tears sting my eyes. I'm not going to lose him, not like this.

Desperately, I take a deep breath and try again, bracing my legs, using every bit of strength I have left to push against the boulder. There is a creaking sound as it moves and the ceiling above us begins to give.

"Now!" He wrenches his leg free and I yank him to his feet. But then he freezes, staring downward at the crumbling ledge. "Don't look, just follow me," I lock my hand in his, pulling him forward.

As we reach the far side of the gorge, the rumble behind us explodes into a deafening roar. I can see light ahead, smell the salt air.

"Run!" Ari cries and we leap forward through the entrance,

landing facedown in the shallow surf. A second later, the entire cave seems to shudder and a wall of rock comes tumbling down, sealing off the opening behind us.

We lie motionless, side by side in the sand, breathing hard as the water laps against our skin. I study his face: there are cuts on his forehead, a fresh bruise at his cheekbone. Our eyes meet.

"I'm so sorry I left," I reply. "When I found out that you were Mosaad, I thought . . . "

"You thought that I betrayed you, despite everything we promised."

"Yes," I admit, touching his arm, feeling the warmth of his skin through the fabric of his ripped T-shirt. "But I found Nicole and she told me the whole story, including the fact that you and she are cousins."

A wary expression crosses his face. "I'm sorry I didn't tell you. But I thought if you knew . . . "

"It's all right," I say, meaning it. Though I hate the fact that he kept the truth from me, I would have done the same if the situation was reversed; I won't be hypocritical by holding it against him now.

He draws me close, strong arms circling around me, and then his lips are on mine. I inhale his familiar scent beneath the layers of blood and sweat.

Nicole, I remember a moment later, pulling away. She stands respectfully a few feet away, facing so that Noah cannot see us.

I turn back to Ari. "What were you thinking, picking up the dynamite like that?" I demand. "You're insane—and you could have been killed."

"Thanks," he replies, as if I'd given him a compliment. "Nice hair, by the way." I raise my hand, recalling my bleached-blond locks.

He reaches for me again, but before our lips meet, Nicole is over us. "Aaron, thank God," she says, kneeling and setting Noah down.

Ari sits up and reaches for the child, running his hands over Noah's torso and limbs, checking for injuries with a swift, smooth touch. Satisfied, he turns to Nicole. "What happened?"

"They grabbed me outside the bank."

"I figured as much," he says grimly. "We never should have split up."

"It wouldn't have mattered. They had Noah. And they didn't want money, just the wine," she adds.

A strange look crosses Ari's face. "Did you give it to them?"

"I had to," she replies. His face falls with disappointment. "It's the strangest thing, though," she adds. "They didn't take the wine, they broke the bottles. Why would they do that?"

"And what does your government want with the wine anyway?" I interject.

He turns to me. "Remember what Signora Conti told us about the wine, about how it was part of a shipment that was supposed to be delivered to the Germans in exchange for the lives of the Jewish workers?"

"Of course. But a lesser wine was substituted for it at the last minute and the Jews were killed."

"Right, but what she didn't say was that François Mercier, Cerfberre's longtime friend, was also a secret Nazi sympathizer and war profiteer."

"The mayor?"

Ari nods. "He's the one who brokered the deal to get the Jews out. He's also the one who substituted the inferior wine and stole the Cerfberre 43. Later in the war he was more overt in his collaboration, permitting his town to serve as a staging point for the transport of Jews to the concentration camps. He was responsible for sending thousands of Jews to their deaths.

"For over sixty years, no one has been able to link him directly to any acts, and he's lived a comfortable life on his government pension, not to mention the wealth he pillaged from the Jews. But recently the Israeli and French governments have been working together to build a case against him, planning to try him as a war criminal. The Cerfberre Bordeaux, which Mercier claimed never existed, is a key piece of evidence in that trial."

Nicole gasps. "I had no idea. I thought it was just a valuable shipment of wine and I was eager to be done with it as soon as possible. I didn't know about the war crimes prosecution."

"No one did," Ari reassures her. "We've kept the indictment top secret so that Mercier wouldn't grow wise and flee to a country that doesn't have extradition."

"So the men who took Noah and wanted the wine destroyed . . . "

"Must be somehow connected to Mercier," I finish for her.

"Mercier must have learned that the Cerfberre Bordeaux had been found," Ari adds. "If only I had gotten here sooner, they wouldn't have been able to destroy all of the bottles and—"

"No," I interrupt. "That is, they didn't destroy all of the bottles." His jaw drops. "Almost all of them were lost," I add, gesturing toward the collapsed entrance to the cave. "But I think that the guy who got away still has one."

Ari leaps to his feet, grimacing at the pain in his leg, then turns to Nicole. "Wait here with Noah." She clutches the child more tightly in response. "You stay here, too," he says to me.

I jump up. "No way."

He looks at me as if he wants to argue before realizing it will just delay him further. "Come on." He starts down the beach.

"Where are we going?" I ask, following.

"I saw the yacht those men came in on when I was on my way here—it's just past that next bluff."

"Should we go to your boat?"

"There's no time. It's back by Jared and Nicole's cottage." I think of Jared. He doesn't know yet that his son has been rescued.

Ari breaks into a run and I follow, neither of us speaking further. He is still surprisingly swift despite his limp and my shoulder throbs as I struggle to keep up. We round a curve reaching another inlet, one that I had not seen coming over land with Jared. There is a small harbor here, seemingly deserted.

At the far end of the lone dock sits a yacht, larger than the one on which Ari and I sailed from Trieste. *Ella,* the name on the side of the boat reads in blue cursive. Something familiar in me stirs.

Ari sprints forward toward the yacht. "Wait here," he calls over his shoulder as he boards. Ignoring him, I press forward. As I reach the edge of the dock, Ari climbs the ladder to the rear deck, pauses for a second to survey the boat and, seeing no one, hoists one foot onboard.

But before he can finish climbing over, Ivan appears behind him.

"Watch out!" I call in warning. Ari begins to pivot, but his usual speed is slowed, I can tell, by the injury to his leg. Before he can react, Ivan grabs him and throws him to the deck. I speed up, racing toward the boat.

A shot rings out. "Ari!" I cry, fearing he has been hit. But the bullet was intended for me, not him, I recognize as a second shot whizzes past my head, closer this time.

I duck, scanning the deck of the yacht. Ivan is still grappling with Ari—the shot must have been fired by someone else on board.

I hesitate, wishing I had my gun—any gun. Continuing forward, I crouch near to the ground. Then I break into a low run, climb onto the rear of the boat.

Ari is on his back now, wrestling Ivan for control of his gun. The last bottle of wine lies on the deck a few feet away from them. I start forward, uncertain how to help. Ari waves me back, then reaches for his waist, his hand closing around air. He must have lost his gun in the explosion. He glances down in my direction, but I shake my head helplessly, as if to say, "Mine is gone, too." His eyes widen as he realizes that both of us are unarmed.

Seeming to find new strength, Ari rolls on top of Ivan, pinning him and grabbing him by the neck and twisting. There is a sickening crunch and Ivan goes limp. An expression of horror and self-loathing crosses Ari's face and in that moment I know all that I will ever need about the work he did for the Israeli government, the things they taught him.

Ari jumps to his feet and picks up the bottle of wine from the spot where it lies on the deck beside the lifeless Ivan. "Let's go."

Before I can respond, there is a noise behind me. I start to turn and suddenly another man comes out of the cabin. He leaps on me like a cat and I freeze, feeling the blade of a knife at my neck, cold and steely. "The wine," he hisses at Ari.

Ari looks toward Ivan's gun where it lies on the ground beside him, realizing he should have picked it up before retrieving the wine. Then he turns back, faltering, ready to give up the bottle if he thinks it will save me.

"Don't do it," I say, remembering how Ivan and his men were planning to kill us anyway, even after they had the wine.

He holds out the bottle and as the man reaches to take it, Ari grabs for me. But the man tightens his grip, drawing the knife closer to my neck, ready to finish this once and for all. I close my eyes, bracing for the pain.

"Enough," a familiar voice calls from the bridge. The man's grip suddenly loosens, his arms going slack. Surprised, I open my eyes, look up in the direction of the voice.

And suddenly I recall where I have heard the name *Ella* before. Above us stands Signor Conti.

What is he doing here? "It's all right, Kristof," Signor Conti says, coming down to the deck. "There's no need to be uncivilized. Let her go." The man releases me and I scurry toward Ari, who stands motionless, too surprised to move.

"Signor Conti?" Ari asks, his face a mask of confusion and disbelief. "I don't understand."

Signor Conti must have been behind this all along, I realize, the pieces coming together. He was the one who had sent the men to destroy the wine. And he must have somehow fed Ari the bad information about Nicole's whereabouts through a third party—he sent Ari to the Mafia stronghold in Zante town deliberately. But why? Because for some reason, he wanted the evidence of Mercier's treason destroyed. And now that we had seen him here, he would want us gone as well.

"Ari . . . " I warn, trying to convey the urgency in my voice. But Ari still watches Signor Conti blankly, unable or unwilling to see the betrayal of his longtime friend unfold before his eyes.

Signor Conti advances toward us and takes the bottle from Kristof, who does not protest. "And the knife, please," he says, his voice cajoling. Kristof hands the knife obediently to Signor Conti, who turns it around.

Then, in a single, smooth gesture, Signor Conti slits the other man's throat.

I stifle a scream as we are sprayed in blood. Kristof clutches his neck and falls to the deck, bright red gurgling from the wound through his fingers.

Signor Conti releases the knife, which clatters to the deck. Then he steps over the dying man toward Ari. "It's all right, my boy. I came to help and thank goodness I did. I wanted to save the wine from these men, the same as you."

Ari's eyes flicker as if, in spite of everything, he still wants to believe the older man. "He's lying," I call out. Both men turn to me. "He sent the men who were trying to destroy the wine."

"Is that true?" Ari asks.

I watch as Signor Conti wrestles with attempting a denial, then decides against it. "You are correct, my dear," he says, as calmly as though we were sampling wines over breakfast at his home once more. "The woman is both smart and beautiful, Aaron. You should keep her."

"Enough." Ari tries to sound commanding, but his voice wavers. "Tell us everything."

Signor Conti's shoulders slump in resignation. "Ella. I did it for her."

Ari's brow wrinkles. "I don't understand."

"When I heard that the wine had resurfaced, I knew it was just a matter of time before it was connected to her family and the truth saw the light of day. I couldn't bear to let my darling Ella go through the humiliation."

Ari and I exchange puzzled looks: Signora Conti's family had perished because the wine disappeared. How could its reemergence possibly be harmful to her?

"I only have a few months to live, you see." He coughs, as if to illustrate his point. "I wanted to take care of this for her once and for all."

"But what about my grandfather?" Ari demands. "The debt?"

"Your grandfather helped my family and for that I will always be grateful. But that was many years ago. He's gone . . . and I have to put my Ella first. I never anticipated you becoming involved, though. You're a good boy and I'm sorry it's come to this."

A light dawns in Ari's eyes as he finally understands the full extent of the older man's betrayal. "It's over, Signor Conti," Ari says calmly, taking a step forward, respectful even now. "Give me the wine." He moves slowly but swiftly, not wanting to startle the old man and provoke him into dropping the last piece of evidence.

"Let it go, my son," Signor Conti says, using his cajoling voice once more. "What good is there in stirring up the past? Just let this go. Then you and your lovely lady friend can walk away."

Ari glances at me out of the corner of his eye, as if weighing Signor Conti's promise, debating whether even after this the old man might possibly be as good as his word. But he cannot leave us alive now that we know the truth about his wife's family. He will have to kill us to keep her secret safe. "Don't do it, Ari," I say.

Ari grabs the bottle of wine, trying to pull it from Signor Conti's grasp. But the older man holds on with surprising strength, clutching the bottle close to his body. Then with his other hand, he reaches inside his jacket. "Gun!" I cry.

But he draws out something small and round. A grenade, I realize as he pulls the pin. If he cannot escape with the wine, then he means to destroy it here—and take all of us with him.

"No!" Ari shouts, lunging for the grenade. Signor Conti raises his hand, pulling it out of reach. As he does, the bottle of wine flies from beneath his arm, sails over the side of the boat. "Jordan . . . " Ari cries, still struggling to get to the grenade.

Suddenly it is as if everything is happening in slow motion. I look hesitantly from Ari to the wine, then back again. My first instinct is to keep him from going after Signor Conti, to pull him away from the grenade to safety. But even as I think this, I know that I will not be able to prevent him from trying to stop the old man, that he would want me to go after the wine instead.

I run to the side, scanning the surface. The bottle is about ten feet from the boat, drifting out to sea, and in a few seconds this lone piece of evidence will be gone forever. I search the beach for Nicole, hoping that she might have come after us, despite Ari's instructions, and can help me retrieve the bottle. But she is not there.

I take a deep breath, then climb over the side of the boat and jump in, trying to ignore the icy water as it soaks through my clothes. I concentrate instead on not flailing, but moving my arms and legs smoothly in what I imagine to be a treading motion, struggling to keep my head above the rough surf. Fighting the urge to look back at Ari on the yacht, I try to swim in the direction of the wine.

I reach the bottle, grasp at it, but it slides away, bobbing a few feet out of my reach. Panting, I start after it again, holding it firmly by the neck. Then, using only my free hand and swimming better than I thought I could, I start back toward the boat.

A second later the world explodes.

There is an enormous bang, followed by searing white heat as I am thrown backward by the force of the blast. Instinctively, I plunge beneath the surface, the water now a refuge from the shower of debris raining down upon me. Salt water floods my nose and mouth. I flail, all pretense of technique gone, desperately reaching for the daylight. Then I break through the surface and gasp, my lungs filling with thick black smoke. The yacht is gone, except for a skeletal shell and splintered wood across a wide swath of water.

Ari, I think, panicking. I scan the debris but do not see him.

"Jordan!" a voice calls. I turn to see Ari, swimming toward me with long, sure strokes. I manage to tread until he reaches me, then I collapse into his arms.

"Signor Conti?" I ask.

"Gone," he replies with a shake of his head, gesturing over my right shoulder.

"I had the wine," I begin apologetically. "But then there was the explosion and it floated away. Maybe there's another way. I mean, I could testify that I saw it . . . "

But he brings his lips fully to mine, silencing me. A second later, he breaks away, smiling.

"What?" I demand.

He points over my shoulder. Ten feet away, wedged between two pieces of floating debris, is the final bottle of wine.

chapter TWENTY-ONE

A N HOUR LATER we round the corner and the cottage comes into
view. Jared is standing on the front porch, hand shielding his
eyes from the sun as he scans the horizon. He sees us, breaks into a
run. But when he nears he rushes past, seemingly not seeing me,
and I am reminded of my dream of him on the bike, riding through
me like a ghost. He sweeps up Nicole and Noah in a single gesture,
spinning them around and drawing them close, a family reunited.

I turn away, an intruder in this private reunion. Ari comes up
from behind and though he does not touch me, I can feel his breath
warm atop my head.

I look up at Ari and we stand facing each other awkwardly. So
he really was working for the right side. I had been so scarred by the
past that I was ready to leap to the conclusion that I was being betrayed again. This time, I was not.

But I still have questions. "Why didn't you tell me?" I ask.

"I couldn't. At first, I didn't know whether or not you could be
trusted. And later . . . " He bites his lip. "Well it seemed like I had
waited too long, kept something from you that I should have already shared. Plus I knew you had issues with Nicole, because of

Jared. I wasn't sure how you would react to knowing that she and I were related—or to the fact that I was working for Mosaad."

I consider his response. Part of me is still hurt that he hid these things from me. It's what we do, I remind myself. Working in intelligence, secrets are our medium, the currency in which we trade. I would have done the same thing. "It's okay," I reassure him.

"Really? Because when you left, I thought . . . " He does not finish the sentence.

"I know." He is trying to say that he thought it was over, that I was gone forever. "So did I." I want to ask if he was planning to come after me, or whether he would have just let me go. "When I found out that you had lied to me—"

"I didn't," he interrupts. "That is, I tried to tell you as much of the truth as possible—that I was working for someone who wanted to find Nicole, and that it had to do with the wine. I just couldn't tell you all of it."

"Were you always Mosaad?" I ask.

"No, I really was in the army. After the school bombing, they sequestered us for several weeks. First, they debriefed us, then later warned us to keep silent about what had happened. The story hadn't leaked to the media and they said if anyone found out, we would be tried as criminals. The stress was too much for me to take. I was depressed and I wound up in a facility for several weeks." I can tell from his expression that he is still ashamed of what he regards as a sign of weakness.

"Shortly after I got out, two high-ranking officers came to me. They said that because of what had happened, the career I dreamed about in the military was out of the question. But I could be trained in intelligence. At first I said no; I wanted to go home to my family.

Then the ordnance exploded, killed my wife and daughter. I had nothing. So I agreed."

My breath catches. "You don't think that they . . . "

"That the government killed my family to isolate me, so I'd have no choice but to work for them? I suppose in the early days I wondered. But I'm not that much of a conspiracy theorist. I mean, it was so random . . . there's no way they could have done that, right?"

He's asking the wrong person. There's no limit to what I believe a government could or would do anymore. But of course I cannot say this to him. "So you stayed."

"Yes. They trained me in special operations. I've worked all over the world since, training paramilitary squads, undertaking assignments. The things I've done . . . " He looks away. "I thought I had no choice."

There's always a choice. But I understand what he means. When you're alone, the mission becomes your purpose in life, covers up the pain.

"What I told you about my leaving the government was true—I did retire from Mosaad last year," he says, eyes haunted by the memories. "I couldn't take it any more. The work was tearing me up and I could feel the depression coming back, breaking through the numbness. I knew if I kept going I would wind up sick or dead. So I left, spent some time on the water just sailing and trying to figure things out. Then a few months ago, when I was docked in Sicily, I was approached by the agency."

That sounds familiar, I think, recalling my own encounter with the CIA agent in Vienna. I should tell Ari about that, and I will, when the time is right. But I don't want to interrupt him now.

He continues, "They asked me to come back inside, to take on this one last assignment. It wouldn't have normally been my area of expertise, but because of my connection to Nicole, I was a natural fit. They needed me because I was the only person who could get to her and persuade her to turn over the wine.

"I didn't want to do it, but I understood the importance of the mission. I said no, but they offered me a staggering sum to do this, many times more than what I normally got paid. I told myself that this was the last time. I thought I could bank the money and walk away forever."

Except you can never really walk away. The things we have done are so much a part of who we are. They change our shape, make us unable to fit in with the rest of the world.

"And I was worried about Nicole," he adds. "What might happen if they sent someone else to try to persuade her and she refused to cooperate."

I see how the pieces must have come together for him: a challenging mission, handsome compensation, and the chance to keep Nicole safe. "What about me?"

He shifts uneasily. "The fact that we met in Monaco wasn't exactly a coincidence. Our government had picked up some intelligence about your assignment in London, the fact that you left your job. We knew that Jared and Nicole were connected and thought that you might be able to lead us to them since I didn't know their exact whereabouts. I never counted on this, though." He waves his hand between us and I know that he is referring to the unexpectedness of our feelings for each other.

"But . . . " I falter, caught somewhere between anger that he had not been honest and surprise that he has acknowledged his feelings for me. "Okay," I say finally.

His face relaxes slightly. "So you understand?"

"I don't know if I understand everything. But I accept it." I shift uneasily. "What happens now?"

Before he can answer, Jared and Nicole break from their embrace, carrying Noah between them as they had in the photograph on their mantelpiece. "Jo," Jared says. My mind reels back to the previous night at the cottage, our almost-kiss. I glance at Nicole, catching the expression of angst that flashes across her face, and I can feel her measuring me with her eyes, assessing what happened while she was away. Then the look is gone, so quickly that I am certain no one else noticed. She blinks dismissively, drawing Noah closer to her.

"Are you okay?" Jared asks.

I look down, remembering that Ari and I are covered in the blood of the man Signor Conti killed on the boat. "I'm fine," I reply quickly. "It isn't my blood."

"Jared," Ari says, extending his hand, but Jared does not shake it. Instead, he stares at Ari, jaw clenched. He's angry, I can tell. For a moment I wonder if it has to do with me, the history I share with both men. But it's more than that: Jared holds Ari responsible for jeopardizing his family's safety, still unwilling to see Nicole's part in the affair.

Noticing the exchange, Nicole puts her hand on Jared's arm, communicating with him silently, soothing him as I cannot. Reluctantly, Jared shakes Ari's still-outstretched hand.

"Come to the house for a meal," Nicole says.

"We should get going," Ari demurs.

But Nicole persists. "Some coffee, at least."

"I don't know . . . " Ari looks at me, questioning. The idea of the four of us sitting down together seems unbelievably awkward, but it will buy more time before I have to say good-bye to Jared. I shrug. "All right," Ari replies, too polite to refuse.

We walk in silence back to the cottage. "I'll join you in a second," Ari says, pulling his phone from his pocket and stepping around the side. I know that he is checking in with his agency, reporting that he secured the wine.

Inside, I retrieve my bag from the bedroom where I left it earlier, then go into the tiny bathroom, cleaning up the blood and dirt as well as I can. Back in the main room, Jared talks on the phone in a low voice. Nicole is preparing a plate of salted fish and meats, more artfully than Jared had done with the previous meal.

A few seconds later Jared hangs up the phone. "That was Myron," he says to Nicole. "He and Eleni are fine." Then he turns to me. "Our friends who were watching Noah. They were found tied up in their cellar but unharmed."

"That's great news."

Ari returns and we sit at the table as Nicole and Jared move around the small kitchen in the easy, familiar way of a couple used to sharing a space, speaking in low voices and laughing. Noah plays at his parents' feet, seemingly unaffected by the earlier trauma. Ari drums his fingers on the table, watching. It must be such a painful reminder of his own daughter. I can think of the child I gave up, imagine what he or she would have been like. But for Ari there are memories of smiles, a warm body that he held.

I reach down, taking his hand beneath the table. "I'm sorry if this is hard for you," I whisper.

His face clears as he realizes I am watching him. "Do you like children?" he asks.

"Yes." I bite my lip. "I don't know, though, if I could ever have my own."

"Why not?"

"I think that ship has sailed. No pun intended."

"You're not too old," he presses.

"I know," I say, hearing the sharpness in my voice. For a minute I consider telling him about the baby I gave up but now, with Jared just a few feet away, is not the time. "I've always lived such a solitary, selfish life," I offer instead. "Moving from place to place, doing what suited me. The thought of having someone constantly dependent upon me is terrifying."

"You can't picture yourself doing it, but once you have you can't imagine life otherwise," he replies. "My daughter was the most wonderful thing in the world. How she looked at me, the way she saw the world. But to lose that . . . " He shudders, not finishing the sentence. I squeeze his fingers harder in my own.

"I still can't believe it was Conti," Nicole says as she and Jared join us at the table.

Ari shakes his head, at a loss for words. Despite the old man's confession, he is having trouble accepting that this lifelong family friend was the culprit. "It seems that he did it to protect his wife."

"But I thought Signora Conti was the daughter of the winemaker," Nicole says, her brow furrowing.

"Apparently not," Ari replies. I stare at him, surprised. "I spoke to a friend of mine who is a researcher at Yad Vashem just now and they're still trying to piece it all together. But it seems that the real Ella Cerfberre died in Terezin during the war. So Signora Conti was not who she claimed to be, and that, whoever she was, she was somehow implicated by the wine."

I remember then how nervous the Contis had seemed when we visited their home that morning. I assumed it was because of the mob, but they were really terrified of us and the possibility that we were getting too close to the truth.

"Signor Conti must have wanted to destroy the wine to hide his wife's secret," Jared offers. "He knew he was going to die in a few months anyway. So he did the only thing he could do, protect her while he was still able."

"No, he didn't," I blurt out, more sharply than I intended. All heads turn in my direction. "Killing himself and leaving her alone isn't protecting her." I stare at the table, feeling my cheeks flush.

"He could have surrendered," Ari interjects, as if interpreting for me. "An older man like him, he might not have even gone to jail. Instead, he took his own life . . . "

"Leaving her to deal with the consequences," I finish pointedly, and I know then that for all of the answers I might get here, some part of me would always be angry at Jared for abandoning me.

"He almost got away with it, too," Jared observes, either not getting or choosing to ignore the parallel I've drawn. "Fortunately, the last bottle wasn't destroyed."

"Thanks to Jordan," Ari remarks, his voice full of admiration. "That was really something, the way you dove after that."

"Rather impressive for one who can't swim well," Nicole adds drily.

"Well, I had to get the wine," I reply.

"Seems like a lot of trouble to go to for a fight that isn't yours," she observes evenly.

"It wasn't, I mean isn't," I fumble, feeling my cheeks grow warm. "But Ari needed . . . " Despite all that has happened to ease the tension between us, Nicole still enjoys setting me back on my heels, feeling in control. "Anyway, I remembered what you said about the water being shallow."

"Oh, that was a different part of the harbor entirely. The place where you jumped in was at least fifteen feet deep." I scan her face for some sign that she is joking and find none. Suddenly, the magnitude of what I had done crashes down upon me.

"You in the water, me on the ledge in the cave," Ari observes. "I guess we both overcame some fears today."

I nod in agreement. Of course our biggest mutual fear—of commitment, of getting close to someone again, lies unspoken between us, a giant question mark.

We eat in silence for several minutes. "So what now?" I ask.

"I'll arrange to have the bottle securely transferred to Tel Aviv," Ari replies. "It should get there in a few days. And with the wine as evidence, the prosecutors should be ready to issue an indictment. I expect to see it announced in the press in a week or two."

"So that's it?" I ask.

Nicole's brow furrows. "Not exactly. I'm sure the Austrian police are investigating Heigler's death." A strange look crosses Ari's face and I wonder if he has done something to make that go away. Nicole continues, "The debris from Conti's yacht in the harbor likely won't go unnoticed, either. And eventually someone is bound to realize that the cave imploded."

"And then there's the question of the money from the original sale that Heigler stole," Jared points out. "It's still out there somewhere."

"I can file a report with Interpol on that," I suggest, knowing Lincoln would help me. Ari could do it as well, but I'd hate to ask him to do anything that might enmesh him further with Mosaad when he's trying to get out.

"No," Jared protests and I see the conflict on his face, the unwillingness to risk putting me in harm's way once more.

"We can do it," Ari intercedes, touching my forearm lightly. We.

My heart quickens. There is a moment of silence as he and Jared exchange competitive looks. Jared is jealous, I realize, that Ari can be with me and protect me in a way that he no longer can. "I'll make sure everything is okay," Ari adds.

For a second I am annoyed. I don't need either man to protect me. I'm not a child; I'm a trained government operative, or was anyway. It's all right, a voice inside me says then. To have someone want to look after you is hardly the worst thing in the world.

Out of the corner of my eye, I see Nicole. Her face is impassive, but she grips the edge of the table, knuckles white, as she watches the two men, her husband and her cousin, vying to protect me. No wonder she hates me so.

I clear my throat. "Ari's right. Let us do this for you. We'll be fine."

"No," Jared insists, unwilling to let go. I am aware for the first time his need to be right, to control the situation, no matter what. In my memories, blurred by the passage of time, Jared had been perfect. Seeing him here in the cold light of present day, his flaws loom into full view, impossible to ignore. I understand now that no matter how much I loved him, we would not have worked out in the long run; even if he had not disappeared, our relationship would never have survived in the cold realities of the real world, stripped of the downy cradle that was Cambridge. Part of me wishes I had not come here and learned the hard truth that was the price of our reunion.

I look from Jared to Ari and back again, remembering the question Ari posed on the boat: If Jared were not married, who would I choose? I know the answer now. My feelings for Ari, imperfect and messy, are real, not based on a memory kept beneath glass, like those I have for Jared.

But that does not mean I do not care about him. "Jared," I say, catching his gaze and holding it. And then it is as if we are alone in the room, speaking in the wordless way we once had. Let me go, I tell him silently. Let me do this; I can help.

I see his protestations—putting me at risk is contrary to everything he fought for years ago. But then his gaze darts around the cottage as he reminds himself of Nicole and Noah and all of the things that must come first now. It isn't his job to protect me anymore. His shoulders slump in defeat and I can tell that he has heard me and accepts what he has to do.

"You won't stay here, of course," Ari says. It is not a question.

"No," Jared agrees. "Too much has happened. We'll move on as soon as you go."

"The quicker the better," Ari replies. It seems that on this point, at least, the two men can find common ground.

I look around the room. The beloved cottage that had become home to Jared, allowed him to finally stop running, is no longer safe. For a moment I am filled with remorse. Had my quest to find him destroyed his sanctuary? No, it was Nicole's actions that brought danger here.

"So where will you go?" But even as I ask this, I know that he cannot tell me.

He gives a faint, almost imperceptible shake of his head, unwilling to jeopardize my safety, or theirs. "I'll get in touch with my contacts again," he says, referring to the Master. "They'll help us figure out where to go."

Sadness washes over me in great waves. Part of the comfort I found in seeing Jared again was knowing where he was, where he would be after I left. Even if I could not come here again, I could see him in my mind's eye, imagine his life from afar. But now he will disappear once more, like smoke, and it will be as if I had never found him at all. As if he were still dead.

Ari clears his throat. "I don't mean to be rude, but we have a long journey ahead of us and we should get started. I'm going to get the boat ready," he says to me. "I'll meet you there."

He is giving me time to say good-bye to Jared. He walks to Nicole, kisses her on both cheeks. "Be well, my cousin."

As Ari leaves the cabin, Nicole busies herself in the kitchen, filling a small sack. "For you," she says, bringing it to where I sit and setting it down on the table. "Some food for your return journey."

It is my cue to leave. "Thanks." I stand and pick up the sack.

"No, thank *you*," she says, grateful to me for letting Jared go as much as for helping to save her son's life. I nod. We will never be friends, but we care about the same men and that, at least, is something.

"I'll walk you out," Jared says, picking up the sack. Neither of us speak as we leave the cottage and start down the rocky hill to the beach.

At the bottom, he stops and hands me the sack, an indication that this is as far as he will go. "Here," he says. From behind his back he produces the copy of *The Two Towers* I had seen on his bookshelf. "You should finish it, and the last one, too, when you can get a copy."

Time for the story to finally have an end. "Thanks," I say, taking it from him and tucking it in my bag.

We stand facing each other for several seconds. "So how do we do this?" he asks, his voice slightly jagged at the end.

"You go first," I say. Even with the passage of time and the questions answered, I still do not have the strength to walk away from him.

"Thank you, Jo," he says.

"For what?"

"For coming all this way. Caring enough to find me."

And enough to let you go. All of the doubt and regret rises up anew. Don't go, I want to shout. Stay with me. No matter how much has changed, how much time and distance has come between us, the notion of saying good-bye for good is still unbearable. I wish I could stop the clock, hold on to this moment for which I have waited a lifetime. But then what? Even if I could keep him from going for a minute, an hour, nothing would change. His life would be waiting, and mine, and we would have no choice but to walk away.

This is England all over again, I think. Forces beyond our control, pulling us apart.

No, this time is different, a voice not my own seems to say. We are no longer children. This time we are making the choice to say good-bye, because it is the right thing to do. We cannot hold on to the past by refusing to move forward. Only by choosing to take that step can we reclaim what was taken from us so many years ago.

And suddenly my relationship with Jared is no longer a gaping loss or a larger-than-life should-have-been. I see it for what it was: a sweet, simple love in a more innocent time. The final piece of the puzzle snaps into place and I understand where Jared fits in to the larger tapestry of my life and what people really mean when they speak of closure.

Over his shoulder I glimpse a figure at the cottage window. It is Nicole, watching us, and even from this distance I can feel her tortured expression, as though her fate hangs in the balance, wondering what we are saying, whether I will walk away. Then she is gone, darkness filling the spot where she once stood.

Suddenly weary, I swallow. "Go. Go now." Jared opens his mouth as though he wants to say something else, then closes it again and starts to turn.

"Wait," I call a second later, before he can complete his first step. He looks back and in his eyes I see a light, a certain hope that I will try to keep him from leaving. I know then that he shares all of my doubts about letting go of what we shared, that he is fighting the same current as I am in order to keep moving forward, away from each other.

But that is not why I have stopped him. "Here." I reach into my pocket and pull the ring from the chain. "I think this belongs to you."

I watch as he recognizes the engagement ring he left in the bank vault so many years ago, his face a mix of confusion and surprise. "Keep it," he says. "It's yours. It always was."

But I shake my head. The ring is a piece of Jared and it doesn't belong with me any longer. I press it into his palm, close his fingers around it. "It was real, you know," he says. "Not just a clue to finding my research. I did want to ask you to marry me."

And though some part of me already knew, it is still good to hear. "Good-bye, Jared." I reach up and brush my mouth against his.

He hesitates, then presses his lips smooth and warm against mine, a promise sealed. A second later we break apart, and he turns away, this time for good. I watch as he walks down the beach, shoulders low, not looking back.

There are questions I did not get to ask him, I realize. Was it him beneath Hammersmith Bridge that day, following me through the London mist as I ran, checking to make sure I was all right? Could he possibly have cared enough to risk everything to protect me? And if so, how could he bear to have gotten close enough to touch me, yet still not have let me know that he was there? I take a step toward him, then stop, closing my mouth again. There was a time when I needed all of the answers, but it doesn't matter anymore. The things that I have learned are enough.

I fight the urge to call after him again as he climbs the hill. But I do not, and a moment later the impulse subsides. It is replaced by a pang of longing and loneliness that hits my stomach and breaks wide open, threatening to swallow me whole. This time, though, the ache is not for Jared, but someone else.

Taking a deep breath, I turn and start in the other direction, retracing my steps toward the dock. In the distance I can see the boat, Ari silhouetted against the late-day sun, waiting for me.

An hour later the island has receded behind us and we are surrounded by calm blue waters once more. The afternoon sun is still high in the cloudless sky.

I drop to the deck where Ari lies shirtless. "You ought to consider some sunscreen," I remark, taking in his bronzed torso. I open my bag and pull out the tube he had given me on the boat. He opens one eye and stretches his arms above his head, ignoring me.

As I start to return the tube to my bag, the Tolkien book that Jared had given me falls out. Ari looks from me to the book, then back again to the place around my neck where the ring once hung. A strange expression flickers across his face and I wait for him to say something about it, but he does not.

I gaze out across the horizon. In my mind, I see Noah, playing on the beach in front of the cottage. Then, as if in a dream, another boy appears beside him. Though the resemblance is strong, he is several years older, with my coloring instead of Nicole's.

"What are you thinking?" Ari asks, jarring me from my thoughts.

I look down at him. "Children." He wrinkles his brow, not comprehending. "Earlier you asked if I wanted a child. I'm sorry I snapped."

"I shouldn't have asked such a personal question."

"It's not that." And then I am telling him everything, about the secret I have never shared, the pregnancy I ended. "I wasn't brave enough to have a child on my own," I conclude, watching his face for signs of judgment.

But I find none. "You were very young and you made the decision you thought was best at the time," he says. "It couldn't have been easy."

"It wasn't. But if I had told Jared . . . "

"You thought he was dead. There was simply no way you could have known." There is a firmness to his voice, and while I know that the absolution he offers is not really his to give, I welcome it nevertheless.

I gaze up, seeing again the little boy, this time against the clouds, and ask a silent prayer of forgiveness of him for having been too young and afraid to believe. Then I set him free on the wind. "I should have been braver," I add.

"We all have times when we wish we'd been stronger," Ari replies, and I can tell by his faraway expression that he is lost in memories of his own. "After my wife and daughter died," he says softly, "I didn't want to go on, that is, I tried . . . "

"Oh!" I exclaim aloud in spite of myself. Ari had tried to kill himself. How far had he gotten? Suddenly I can see the depth and blackness of his pain. I throw my arms around him, as if trying to smother out the sparks of anguish that seem to dance around him like fireflies. He drops his head to my shoulder and I hold him tight, rocking him like a child.

A few minutes later he looks up. His face is calm now, his eyes clear. "So what are you going to do now?" he asks.

"You mean, with the rest of my life? No clue."

"Would you ever go back?"

He is talking about returning to government work, I know. I consider the question. "That's a tough one." A day earlier, I would have said no. But helping Ari set things right with the wine made me realize how big a part of me that really was. "I couldn't go back to State after the things that have happened. But . . . " Taking a deep breath, I tell him about the encounter in the taxi in Vienna with the CIA agent, the entreaty from Van Antwerpen to return in a different capacity. "I'm sorry I didn't tell you earlier."

"It's okay. We were both feeling each other out, and I don't think learning to trust is instinctive to either of us. I'm glad you told me, though. Would you consider his offer?"

"I don't think so, at least not now. I think it was Isaac Newton who said, 'If I have seen further, it is by standing on the shoulders of giants.' That's what I've done. Don't get me wrong, the Director has been a great mentor and I'm grateful for the places that he's enabled me to go, but I think it's time to stand on my own for a while."

"Agreed."

I look up at him. "Really? Does that mean you're out, too?"

"For good this time. Plus, I don't know how either of our agencies would feel about this . . . " He waves his hand between us, his voice trailing off. A faint blush creeps up from his collar. "That is, maybe it isn't too late, even for two old adrenaline junkies like you and me, to really have something."

"What, settle down, have a normal life?" I can hear the disbelief in my own voice.

"Normal?" he laughs. "I wouldn't go that far. But it seems like we've both been searching for something, trying to get out from under. I haven't believed in fate in a very long time, but maybe that's why we found each other."

I am caught off guard by his directness. We've known each other for days. But at the same time, I understand what he is saying: that after everything we've been through, there's no need to waste time playing games.

A life with Ari. I try the idea on for size. A fresh start, one that would allow for all of the scars and baggage we've accumulated along the way. With someone who understands, because he, in his own way, has been there, too.

The idea of really trying to make a go of it with him, with anyone, is as terrifying as anything I've ever contemplated. But at the same time, being with him feels right and I cannot imagine walking away.

"So what do you think?" he asks.

Before I can answer, my cell phone rings. I glance down, preparing to turn it off. But then I notice the number. "I should take this," I say, opening it.

"Jordie," the voice on the other end of the line says, squeezing my heart. And as I listen to her words, I know it is the one call for which I was not prepared: Sarah reaching out for me, calling me home to her once more.

chapter TWENTY-TWO

I GAZE OUT ACROSS the rolling green hilltops to the snow-covered peaks that dance along the horizon. The morning sun is just beginning to break through a thick veil of low gray clouds, bathing the valley below in pale yellow light.

Ahead, a small group of people shrouded in dark coats against the dampness have gathered beneath a cluster of pine trees. As we make our way across the flowered field toward them, Aaron takes my forearm, supporting me so that my heels don't dig into the muddy earth.

We reach the gathering and I inhale the sweet smell of dewy grass, searching the crowd for Sarah's familiar face. But of course she is not there. My eyes fill with tears. I see her by my side at Cambridge, licking an ice cream cone as we strolled along the path by the river, laughing and talking. Then the image fades and is replaced by one of her in London last month, watching the world through the window as she sat alone in her flat, a prisoner of her own body. I'm sorry I left you, I think. Sorry I waited so long to come in the first place.

I look up at Ari, who is staring out across the hills, processing, I

am sure, all that has happened these past few days. "Signora Conti
has been arrested," he told me grimly the previous evening, returning to our hotel bedroom from the balcony where he had taken a
call. "She confessed everything. She was really Madeline Mercier,
the niece of the mayor who betrayed the Jews. As the end of the war
neared, she knew that there was no one to carry on the winemaking
dynasty, as all of the Cerfberres had died in the camps. So she took
the papers that Ella Cerfberre had left behind and assumed her identity, moved to Italy where no one would know her or look too
closely."

"And the part about her meeting her husband in the camp?"

"Also a lie. I don't know where they met or when she told him
the truth. But he loved her enough to protect her all of these years,
right to the end."

And with that final piece of information, the puzzle of the Cerfberre Bordeaux, of who had wanted it and why, was complete.

Not that the Contis' secret was the only thing for us to process;
there was my reunion with Jared, too. Ari asked me about it yesterday, as we wound our way through the mountains to Geneva. "Was
it what you expected?" he asked abruptly, not taking his eyes off the
road. "Seeing Jared again, I mean."

I considered the question. "I don't know," I admitted finally. "I
think I got the answers I was searching for, at least most of them.
Things are just so different now."

"It's like you've spent the past decade grieving for something
that really isn't there to mourn anymore," he observed.

I nodded, but in truth I knew it was more than that. Even for all
the years I thought Jared was dead, the mourning was never really
just about him, but for a time and a place, carefree and youthful,
that was ripped away in an instant. Leaving Cambridge was the end

of childhood, and forever after life would be broken into two segments: Before and After. Jared's death might have marked the turning point, but it was the loss of innocence I mourned. I had spent the past ten years crafting an elegy to Camelot.

Perhaps I was being dramatic, I thought. Everyone has pieces of the past that they cannot let go. But the hold Cambridge has on those who have passed through seemed stronger somehow, almost mystical. There were people I knew who had never been back, not wanting to see the place a shell of its former self, bereft of all the memories. Still others could not seem to tear themselves away, went back for every race and event, retelling the stories of the past as if it would keep them alive. One classmate spent nine years completing his doctorate, then tried to leave, only to be drawn back to marry a local woman and live in the town forever. No, Cambridge was different, and the ties that bound us there stronger and more enduring in a way I could never make Ari understand.

And then there was me—I had run as far and fast as I could, but in my mind, I'd never really left. Until now. Having found Jared, perhaps I can finally put the memories in their proper place, like a box on the shelf, to be taken out and dusted off when the time is right, on special occasions like the reunions that I might actually attend, or perhaps someday to share with my children.

My children. I stop, surprised by the thought I'd never allowed myself to have. Ari had said it was not too late. I turn to him, remembering his proposal on the boat of making a life together somewhere, starting over. He has not mentioned it again since we were interrupted by Sarah's urgent call. But the question lies unanswered between us: Could we build a life together?

I imagine it, free of our pasts, no more ghosts or doing the bidding of others and their agendas. No longer pieces on someone else's chess set, we would play our own game. I have no idea where we would go, how we would spend our lives. There was a time when that uncertainty might have terrified me. Now it fills me with excitement—and undeniable hope.

I run my hand through my hair, which I'd taken time to dye brunette again, then take a deep breath. "Your offer . . . " I say, faltering. He looks down at me. "Is it still good?"

He licks his lips and I brace myself for the disclaimer, that it was a statement made in a moment of impulse, or that we barely know each other or aren't the kind of people who can settle down. Then he nods slightly. "It is. I didn't want to mention it again for fear of pressuring you." He gestures with his head to the assembled crowd. "Especially with all of this . . ."

I reach up, silencing him with a kiss. "Is that a yes?" I ask, when we break apart a moment later.

"Yes." He smiles. "What shall we do?"

"I may have to go back into government work," I say. His eyebrows rise. "Being a civilian is just too dangerous."

His face breaks into a smile as he comprehends my joke. "Seriously, what are we going to do?"

There are so many questions embedded in that one: Where will we go? What will we do for a living? And more important, what will we be like as a couple, away from all of the adrenaline? I wonder if we will flourish with the intimacy, or become bogged down by the familiarity that comes from a shared everyday life. Will I feel liberated by unconditional acceptance or caged by the commitment?

I silence the voices that scream inside me, and shrug. "Let's live somewhere by the water. And somewhere we can see snow each year, too."

"The geography might be tricky. But it sounds good to me." He smiles, looking as relaxed and happy as he has since I have known him. Maybe we really can move forward.

As if to prove me wrong, Jared appears unbidden in my mind. I wonder if he, Nicole, and Noah have left the cottage, how far away they have gotten. Perhaps the mantle of the past I have carried around with me all of these years is not that easily shed, but slowly, a bit more each day.

From over the hill comes the haunting sound of a bagpipe, tearing me from my thoughts. My eyes begin to burn once more as a black limousine appears in the distance, moving slowly toward us. Then, a few feet from the gathering, the vehicle stops and the door opens. Ryan Giles steps somberly out of the far side of the car, looking more dignified than I remembered in his dress uniform. He seems to have aged years in the weeks since I have seen him, new wrinkles lining his face. I imagine what he must have been through, falling in love with Sarah, caring for her.

He walks to the near side of the car and there is a momentary pause, and the onlookers seem to hold a collective breath as the door opens.

Appearing there, as if in a dream, is Sarah.

My heart lifts as I take in the simple white-lace sheath that seems to swallow her tiny frame, the wreath of tiny matching flowers that rings her head like a halo. Her face is radiant and her eyes do not leave Ryan's as he brings a wheelchair to her side, helps her into it. He pushes her with great effort over the sodden earth to this most beautiful-but-difficult-to-reach site that she herself had insisted upon for the ceremony, the same place he had brought her just days ago to propose.

The news had come hurriedly by phone on the yacht with an apology for the informal invitation, as well as the last-minute nature of the event. "A week from tomorrow. We want to have the wedding before I start my course of treatment," Sarah explained, but I knew it was more than that. She was not sure how much time she had left, but she wanted to spend every minute of it married to the man she loved.

So after a quick stop at the Israeli embassy in Athens to ensure safe transit of the wine, Ari and I made our way north, stopping for a few unforgettable nights at a private chalet by Lake Cuomo before reaching Geneva. Our conversations were meandering and unhurried and even as we got to know each other better, there was a sense that we'd been together forever.

The crowd parts to make way for the couple. As she is wheeled past me, Sarah lifts her face and smiles as broadly as I have ever seen, mouthing something to me. And though I cannot quite make out her words, I know that they are an expression of gratitude that we have both made it to this point in our lives and that we are together for this special day.

I recall the Jewish prayer Shehecianu, the blessing that is said on all joyous occasions to thank God, and suddenly the words, which I have not uttered in years, flow silently from my lips: Baruch Atah Adonai Eloheinu Melech Haolam Shehehcheyahnu Vekiyimanu Vehegianu Lazman Hazeh. *Blessed are You, Lord our God, King of the universe, who has kept us alive, and sustained us, and enabled us to see this moment. Amen.*

I think of all that was sacrificed to get here, the people who suffered or died, the loss of friendships, career. Was it worth all of the pain? I'm not sure there was any other way; the truth had to be found, the questions answered. I could not have stayed at State knowing what I did. And if I had remained a prisoner of my past instead of setting out on this quest, I would not have met Ari. But there had been an irreparable price of lives and innocence lost that had been paid to get to where we are now and I would try, at least, to remember that with gratitude.

The bride and groom reach the front of the crowd, where the minister waits. Sarah reaches up and smiles at Ryan. He holds out his arm to her and there is a faint gasp from the guests as he helps her to her feet. Sarah, with great effort, stands tall and straight, and I can see the faint tremor of determination as she grasps Ryan for support in this simple act of defiance against the disease that has taken so much. Today she is not sick or defeated, but is taking her first step forward in her new life.

I reach down and grasp Ari's hand in my own, taking my own stand for the future as the music ends and the last note fades into the hills.

Acknowledgments

I'M GOING TO modify the perhaps-overused phrase, "It takes a village to raise a child," and say instead, "It takes a village to write a book when you have a child." My son was born three weeks early in the midst of finishing *A Hidden Affair* and everything I thought about being a busy writer with two jobs proved to be laughable as I tried to navigate the waters of novelist-under-deadline-and-sleepless-new-mom. I wrote much of this book lying down with The Muse (then-infant Benjamin) sleeping on top of me, the laptop perched on a pillow behind his tiny feet. But finishing this book would have been impossible without the village: my beloved husband, Phillip; parents, Marsha and Gene; brother, Jay; and in-laws, Ann and Wayne, who gave me countless hours for both the work I needed to do and the rest that kept me functional.

The experience reminded me of the fact that every book takes this level of support to bring it to life and I've been so fortunate to work with the most wonderful people in the business. To that end,

I would like to thank my talented editor, Emily Bestler; her assistant, Laura Stern; publicist, Jess Purcell; and the entire team at Atria for their remarkable work. I would also like to recognize Rebecca Saunders and Tamsin Kitson and their team at Sphere for their outstanding efforts promoting my books in the UK. And, of course, my boundless gratitude to my friend and agent, Scott Hoffman, at Folio Literary Management, whose unmatched instincts and tireless representation have made my career.

Warm thanks also to my closest friends (you know who you are) and also to my present colleagues at Rutgers School of Law–Camden, as well as my former colleagues at Exelon and Morgan Lewis for their enthusiastic support.

A Hidden Affair covers a wide range of locations and topics and I have taken some fictitious liberties with both for the sake of story. However, the depiction of the sea journey taken by Jordan and Aaron was greatly enriched by the factual expertise of Peter Vassilopoulos. My appreciation to Peter for his generous counsel on yachts, and to his nephew, John Papianou, for putting us in touch. Also, while my depiction of the history of the wine was entirely fictitious, I greatly enjoyed learning about the true history of wine during the war from *Wine and War: The French, the Nazis, and the Battle for France's Greatest Treasure* by Donald and Petie Kladstrup. As always, the mistakes are all mine.

Finally, I'd like to say that once again, I didn't set out to write a sequel. I set my pen down (metaphorically speaking) at the end of *Almost Home,* content to let Jordan ride off into the sunset. But she came calling again, asking questions that piqued my interest and demanding to have her story told. If *Almost Home* was about coming to terms with the past, then *A Hidden Affair* is the other half of the story, the future and the destiny we shape for ourselves out of the unexpected and poignant moments of our lives. I'm delighted to continue the journey with you and I hope you enjoy it.